Books by L.M. Brown

Mermen & Magic

Forbidden Waters
Tempestuous Tides
Dangerous Waves
Shifting Currents

Heavenly Sins

Between Heaven & Hell
Between Good & Evil
Between Life & Death

Single Titles

My Boyfriend's an Alien
Falling Into Darkness

Shifting Currents

ISBN # 978-1-78686-145-0

©Copyright L.M. Brown 2017

Cover Art by Posh Gosh ©Copyright 2017

Interior text design by Claire Siemaszkiewicz

Pride Publishing

Published in 2017 by Pride Publishing, Think Tank, Ruston Way, Lincoln, LN6 7FL, United Kingdom.

Mermen & Magic

SHIFTING CURRENTS

L.M. BROWN

Prologue

Delwyn brushed away the dirt from the wall mural as carefully as he could. Time and the ocean had taken their toll on the city of Atlantis and he didn't want his actions to cause any more damage.

"What does it say?" Prince Finn asked.

Delwyn's best friend was the only merman in the whole of the sunken city to show any interest in the Atlanteans who had once lived there alongside the mer. Delwyn delighted in regaling him with the stories written on the walls of the buildings.

"It's a story about a great hero, who fought a three-headed monster to rescue a princess." Delwyn pointed to the tall hero wielding a sword. *"This is him."*

Finn leaned in closer. He hovered perhaps a little too near. Delwyn's heart raced. Finn had been doing that a lot recently. Delwyn hadn't yet figured out if it was intentional.

"He's very handsome," Finn commented. *"Don't you think so?"*

"I hadn't really thought about it."

Delwyn could tell Finn wasn't happy with the answer, from the slight downturn of his lips. However, he quickly returned to his usual self and concentrated on studying the mural.

"How is it you can read the stories?" Finn asked, not for the first time. *"Did someone teach you the Atlanteans' language?"*

Delwyn didn't know how to answer Finn's question. He hadn't learned the language at all — he simply knew it. When he looked at the pictures and symbols on the walls he could tell what they meant. He always had. At first his mother thought he had made up the stories, but even she'd become convinced when Delwyn had repeated the same stories back to her, sometimes several years after he had first told them. He didn't vary even the smallest of details.

"I don't know. I can just read them."

The mer didn't have a written language of their own, which made Delwyn's ability to read another even more unusual.

When he thought about it, it was as if he had the knowledge hidden somewhere deep within his mind, easily accessible whenever he needed it.

There were other things in his head, too, that he only saw when he closed his eyes to sleep at night. They were almost like memories, except they weren't his. He had never spoken to anyone about them, not even Finn. He wondered whether to mention them now but decided against it. Finn sometimes teased him for his strange ways. The last thing Delwyn needed was to give him even more reason to do so.

Finn swam farther into the chamber. There was little illumination there, but the mer could see as well in the dark as the light.

Delwyn followed him, just as he always did. It was how it had been for as long as Delwyn could remember. Where Finn went, Delwyn followed.

They swam through the tunnels and chambers beneath the palace, exploring every nook and cranny of the vast building where once the kings and queens of Atlantis had lived.

Eventually they came to rest in an abandoned private temple which Delwyn told Finn belonged to Medina, the Atlantean Goddess of Love.

"Do you believe in love?" Finn asked.

"I guess." Delwyn gazed at the stone features of the woman who the Atlanteans had once prayed to. *"Do you?"*

Finn smiled and nodded. *"Yes."*

"You sound pretty sure about that."

"I know it's real because I've fallen in love with someone."

Delwyn's own smile froze. Finn was in love? How had he failed to notice this? Who was the mermaid the young prince had given his heart to?

Finn continued to watch him, quietly waiting for him to say something but Delwyn couldn't seem to find the words.

His stomach cramped and his eyes stung. He wanted to ask Finn so many questions, yet he couldn't summon a single word.

"*Are you angry with me?*" Finn finally asked, his voice barely a whisper in Delwyn's mind.

Delwyn found his words. "*No, of course not. Where would you get that idea?*"

"*Because you've not asked me who I'm in love with.*"

Delwyn forced a smile back onto his face. "*Tell me then. Or do you want me to guess?*"

"*You'll never figure it out.*"

Finn didn't even wait for Delwyn to try. Before he could even bring to mind a single mermaid he had seen keeping company with Finn, he knew. How could he not, when Finn pressed his lips hesitantly against his own?

Delwyn sighed into the kiss, opening his mouth and letting Finn's tongue enter.

"*It's you.*" Finn wrapped Delwyn into a close embrace. "*My best friend, and now, my love.*"

Delwyn shivered as Finn lowered his hands to stroke his fins. An unfamiliar feeling washed over Delwyn and he wanted — needed — to go to land with the merman in his arms. "*The mating season isn't for another two months. Do you think your parents will let you come to the island with me before then?*"

"*I'll just give my guards the slip. They won't be able to stop me.*"

Finn had long since become an expert when it came to hiding from the mermen assigned to protect him. Calder, the gruff leader of the guards, often spoke of his despair at ever finding someone who could keep up with Finn.

Unfortunately, Prince Finn had the most protective

parents in the city. The king and queen would not allow their precious son to pass the city boundaries for any reason.

Delwyn loved going to the island. Although he had never visited during the mating season, he knew the time would come soon. He was a young man now, or near enough.

He and Finn would go there together. They would learn each other's bodies on the sandy beach and when the mating season arrived they would break their first fevers together.

Their kisses grew more passionate. They stroked each other, entwining their fins as they rolled around on the stone floor.

"We could go to the island right now," Finn suggested. *"No one would miss us until nightfall."*

Finn pulled out of the kiss and Delwyn opened his eyes, or at least he thought he did. Now that he came to think about it, he didn't remember closing them.

Except he must have, and they were still closed, because he couldn't see a thing.

"Delwyn, what's wrong?" Finn asked.

"I can't see," Delwyn replied. He tried, without much success, to keep his voice calm.

"But you were fine before."

"I know. I saw you lean in to kiss me, but now I can't see anything. I don't know what happened."

"You're not just saying this to avoid going to the island with me, are you?"

"No, I want to go with you. I swear it."

"Maybe I should take you home," Finn suggested. *"What if you're unwell?"*

"Delwyn is not ill," a female explained.

Delwyn didn't recognize her voice.

"Who are you?" Finn asked. *"What are you? How are you alive under the ocean?"*

"I'm a goddess."

"Do you know what's the matter with Delwyn?"

"There is nothing wrong with him. He has now become what he was always meant to be."

8

"Who are you?" Delwyn asked.

"My name is Cari, and I'm the Atlantean Goddess of Prophecy. And you are now one of my Oracles."

"What? I can't be. There are only ever three Oracles and they were all alive and well at the palace dinner last evening."

"They were," Cari agreed. "However, my Oracle of the past left this world a short while ago. His passing means a new Oracle must be appointed and the honor falls to you."

"But I don't want to be an Oracle," Delwyn argued.

"It is too late. It is what you are, what you were always meant to be. This is your destiny. Come with me. Let me escort you to Ula and Kai. They're waiting for you."

Delwyn felt a hand take one of his and squeeze it. It wasn't Finn's hand — he knew the touch of his friend's hand. He let the goddess lead him from the temple to his new home.

He thought Finn swam with them, but when he tried to speak to him, the reply came from a distance. Finn had clearly remained in the temple of the Goddess of Love.

"I'll fix this," Finn called. "We'll be together. I promise."

"Do you have a plan?"

Finn's reply sounded firm and sure. "The Goddess of Prophecy has taken you from me, so I'm going to ask the Goddess of Love to bring you back. I love you, Delwyn."

While Delwyn didn't know whether the Goddess of Love could help, he supposed it wouldn't hurt to try. He didn't want to be an Oracle. He didn't want to be blind. He wanted Finn.

Chapter One

Delwyn wasn't sure why he kept replaying one of the worst moments of his life over and over in his mind. He knew what his best friend Kai would say about it if he found out what Delwyn had been doing, but he hadn't confided in anyone, not even him.

With all of history to watch through his visions, why did he keep coming back to this fairly recent event?

"Delwyn?" Kai's voice in his mind let Delwyn know he wasn't alone in the chamber. Being blind whenever he was in his mer form meant it could sometimes be rather difficult to tell.

His lack of sight was the reason he had first watched the events which had occurred on the day the sea dragon had temporarily escaped. He wanted to see for himself just how close he had come to death. The truth had been terrifying.

"What is it?" Delwyn asked. *"Can't you sleep?"*

"I'm fine. I'm just worried about you. The solstice is nearly here."

"You don't need to be concerned. I'll handle it just as I've always done."

"But why?" Kai asked.

Delwyn didn't need to see his face to know Kai was frowning at him. *"I already told you. I don't want to intrude on your time with Dax."*

"It's not an intrusion. Dax knows we come as a pair until you have someone of your own."

"We're not a pair anymore," Delwyn reminded him. *"That*

would be you and Dax."

"We don't want you to suffer through the solstice on your own."

Delwyn signed and shook his head, even though he didn't know if Kai was using his own power of visions to see him.

"King Nereus is finally letting his precious Oracles out of the city and you're choosing to stay here." Kai's frustration echoed in Delwyn's head.

"I want what you and Dax have," Delwyn admitted. *"I've seen the two of you together on land and in my visions. I want someone to care for me like Dax cares for you."*

"And you can, when you find the merman for you, but it doesn't mean you have to go through the solstice alone."

Delwyn didn't expect Kai to understand.

The Oracles were three mer who had been chosen by Cari, the Goddess of Prophecy. They had been gifted — or cursed, depending on the point of view — with the power to see visions. As long as they remained in mer form, they were blind, unless they were having a vision. When they took human form on land their sight was restored with the appearance of their legs. Ula, a mermaid, and the oldest of the trio, could look into the future. Kai had the power to see anything in the present and often used his ability to appear sighted. Delwyn, the youngest, could see into the past.

For most of their time as Oracles, the three mer had been confined to the sunken city of Atlantis, forbidden to go to land and to engage in sexual intercourse. The problem had been that any child they might have would inherit their powers. This meant the three Oracles had been forced to spend the summer and winter solstices underwater, instead of breaking their mating fevers on land. To go through the bi-annual mating season without having sex could be an uncomfortable experience, and one which became increasingly painful with each passing solstice.

The recent cursing of the Oracles with infertility meant they could now go to land with the rest of the mer. Kai and Ula had rejoiced in their new freedom, and neither could understand why Delwyn wasn't doing the same.

"Delwyn, you don't have to go through this alone." Delwyn could hear the frustration in Kai's tone. *"I'm here for you, and so is Dax. I hear Marin offered to let you join him and Calder, too."*

"I'd rather stay in the city," Delwyn insisted.

"Is there someone else you'd prefer be with?" Kai asked. *"Is that it?"*

Delwyn shook his head before he remembered Kai and Ula were blind, too. *"No."*

The sight of a human man he had watched in his visions sprang to mind. He pushed the thought of the tempting male aside.

Kai sighed loudly. *"Okay, I'll leave you alone, but if you change your mind, come and find me, promise?"*

"I promise."

Delwyn felt the water change around him and could tell Kai had swum away from him. He closed his eyes and summoned the vision he suspected would haunt him for years to come.

* * * *

Delwyn had long since become accustomed to seeing himself from outside of his body, however strange it had been at first. When he had initially come into his powers, he had watched himself swim blindly through the water, banging into walls and furniture whenever he tried to navigate his way around. Over time, he had become more adept at handling his lack of vision. Now he could almost forget that the merman he observed could not see. Most of the time, at least.

Delwyn's blindness and vulnerability had never been as obvious as during this particular event.

The ground shook with the force of the earthquake, the water rippling around the mer. Everyone swam for safety, away from the less structurally sound buildings.

Delwyn saw his guard pull him aside the moment the

columns of the building beside them toppled. They dodged the nearest column, only to find a second one swaying dangerously. The first of the aftershocks sent the second column tumbling and this time there was nowhere to swim to.

Delwyn stared at the sea dragon circling above the city, protecting the inhabitants from the predators of the ocean. The sea dragons had been hiding the sunken city from prying eyes for centuries. Their power of invisibility meant no humans would ever find Atlantis for as long as the sea dragons remained at their posts.

The large orange sea dragon batted aside his guards with one harsh swipe of his tail. The creature swooped down toward the city at a speed faster than any other animal of the sea. He headed straight for Delwyn and his guard, his jaws wide. He made a sound reminiscent of a scream of triumph.

Delwyn cringed, even though he knew what would happen.

As the dragon neared them, the column lost the fight to stay standing and crashed down. One of the larger stones hit the sea dragon on the side of the head, distracting him from his target.

Delwyn's guard stepped between the Oracle and the sea dragon, and the other guards joined him. Together, they forced the sea dragon back above the city while Delwyn felt his way around the rubble, searching for the safety of an open space.

* * * *

Delwyn ended the vision and let the darkness envelop him once more. He wondered how close he had come to being crushed by the columns or, worse, eaten by the sea dragon.

Realistically, he knew the sea dragon was unlikely to have eaten him. They survived on small fishes and huge portions of sea fruits. Delwyn just wasn't sure whether their diet was because they preferred such food, or if they simply hadn't had the opportunity to taste mer yet.

Whatever the truth, Delwyn had been giving the sea dragons a wide berth since the incident. Not that he had been getting particularly close to them before, but now he stayed well out of their way.

At twenty-four years old, he might have been the oldest male virgin in the city of Atlantis — a crown recently handed down to him by Kai — but he had no intention of dying before he managed to find a love of his own.

Chapter Two

Delwyn groaned, recognizing the voice of the guard in his head. Their guards changed on a regular basis when they rotated in their duties. Some were more pleasant than others, and one in particular was best avoided. Otus.

A clan leader before he arrived in the sunken city, Otus had made it clear from the start he didn't enjoy taking orders from Calder, the leader of the guards. He wanted to be the one in charge and had done everything in his power to try to bring that about, even going so far as to inform King Nereus about Calder's relationship with Marin, back when same-sex relations were still forbidden in the city.

Delwyn was pretty sure Otus didn't take pleasure in any aspect of his job. The guard had made it clear on numerous occasions that he saw the task of babysitting the Oracles as beneath him.

"So, what do you think?" Otus asked. *"You want me to help you get rid of your virginity tomorrow night?"*

Delwyn ignored him. If he had been inclined to go to the island tomorrow, Otus wouldn't be his first choice of companion. He would probably be his last. Otus had a reputation for being brutal and uncaring for his partner's pleasure. Delwyn was one of a limited number of mermen who knew just how cruel Otus could be.

Although Kai chided Delwyn for misusing his powers, Delwyn had long since fallen into the habit of watching mermen pleasure each other on the nights of the solstice. He often watched Marin and Calder together, while stamping down the feeling of envy over the love they shared. He had only watched Otus once and that had been enough.

Although his partner had been willing, he had clearly found no pleasure in the way Otus had taken him.

Delwyn had no intention of letting Otus anywhere near his arse. The truth was, while he sometimes wondered what it might be like to feel another man enter him, he wasn't sure whether that was what he wanted. His attraction to other men didn't automatically mean he was enthusiastic about the idea of anal sex. Some of the other methods of pleasuring each other appeared far more to his liking.

"*Are you even listening to me?*" Otus pressed.

"*I'm trying not to,*" Delwyn complained. "*You're distracting me from my work.*"

"*What work is that?*" Otus's sneer came through loud and clear. "*Sitting around all day while being waited on hand and foot?*"

"*Honing my powers, actually. In case you hadn't noticed, King Nereus is anxious for a solution to the current population crisis. He wants to know why our mermaids find it difficult to conceive and why our numbers are falling so rapidly. Our race is on the verge of extinction. The more I search into the past, the more likely it is I'll discover a solution to the problem. Unfortunately, that requires me to be sitting around all day, as you so nicely put it.*"

Otus snorted. "*You could at least answer my question.*"

"*No.*"

"*No, you won't answer my question?*"

"*No, I won't be going to the island with you,*" Delwyn clarified.

"*Maybe I'll search for you once you're there,*" Otus suggested.

"*I wasn't planning on swimming to the island at all,*" Delwyn told him. "*So save your threats for someone else, or better yet, keep them to yourself in future.*"

"*Good idea,*" Ula interrupted. "*Otus, why don't you return to your duties and leave Delwyn to get on with his work?*"

"*Got a mermaid fighting your battles for you now, have you?*" Otus asked. "*She's probably got more balls than you, anyway. Is that why you aren't going to the island, Delwyn? Ashamed of how little you have down there?*"

Delwyn bristled at the insult.

"Get out of here," Ula snapped. *"Or you might find I tell you a little about your future, and I doubt you'll like what I have to say."*

Otus didn't reply, but the waters shifted around Delwyn when the guard swam quickly away.

"Are you all right, darling?" Ula patted Delwyn's arm.

Delwyn tried not to be annoyed at her interference. She had his best interests at heart. Ula had been something of an older sister to him and Kai, and an overprotective one at that.

"Otus was just being his usual charming self. I don't intend to be anywhere near him on the solstice."

"From what you've said, you still don't intend to go to land at all," Ula reminded him. *"Are you sure you've thought this through?"*

"Yes, I'm sure. I'm not ready for this yet. I'd rather wait until the right merman for me swims along and sweeps me off my fins."

"It might help him find you if you made a little effort to swim out there and look for him."

"Bit hard to see him when I'm blind as a cave fish."

"You know what I meant."

Delwyn did know — not that he would admit it.

"At least think about Kai's offer to join him and Dax on the solstice," Ula urged.

Delwyn had already thought about the offer and made his decision, but for the sake of peace and quiet he agreed to reconsider the idea.

* * * *

The next day, Kai cornered Delwyn in the palace kitchen. Their temple home had finally been declared safe for them to return, following repairs after one of the recent earthquakes, but Delwyn had taken to eating in the palace, especially when he wanted to avoid his fellow Oracles.

"There you are," Kai said. *"I've been searching all over for*

you."

"And now you've found me."

"Have you been avoiding me?" Kai asked.

"No." Delwyn shook his head, suspecting that Kai might be using his powers to determine if he was lying.

"Have you changed your mind about coming to the island tonight?"

"No. I already told you, I'd rather stay here in the city, like I always do."

"You know you'll be in pain if you don't come to land and have sex."

"I don't mind. I'll retreat into the distant past. I've told you before, the farther back in time I go, the less connection I feel to my own body. On the solstice, I go back so far I can barely feel the pain."

"Barely," Kai reminded him. *"But you still feel some."*

"It's not so bad."

"I don't understand why you'd put up with any pain at all when you have another option."

Delwyn reached out blindly until he found Kai's hand. *"You're kind and sweet to worry about me like you do, but there's no need. I'll be fine. And maybe by next solstice I'll have a merman of my own to love."*

"You have plenty of offers already," Kai pointed out. *"Me and Dax, Marin and Calder."*

"And Otus, yes, I know."

"Otus!"

Delwyn frowned. He thought Ula would have told Kai about the guard and his unwanted proposition. *"I told him I had no intention of spending the night with him."*

"Good. You can do so much better than him."

Delwyn smiled at Kai's vehemence. *"You should probably be heading to the island with Dax. You know how impatient he gets on the solstice."*

"That's an understatement if ever I heard one," Kai muttered. *"I'll be back later. If you change your mind, come and find us in the grove to the west of the rock pool."*

"Thank you, but I'm happy to stay here as I've always done in the past."

Kai left him alone with his guard and the two mermaids preparing the evening feast for when the mer returned from land, famished and eager to eat. Delwyn's companions would be going to land themselves later with their own partners, just like everyone else. Everyone, that was, apart from Delwyn.

He knew that wasn't strictly true. Some mer chose to remain faithful to their lost mates by observing the solstice alone, but they were relatively few in number. Delwyn wouldn't be the only merman in pain tonight, though he did wonder if perhaps he was one of the more foolish for his romantic ideals.

Chapter Three

Despite his assurances to the other Oracles, Delwyn had noticed the increasing pain with each passing solstice where he went without sexual release.

Fortunately for him, the farther into the past he wandered in his visions, the easier the solstice became.

Delwyn had gone back centuries in his visions and had seen the city of Atlantis newly built, long before it had sunk below the ocean. He had watched the Atlantean gods and goddesses walk amongst their people, worshipped and adored by their devoted followers.

He had seen civilizations rise and fall, watched battles for land and supremacy at sea played out. With his powers to see into the past he could discover the truth in almost everything. Only those shielded by the gods themselves remained hidden from Delwyn's visions.

Even though he could go farther back in time than the birth of civilization, Delwyn had long since chosen his favorite time period to visit.

For a relatively short span of time, two races had inhabited the city of Atlantis. In the years after it had sunk beneath the waves, both Atlantean humans and merpeople had lived within the boundaries. The Atlanteans had been protected by their gods and granted the ability to survive at great depths under the surface of the ocean. With the help of the mer they had become as adept at living in the water as their half-fish neighbors.

Delwyn, like the rest of the mer, had no idea what had happened to the Atlanteans. They appeared to have vanished overnight. He often wondered why, but try as he might he could not see the cause of their disappearance. He suspected he was simply searching in the wrong place.

Once Kai and Dax had gone to the island, though not without one final attempt by Kai to convince Delwyn to join them, Delwyn relaxed on his sleeping sponge and retreated into the past.

He swam through the city, studying how much it had changed over the centuries. The stones of the buildings appeared clean and securely in their places. Delwyn knew the work of the gods kept them that way.

When the Atlanteans had disappeared, most of their gods had gone into stasis. Only now were they finally waking from their long sleep. Each earthquake to shake the city was a sign of another immortal about to join them.

Here in the past, the gods still walked and their love for their city was evident in their efforts to keep the ocean waters from decaying the buildings.

Murals painted by the people remained clean and beautiful. Sculptures stood intact, without so much as a chip on the smooth stones. Mosaics covered the floors of the palace and temples. There wasn't a tile out of place.

The city survived and thrived underwater as well as it had on land.

Delwyn swam through the marketplace, wishing the stalls of his own time held such a variety of wares. The Atlanteans sold jewelry such as Delwyn had never seen before. He checked out the armbands and necklaces, as well as rings to pierce the ears, noses, lips and nipples. Delwyn watched one merman flinch when the sharp needle pierced his nipple. *Rather him than me*, he thought to himself as he swam on.

His stomach growled at the sight of a stall of scrumptious-looking fruits. Unfortunately, while he was in the past he could only see things, never touch. He had no more substance than a shadow and even less impact. He could move amongst the people, but he couldn't be seen or heard and had no way of making his presence known. The past was over and done with, and all he could do was watch and learn from the history he had been given the privilege of viewing for himself.

Delwyn spotted two Atlanteans from the corner of his eye. He recognized the auburn-haired one as the handsome man he had seen several times before in his visions. A black-haired man tugged the other into an alleyway between two buildings, taking him by surprise.

Delwyn swam over, wondering whether the object of his desire might be in some form of danger. Even though he couldn't do anything about it, he instinctively hurried to help.

When he rounded the corner, he realized his mistake. The two men clearly knew each other. It wasn't a case of one man being assaulted by the other, just the teasing play of someone catching his lover unawares.

Delwyn followed the two men down the alley and out onto a street. He had already explored the buildings in the area numerous times. He loved seeing them as they used to be, before they had fallen into disrepair. The two men entered the temple of the Goddess of Sea Creatures, with Delwyn close behind.

He watched one of them touch a crystal with his thumb, pressing into the jewel. A passage of light appeared and the two men swam through the opening.

Delwyn's curiosity kept him close by the two men. He didn't notice quite how close until a flash of light blinded him momentarily. When his vision cleared, he realized he had been caught up in whatever power had transported the Atlanteans from the temple and he had arrived on land with them.

It was strange to be on land in his mer form. The first time it had happened to him he had wondered if he might take human form. Of course, he soon found out that wasn't going to happen. His actual body remained underwater.

Delwyn moved around on land simply by thinking about where he wanted to be. Just as his thoughts about the past took him to other times, by concentrating on the places he could see about him, he navigated with ease.

The building they had arrived in seemed to be an exact replica of the one they had just left. Delwyn peered out of the window and saw beautifully laid out gardens and winding paths. In the distance the ocean stretched out to the horizon. He was tempted to explore, but if he did that, he would no longer be able to observe the two Atlanteans.

Delwyn followed them along a passageway and through a large open room where several men lounged on furniture in various states of undress. Delwyn took a moment to enjoy the view. It always struck him as amusing that the Atlanteans chose to remain clothed, even though their mer neighbors walked around naked.

The two men he followed didn't linger in the room. Delwyn trailed after them until they came to a halt in what seemed to be the private quarters of the dark-haired man.

Delwyn studied the two men more closely and spotted the symbol of the Goddess of Sea Creatures on the black-haired man's shoulder. He recognized him as one of the goddess' priests.

All those who had been blessed, or cursed, by the Atlantean gods bore the symbol of a trident on their body. Delwyn, having been blessed by the Goddess of Prophecy, as well as cursed by her mother, the Goddess of Fertility, had two marks on his own body. They were almost identical, but not quite. Only the most observant could tell the difference. Delwyn had always had a keen eye. He checked the body of the second man and saw one which matched his own exactly. It seemed the auburn-haired man had sworn allegiance to Cari, just like Delwyn.

"Isander, you are temptation itself," the auburn-haired man teased.

Isander laughed and dragged his lover over to the bed. "What's the matter, Fabian? Are you tiring of me already?"

"Hardly," Fabian replied. "Now, what did you have in mind?"

"Hmm, let me think. How about you take me hard from behind?"

Delwyn gasped as his blood quickened. *What a stroke of luck.* Although Kai and Ula frowned upon the way he used his powers to watch men making love, he had no scruples about what he did.

Ula called him a voyeur and Delwyn relished in his title.

Fabian tumbled Isander onto his back.

Delwyn moved closer to the bed, which appeared even more comfortable than the sponges the mer slept on.

Isander wrapped his legs around Fabian and trapped him between them. "I have you right where I want you now."

"Do you indeed? I might find it rather difficult to claim your arse from behind now."

Isander smiled wickedly. "I'm sure you'll find a way to please me."

Fabian reached between them and took both their cocks in his hand, stroking them together.

Delwyn peered closer. Fabian's cock was long and thick. Isander, by comparison, was both shorter and slimmer. Delwyn licked his lips, watching the first traces of seed appear at the tip of Isander's cock. Fabian seemed to echo Delwyn's thoughts and he eased his way out of Isander's embrace so he could lean down and take him into his mouth.

Delwyn groaned loudly while Fabian pleasured his lover. When he watched them he could almost forget the solstice and the mating fever.

Fabian drew back, licking his lips before crashing them into Isander's in a passionate kiss. Isander tugged on Fabian's hair as Fabian continued to stroke them off. Delwyn moaned at the sight before him.

Fabian let go of their erections and opened his lover's legs wide. Isander inched closer, sliding up against Fabian, winding his arms and legs around him, clinging to his lover like a vine.

Hovering nearby, Delwyn sighed and smiled. He touched

his own chest, lightly brushing his nipples, and wondered what it might be like to be one of the two men on the bed.

Both men were handsome and well-built. Isander seemed to be shorter than Fabian by several inches. Delwyn suspected he and Isander could be of a similar height. Fabian's chest was covered in hair, Isander's less so. Delwyn himself was perfectly smooth, just like the rest of the mer.

More and more, Delwyn's attention was drawn to Fabian. The man was magnificent. He maneuvered Isander around the bed with ease. The strength in his body made Delwyn crave to be carried in his arms. It was impossible, of course. Fabian had lived and died centuries before Delwyn had been born. They couldn't touch hands or interact in any way at all. But such minor inconveniences didn't stop him from wondering what it might have been like.

Things heated up between Fabian and Isander. Their words became incoherent until the only sounds they made were moans of desire and the occasional whine.

Finally, they fell onto the bed together, panting and sticky.

"Are you coming to the ceremony this evening?" Isander asked.

Fabian shook his head. "I have duties to my own goddess tonight."

"Your mother would wish you to attend *her* temple."

"No doubt, but she'll be disappointed once again. She's used to that when it comes to me." The bitterness in Fabian's voice took Delwyn by surprise. It was a stark contrast to the playfulness of earlier.

Isander rose from the bed and picked up his robe. "Come bathe with me?"

Fabian leaned up on his elbow. "You go ahead. I'll follow in a moment."

Isander raised an eyebrow.

"You exhausted me," Fabian added.

Isander chuckled as he wandered from the room.

Delwyn watched him go. The view of his pert backside was as delectable as the rest of him.

"Enjoying the view?" Fabian asked.

Delwyn tore his eyes from the retreating man to glance about the room, wondering who might have entered. There was no one there. When he faced Fabian once more the man appeared to be studying him.

"Yes, I'm talking to you," Fabian said with a laugh. "Did you enjoy the show?"

Delwyn squeaked and looked behind him. No, they were alone. But what was happening was impossible. Fabian *couldn't* be speaking to him.

The moment he realized Fabian had indeed spoken to him, the shock yanked him right out of his vision, plunging him back into darkness.

What? How? That's not even…

Delwyn tried to calm down and gather his thoughts. It wasn't possible. It simply *couldn't* be. The past was over and done with. All he could do was observe events that had already happened.

He tried to stop his racing heart.

Finally, he managed to convince himself he had imagined the last few moments of his vision. There must have been someone else there who Delwyn hadn't noticed. It was the only explanation for what he had seen and heard.

Next time he went into the past, he would find Fabian as oblivious to his presence as everyone else. The fact that he was already determined to visit Fabian again didn't worry him even half as much as he knew it probably should.

Chapter Four

The merman vanished in the blink of an eye. Had Fabian been a fanciful man he would have thought he had imagined his presence. After all, mermen didn't simply float around on land. They changed to human form and walked on their feet, the same as mortal men.

He had first spotted the silver-finned merman as he and Isander had arrived on land via his mother's portal. Strictly speaking, Fabian wasn't supposed to use the portal. It was for the goddess' priests alone, but Fabian had never been one for abiding by the rules. He suspected his mother knew her priests brought their lovers through the portal, since they made no secret of what they did, though whether she was aware Isander had taken her son into his bed was another matter entirely.

When the merman had appeared behind them, Fabian had thought him merely caught up in the vortex. Only when he didn't take human form did Fabian realize their spy was not of this world.

None of the Atlanteans were particularly shy when it came to their affections and Fabian saw no reason to alert Isander to their guest. He doubted his lover would've minded being watched, but he would have been distracted from their pleasure and more interested in why Fabian could see the merman while he couldn't.

Although he usually played in private with his lovers, Fabian admitted to himself that he had been more turned on today than he had been for a long while, just from the gaze of the silver-eyed merman.

Fabian wished the merman had stuck around a little

longer so they could've talked. Fabian was curious to know more about him and maybe figure out why he could see him. He had a couple of theories he would've liked to investigate further.

Unfortunately, Fabian had never seen the merman before and was fairly certain he was not a resident of Atlantis. Clearly, he had been observing them through some kind of magical means, and Fabian had met all beings in the city with such powers.

He wondered whether the merman would come back again. The thought plagued him enough that he took his leave from Isander sooner than he had intended.

Cari's temple on the island was a short walk from the one belonging to his mother. Hidden from everyone, the Isle of the Gods had only a tenuous link to the world. The island was for the exclusive use of the immortals and those who had sworn to serve them. Located in the realm of the immortals, it was impossible for anyone else to see it or visit it without permission from one of the gods, which made Fabian even more curious as to how the merman had managed such a feat.

He found Hiron, the Oracle of the future, with two of his lovers, a beautiful set of twins who served the Goddess of Memories.

Fabian coughed deliberately and Hiron glanced over at him.

"Fabian, is it time for the ceremony already?"

"No, I wanted to talk to you. Are you busy?"

Hiron gave each of the twins a smack on the arse and the women took that as their cue to leave. "What is it, brother?"

They weren't truly brothers, at least not by blood. But the Oracles were a family of sorts.

Fabian sat on one of the cushions and crossed his legs. "I had a visitor today. I thought you might be able to tell me more about him."

"Who was it?"

"A merman I've never seen before. He had a silver tail

and matching eyes."

"Did he have a name?"

"No doubt, but he disappeared before I could introduce myself. He was here on the isle."

"What?" Hiron sat up straighter. "No one can come here unless they're bound to an immortal. There are few mer who have sworn to serve in such a way, and none of those have silver coloring."

"I know. And that's not even the strangest part."

"It isn't?"

Fabian smiled. "The merman was in the private chambers of my mother's priests, in his mer form, and vanished in the blink of an eye."

"Are you saying he was just flopping about on his fins on land?"

"No, he floated in mid-air."

"Very curious."

"There's one more thing…" Fabian hesitated, knowing this was where even Hiron might doubt his words.

"What is it?"

"Isander couldn't see him."

Hiron chuckled. "You haven't been gorging on the green berries again, have you?"

"You're never going to forget that, are you?"

"No."

Fabian laughed. "I promise the berries are not to blame this time. The merman was right there, I'm sure of it."

"Have you tried to see him? Since he disappeared, I mean?"

Fabian shook his head, cursing himself that he hadn't thought to try finding him in a vision.

He closed his eyes and concentrated on the merman. Unfortunately, for the first time in years, his powers failed him. As the Oracle of the present he should be able to see anyone on Earth.

"Anything?" Hiron asked.

"No. Perhaps he's in another god's temple. You know we

can't see anything taking place in any temple other than Cari's."

Hiron nodded. "Let me see if he's in your future. I assume that's why you came to talk to me."

"If you don't mind."

"Not at all. I believe I'd like a glimpse of this handsome merman, too." Hiron closed his eyes to bring forth a vision of his own.

"I never said he was handsome."

Hiron opened one of his eyes and smirked. "I assumed he must be, otherwise you wouldn't be so eager to see him again."

Hiron knew him far too well. Fabian sat back and relaxed while Hiron looked into the future. When he finally opened his eyes again he frowned and shook his head.

"Did you see him?"

"I think so, but it was strange."

"How so?"

"I saw you with him in your chambers, on your bed, in fact, but he didn't seem to be entirely there. Every time I tried to focus on him, he flickered out of existence. It's almost as though he were some form of spirit."

"Did you see where he resides?"

"No. I'm afraid not. When I tried to see more, there's nothing but darkness."

"Has that ever happened before?"

Hiron nodded and glanced away.

"When?" Fabian prompted.

"It happens when I try to see the future of someone who has none. The darkness is a sign that the person whose future I seek is close to death."

"No!" Fabian felt sick to his stomach. Even though he didn't know the merman, his voyeur had appeared quite youthful. The idea that he didn't have a future, and was destined to die young, was the last thing he wanted to hear.

Hiron leaned over and patted him on the arm. "Destiny can be changed. You know this."

"I know. It was just a shock, that's all."

"A shock?" Cari appeared in the room with a flash of light and a waft of flowery perfume.

Hiron and Fabian rose from their seats and bowed low before their goddess.

"You were talking about a shock," Cari said. "Is this something I should know about?"

"Nothing to trouble you, Goddess," Fabian assured her. "Hiron was just looking into the future of a merman I saw today. I was shocked to find he had none."

"Sometimes the brightest lights burn out the fastest." Cari offered him a kind smile.

"Destiny can be changed," Fabian replied.

Cari patted his arm. "Not all the time."

"But this time?"

Cari closed her eyes and frowned as she gazed into a place only she could see. When she faced him again, he waited for her to tell him what she had seen. When she remained silent, he realized she wasn't going to reveal whatever her vision had shown her.

Fabian didn't press her to tell him anything. He knew she would tell him only what she wanted him to know.

"The ceremonies tonight will require all my Oracles to be present," Cari said, effectively changing the subject.

Fabian let her. The solstice celebrations were amongst the most lavish of the year and they had been preparing for them for days. The feast would last into the early hours of the morning and Fabian looked forward to it.

He recalled that the merpeople had their own way of celebrating the solstice. They went to land, where they mated with each other, and occasionally with humans. Fabian had never had a merman lover, but as a youngster, before he had sworn fealty to the Goddess of Prophecy, he had swum to one of the islands frequented by the mer and watched them from the foliage. That had been the first time he had seen a merman transform to human. Even from some distance away, he had been fascinated by the magic that was nothing to do with the gods and everything to do with them.

As he'd watched two mermen grinding together on the sands Fabian had recognized his own preference for men. The mermaids just didn't hold the same attraction for him.

His mother had been furious when she'd found out where he had been the night before. She had always sneered at the half-human, half-fish race of people and had forbidden Fabian from ever visiting the island again.

To a young man like Fabian, the temptation was irresistible. The more his mother raged at him for his fascination with the mer, the more obsessed he'd become.

When the time had come for him to swear fealty to one of the gods he had balked at his mother's order that he devote his life to her. He had studied each of the immortals and had chosen to serve Cari, the Goddess of Prophecy, instead.

After several years as one of her priests, she had chosen him for an Oracle. Fabian suspected that the rivalry between Cari and his mother had some bearing on his swift rise through the ranks, but he had never managed to persuade Cari to admit it.

As he continued to assist with the preparations for the ceremony and feast, Fabian's mind drifted to the merman who had visited him earlier. If he wanted to track him down, perhaps he might swim to the island tonight and forgo part of the feast. There wasn't a merman alive who wouldn't be taking human form tonight. If he was lucky, maybe he could find him before he found a partner for the solstice. Fabian would be only too happy to get to know the merman better.

* * * *

Fabian left the feast when the second course was being served. Hiron caught his eye as he slipped out past the columns and gave him a wink.

Fabian grinned back and hurried from the room.

With no portal on the island of the merpeople, Fabian had no choice other than to swim there. As an Atlantean he could swim underwater and at great depths, but as a human he wasn't the fastest of swimmers.

Thankfully, he had inherited a few things from his mother apart from her red hair, and one of those things was the ability to speak with sea creatures.

It took almost no time at all for Fabian to summon a dolphin and convince the mammal to take him to the surface and as close to the land as he could get.

When he arrived on the island he found himself surrounded by mermen and mermaids. They mated on the beach, in the clearings and up against the trees.

Fabian soon realized he wouldn't be able to find the merman by searching for the stunning silver fins and tail. He wished he had taken a little more notice of the rest of his body.

He wandered through the trees, catching the eye of several mermen, some of whom beckoned him over with offers of what pleasure they could give him.

Tempting as the offers would have been at any other time, there was only one merman Fabian wanted to find.

He wondered if he had missed him. Perhaps he had come to land earlier in the evening, or returned to the ocean while Fabian had been wandering around another part of the island.

Fabian didn't wish to think of the merman suffering somewhere under the water, so he pushed the distasteful thought aside almost as soon as it had entered his head.

Eventually, Fabian found a spot on the beach where he could see the majority of the mer when they swam back to the underwater city.

One by one, they ran into the surf and dove beneath the waves. Fins of every color imaginable flitted in and out of his view as they transformed and pushed away from the surface. The only color he didn't see was the one he wanted to spot the most. There were no silver fins in sight.

As disappointing as it was, Fabian consoled himself with the knowledge that Hiron had seen the merman in his future and in his bed. Fabian just had to exercise a little patience.

It was too late to go back to the feast, so Fabian stretched out on the beach and closed his eyes. The sun, rising above the waters, warmed his body. He drifted off to sleep with a smile on his face, dreaming about the mysterious merman.

Chapter Five

Delwyn felt rather foolish. Had he honestly believed the Atlantean had spoken to him? *How ridiculous is that?*

The past was the past, over and done with, to be seen but never altered.

Clearly, his imagination had been working overtime.

"Are you okay, Delwyn?"

Dax's voice in his head told Delwyn he had been lost in his vision longer than he had thought. Dax, and presumably Kai, had already swum back from the island.

"I'm well, just a bit of an abrupt ending to my vision."

"Kai says that happens sometimes," Dax replied. *"Er…"*

"What is it?" Delwyn asked when Dax didn't finish his thought.

"Are you sure you don't want to go to land and break your fever? If you want to go alone with Kai, I won't mind."

Delwyn laughed. *"Says one of the most jealous mermen I've ever met."*

"I might be jealous, but I know how much you mean to Kai. We discussed the situation, and it's as I've always said, sometimes sex is just sex, especially during the mating season."

Delwyn sighed. *"I know you think that way, but I don't, and neither does Kai."*

"Kai cares a great deal for you. He loves you."

"I know he does, but not in the same way he loves you." Delwyn struggled to put his thoughts into words. While he loved Kai, he wasn't *in love* with him. He had been in love once, but Finn had long since gone from his life. He had moved on and found a new love, two, in fact. He had no room in his heart for a third lover, even if Delwyn did have a way

of joining him.

"Are you sure you won't go to the island with Kai? I don't have to come with you. I'm sure of Kai's feelings for me, and I know him helping you break your fever doesn't diminish those."

Delwyn navigated his way across the chamber, searching with his hands for Dax.

"Right here," Dax said as he drew Delwyn down beside him.

"Thanks." Delwyn patted Dax's arm. *"I know you and Kai are worried about me, but there's no need. When I say I want what you have with Kai, it doesn't mean I want him for myself. I want someone of my own."*

"I'm not going to talk you into going to land with Kai, am I?"

"No. I've waited this long to have a man of my own. I can wait a little longer."

Kai made his presence known with a snort of laughter.

"And what's amusing you?" Delwyn teased.

"You're the most hopeless romantic, you do know that, right?"

"And you aren't?" Delwyn replied. *"I seem to recall you waiting out a mating season yourself."*

Dax's laughter echoed through Delwyn's mind. *"He has you there, Kai."*

Delwyn swam back to his own sponge and closed his eyes. *"I'm going to retreat into another vision for a while."*

Kai and Dax followed him and settled themselves on either side of him. Kai wrapped him in a familiar embrace and stroked his chest and abdomen. The pain in his gut receded slightly at the tender touch.

Nestled between the two lovers, Delwyn concentrated on Finn for the first time in months. He couldn't see him in the present, but what he wanted to see had already taken place. It was a vision Delwyn had observed several times.

Finn had been on land for a few months and already shared his bed with his two lovers, but Delwyn didn't enjoy watching the trio have sex. Instead he enjoyed observing the men as they swam in the indoor body of water which he understood was inside their home.

Mermen were only ever truly happy in water and even though Finn and his merman lover had made lives for themselves on land, they never strayed far from the water.

Delwyn watched them splashing and playing while their human lover watched them from his seat at the edge of the pool.

As one they turned to their third, darted through the water and pulled the human in with them.

They laughed and squealed, before they kissed, all three of them together.

Delwyn usually stopped watching at this point. It always hurt to see Finn become intimate with his lovers. Yet somehow, this time, he didn't feel the same pang of envy at what his oldest friend had found.

When the three lovers exited the pool, Delwyn ended the vision and concentrated on another moment with Finn, this time an event where he had been present, and one he had never looked back on until now.

Finn and Delwyn were in the temple of the Goddess of Love underneath the palace. Their guards waited outside. Even though the two mermen communicated privately, Delwyn could remember the conversation as though it was yesterday.

"It's been a year," Delwyn said. "I don't think she's going to answer."

Finn frowned stubbornly, his lower lip sticking out in a pout. "I'm not giving up."

"Even if she does answer you, it won't make any difference," Delwyn argued. "Your father still won't let the Oracles out of the city."

"Or me," Finn muttered. "Why do my parents insist on treating me like a child?"

"I don't know. Maybe in a year or two, when they've seen how painful the mating season is for you, they'll relent."

"I hope so. And when I'm allowed up there, I want to go there with you."

Delwyn sighed. "You know it's not allowed. Even if Oracles

were allowed on land, I'm still a merman, and if you were allowed to mate with another merman, I'm still an Oracle. It's not just one law keeping us apart."

"You sound like you've given up on me, on us."

"I suppose it might sound that way. I'm resigned to my fate."

"I thought you loved me."

"I did. I do, which is why I'm asking you to forget about me and find someone else."

"I don't want anyone else."

"Maybe not right now, but I'm sure one day you will."

"No, I won't."

Delwyn watched himself chew on his lip, debating whether to tell Finn what Ula had seen in her vision. The mermaid with the power to see the future had sobbed as she'd told Delwyn there was no hope of him ever being with the young prince.

"I want you to be happy, Finn."

"You make me happy."

Delwyn wrapped his arms awkwardly round his best friend. Even a year later, he hadn't been entirely accustomed to his lack of vision. He hadn't needed to see Finn to know the merman had wept in his arms.

Delwyn's heart had broken that day. Distancing himself from Prince Finn had been the hardest thing he had ever done, especially at first, when he'd been able to see Finn missed him just as much. Now, having seen Finn with his two lovers, Delwyn knew he had made the right decision. Finn had found happiness with Kyle and Jake, and Delwyn was pleased for all of them. He hoped one day soon he would be similarly content.

Thoughts of the Atlantean he had watched in his last vision came to mind. He was startled to realize he harbored more jealousy toward Fabian's bed-mate than he ever had for Finn's lovers.

This time Delwyn ended his vision slowly. He could tell from their breathing that Kai and Dax slept. He snuggled between them and closed his eyes to get some rest himself.

It would be a while before he had the strength to go far enough into the past to see Fabian again, but he resolved to do so as soon as he could.

* * * *

Unlike the other two Oracles, Delwyn had been born and raised in the sunken city and his family still lived there.

Delwyn tried to visit his parents every few days, and if he was a little slack in his duties, they soon tracked him down.

"Has it really been six days?" Delwyn asked. *"It can't be."*

"I promise you, it is," his mother scolded. *"Did you forget to visit because of your excitement about spending your first mating season on land?"*

Delwyn rolled his eyes, earning himself a smack from his mother's fins.

"Or is it that you didn't want to explain to me why you decided to stay down here instead of breaking the mating fever?"

Delwyn should have known his mother would be aware of his decision without his having told her. Thankfully, she didn't require him to respond to her questions.

"All these years you've complained about not being allowed on land with the rest of us, and now, when the law has finally been changed, you stay here. You aren't still pining over Prince Finn, are you? He's long gone and he's not coming back here."

"I know he isn't."

"There are plenty of mermen in the city who would be delighted to help you lose your virginity."

"Mama!"

"I'm just saying. What's the name of that guard who can't take his eyes off you?"

"I don't know. I'm blind, remember?"

"Handsome merman, quite large, a very commanding presence."

Delwyn suspected she might be talking about Otus, but he didn't want to encourage her by giving her a name to cling to.

"Or there's that sweet young gatherer who always brings you

the choicest fruits of the harvest. He obviously favors you."

Delwyn reached out to snack on one of the fruits in question, only half listening to his mother rattling on beside him. She had been fussing over him all his life and he had long since become accustomed to her ways.

His mind drifted while she talked and, as he had been prone to do for the past few days, he began to think about Fabian again.

"Mama, can I ask you something?"

His mother stuttered to a halt in her relaying of his father's latest promotion within the palace. *"Of course, dear. What is it?"*

"Do you think I'm foolish to want to wait for someone who loves me before going to land?"

His mother waited several moments before she answered. *"No, you're not a fool. But, Delwyn, who are you waiting for?"*

"I don't know. Someone special. Someone who loves me."

"You've spent too much time reading the stories in the old Atlantean buildings. All those tales of romantic heroes have built your hopes up too high. You're waiting for something that just isn't real."

"Love is real. Just look at you and father. You've been mates for years and you've never taken other lovers."

"That's different."

"Why is it?"

"Because it is."

Delwyn shook his head and groaned at a typical answer from his mother.

"You'll find the right merman for you, but not if you aren't trying. You need to start looking around you, at the mermen who are right here with you. It's no good waiting for some idealistic romantic hero to come sweep you off your fins, because it's never going to happen. One day, you'll realize you're going to have to settle for an ordinary merman, else you'll spend your entire life alone."

"What if I don't want to settle?"

His mother hugged him tightly. *"I hope you will soon.*

You've said it yourself, having visions on the night of the solstice only helps the pain so much. I hate to think of my baby boy suffering, and it's going to get worse. Please, Delwyn, take up the offer of one of the mermen before even the visions can't help you get through the mating season."

"I'll think about it," Delwyn promised.

* * * *

It took a few more days before Delwyn judged his powers sufficiently restored enough for him to see far enough into the past, to the time when Fabian had lived.

King Nereus wouldn't have been pleased if he'd discovered Delwyn was having such exhausting visions without any set purpose, but he had no intention of letting the ruler of the city find out.

Delwyn concentrated on the Atlantean and within a few moments he hovered behind him.

Fabian kneeled on the stone floor of the temple of the Oracles. A man and a woman were on their knees beside him. Their heads were bowed and they seemed oblivious to their surroundings.

On the far side of them, Cari sat on her throne, smiling softly.

Delwyn wondered for a moment if Cari was aware of his presence. When the goddess stared right at him and gave a small nod, he guessed that answered his question.

"Thank you, my Oracles," Cari said. "You have done well."

Delwyn wondered what they had been doing. It certainly wasn't something he had ever seen before.

The three Oracles stood and turned to leave. Two of them passed by Delwyn as though he wasn't even there, but Fabian stumbled the moment he spotted him.

"It's quite all right," Cari said and Fabian faced her. "I see him, too."

"I'd begun to wonder if I'd imagined him," Fabian

admitted.

"No." Cari walked down the steps from her throne and stood between them. "You are my Oracle of the present, Fabian. You are also a powerful demi-god in your own right. The powers you've inherited from your mother mean you can see a little more than other Oracles of your ilk. You can see *anything* happening in the present, including visitors such as Delwyn here."

"Delwyn." Fabian smiled at him and Delwyn's heart raced. His name sounded good on Fabian's lips.

"Delwyn is an Oracle, too," Cari continued. "He's able to see visions of the past."

"I thought there were only ever three Oracles serving you," Fabian asked.

"That's correct, but Delwyn here hasn't been born yet. He won't be chosen as one of my Oracles for many centuries."

"Centuries?"

"Yes. Delwyn lives in the future. Though he spends rather a lot of time nosing into the past, just as he is doing now. Only immortals can see him, and most will merely ignore him. Well, immortals and you, of course."

Delwyn was glad to hear he wasn't losing his mind and Fabian *could* see and hear him. He still had some questions, though. "Cari, are you the goddess from my time or Fabian's?"

"I'm both," Cari replied. "Though I haven't technically appointed you as one of my Oracles yet, I know one day I will do so, because I've seen it for myself."

"Am I allowed to be here?" Delwyn asked, gesturing to Fabian as he spoke.

"Yes, of course."

"Even though I could alter the past by communicating with Fabian?"

"You don't know what happened in the past, so what could you change?"

"Anything," Delwyn replied. "What if Fabian is supposed to be doing something right now instead of talking to us?"

Cari's light laugh echoed through the temple. "You worry too much, Delwyn. If you wish to talk with Fabian, I won't stop you from doing so. You might find you have a lot in common."

With those words, Cari vanished in a flash of light, leaving Delwyn and Fabian alone in the temple.

"An Oracle of the past, hmm?" Fabian said.

"And you're an Oracle of the present."

"Yes. One who thought he had imagined this sexy silver-finned merman who enjoyed watching me with my lover."

"I thought I was going insane, too," Delwyn admitted. "I tried to convince myself you hadn't spoken to me."

Fabian gestured for Delwyn to follow him from the temple. "I suppose you have questions for me? I certainly have some for you."

"Oh, yes. Are you really a demi-god?"

"Yes, my mother is Mariana, Goddess of Sea Creatures."

"And your father?"

"One of her priests, though I don't know which one he was. She sleeps with most of them."

"Was?"

"I'm not immortal, but I age slower than a regular human. My father is long since gone from this world."

"I'm sorry."

"Don't be. I never knew him, so it wasn't much of a loss."

"I'm still sorry. I can't imagine what it would be like not to know who my father is."

Fabian shrugged. "You don't miss what you never had. Come, let us go for a walk." He glanced at Delwyn's fins and smiled. "Or float, in your case."

Delwyn let Fabian guide him out of the temple and into the sunlight. There wasn't a single cloud in the clear blue sky.

"This way," Fabian said as he pointed to a path winding through beautifully sculpted flowerbeds.

Delwyn gazed about him with wonder. "Are we on the same island where I saw you before?"

"Yes, this is the Isle of the Gods, where they make their homes. Those bound to the gods are able to come here whenever we please and keep quarters on the island."

"By touching the crystal in the temple?"

"Yes. Though if one who isn't bound to a god tries to use the power it will do nothing."

Delwyn guessed that Cari had never told him or the other Oracles about this place so they could not have easy access to land, back when they hadn't been allowed to take lovers.

"It's beautiful here," Delwyn said.

"I'm glad you think so."

Fabian plucked a flower from one of the nearby plants and sniffed it. "Here, for you." He held it toward Delwyn.

"I can't touch it," Delwyn reminded him. "I've no more substance here than a shadow."

Fabian smiled and tucked the bloom into the belt of his robes. "Then I'll keep it for you until such time as I catch up with you."

"What do you mean?"

"As I said, I don't age as humans do. I will live for many more centuries yet, and I think I might like to see you again when I arrive in your time."

"You'll really live as long as that?"

"As long as I'm careful not to get eaten by a shark or something."

Delwyn snapped his fingers. "*That's* what's missing from the sunken city."

"What?"

"The sea dragons. They protect us from the sharks — at least they will one day. They aren't here in your time, though. I hadn't noticed, which is rather foolish of me, considering how enormous they are."

"They sound fearsome."

"They are." Delwyn shivered at the thought of the one that had come so close to devouring him. "But let us talk about something more pleasant."

"What do you want to discuss?" Fabian asked.

Delwyn's face heated and he lowered his gaze.

"What is it?" Fabian urged.

Delwyn avoided Fabian's eyes. "It's nothing. I shouldn't be so nosey."

"Now you have me intrigued, so you have to tell me."

Delwyn guessed there wasn't any harm in asking the question he most wanted the answer to. "Are you and Isander, um…?" Delwyn wasn't sure how to phrase his question. He already knew they were lovers—what he wanted to know was whether their relationship was serious or not.

"Are we what?" Fabian asked.

"Are you mates?" Delwyn blurted.

"You mean, are we committed and faithful to each other?"

"Yes."

Fabian laughed. "Do you think I'd be giving you flowers if we were?"

"I guess not, but you *are* lovers."

"Yes, occasionally, but we both take others into our bed when we wish to. If you were here in the flesh, I'd be inviting you to join me in my rooms, and I assure you, Isander wouldn't mind in the least, though he may wish to join us."

Delwyn's face heated again, only this time there was a warm feeling elsewhere as well, one he didn't want to focus on too closely, not while Fabian remained so far out of his reach.

Fabian smiled and they continued their walk, passing other priests and the occasional immortal. Delwyn spotted Medina reclining on cushions in a green clearing. Devoted followers surrounded her, hanging on her every word.

"That's Medina, Goddess of Love," Fabian commented.

"I know. I've met her."

"What did you think of her?" Fabian asked.

Delwyn had a feeling there might be more to the question than casual interest.

"She helps bring love into the world," he replied. "What's

not to like about that?"

"Just don't get on her bad side," Fabian warned. "She has a dreadful temper."

"Have you been the brunt of it?"

"I once let a gaggle of geese loose in her temple. She was furious about it and made me clean the place from top to bottom."

Delwyn laughed. "It could have been worse. Be thankful she didn't curse you."

"She'd never do that. I'm her favorite nephew."

"You are?"

"Yes. She and my mother are sisters, which makes her my Auntie Medi."

"Are your god powers the reason you aren't blind?"

Fabian gave him a confused glance. "What do you mean?"

"The Oracles are blind under water, unless we're having a vision."

"I've never heard of that happening before. I've never been blind, and I have no knowledge of any of those who came before me being so."

Delwyn, like all Oracles, had the collective memories of all the Oracles of the past who came before him. As far as he had known, they had all been blind when underwater. He concentrated on sifting through the memories of the older Oracles. He soon realized he had no way of telling the difference between visions and memories of something the Oracles had seen for themselves. What he had assumed were visions could easily have been actual memories.

He wondered when they had been inflicted with blindness. Were they being punished, or was it because they were mer?

He didn't have the answers and apparently, Fabian didn't, either.

The memory of Cari and the summoning of her mother, the Goddess of Fertility, came back to him. She had talked about how things had changed on a particular day. Oracle powers had become hereditary and sexual relations had subsequently been forbidden.

From what Delwyn had seen, the law hadn't yet been imposed. The gods who slept were still part of this world. The Atlanteans lived in the city, alongside the mer.

Whatever had happened on what the goddess referred to as *that day* hadn't yet come to pass.

"You seem deep in thought," Fabian commented. "Did I say something particularly interesting?"

"No." Delwyn shook his head before he thought about how his action might appear. "I mean, yes, I mean, er… Sorry, I didn't intend to drift off."

Fabian laughed. "Don't worry about it. I'm only teasing. You're no doubt wondering about the differences in your experience of being an Oracle and my own."

"Yes, I was. It seems things have changed a great deal since your time."

"What else has changed?"

Delwyn wondered how much he should say. Cari had told him he could talk to Fabian, yet he still hesitated. Telling Fabian about what was to come might be dangerous.

"You're worried about telling me something that might alter the future, aren't you?"

"How can you tell? Are you reading my mind?"

"No, just your face. Cari wouldn't have let you linger here if she thought you could tell me something I shouldn't know about."

"You sound sure about that."

Fabian sat on a nearby stone bench and patted the seat beside him. Delwyn waved his hand through the seat, reminding Fabian he couldn't interact with anything in this time.

"Delwyn, do you have faith in the gods?" Fabian asked.

"I believe in them, if that's what you mean."

"Of course you believe in them. You've seen them and spoken to them. I mean, do you trust their judgement?"

"I don't know. Do you?"

"Yes." Fabian gave his answer without hesitation.

Delwyn nodded, his mind made up. "Then that's good enough for me. Tell me what you want to know about the future."

Fabian grinned. "I guess my first question is whether we've met in your time." His face fell as he realized what he was saying. "We haven't, have we?"

"No, I'm afraid not. I wish we had."

Fabian frowned. "Maybe I'm not going to live as long as I thought. I can't imagine ever living anywhere except Atlantis."

"There are no humans living in the sunken city," Delwyn said. "Not a single one."

"What do you mean?"

"Only the mer live there now. The Atlanteans vanished from the city a long time ago."

"Then I must be somewhere else in the world. If I'm still alive, that is."

"I'm sure you are," Delwyn said, though he had no facts on which to base his conviction. "You're probably living amongst humans."

Fabian sighed. "I guess I'll have to come back to the city to find you, then. I just wish I knew when to make the journey."

"The mer have no way of marking time, but humans do."

"What are you thinking?" Fabian asked.

"There's a merman in the city who was raised on land."

"Do you think he could tell you the year you live in?"

"I know he could. Then all I have to do is come back here to you, tell you what he says, and you'll know exactly when to come back to the city to find me."

Delwyn knew he was getting ahead of himself, but now that the idea of finding Fabian in his own time had taken root in his mind he was determined to bring it about.

They talked for hours. Fabian showed Delwyn some of the nearby temples and introduced him to a few of the immortals. Only the gods could see him, as was obvious when others on the island snickered when they saw Fabian apparently talking to himself.

Delwyn in turn spoke of his life in the sunken city, his fellow Oracles and his family. He didn't talk about his feelings for Finn, though he couldn't have said why he chose to remain quiet on that subject.

Only when Delwyn recognized the start of a headache did he know his time was up.

"I've been in the vision too long," he said. "I'd better go back now."

"You'll visit again, yes?" Fabian asked.

"I promise. And make sure you save my flower for me."

They were in Fabian's chambers and he had placed the flower in water earlier. Now he waved his hand over the vase and whispered something Delwyn couldn't hear. "There, it is preserved forever."

"What?" Delwyn stared at the demi-god. *How powerful is this man?*

"This flower will never fade or die for as long as I draw breath."

Delwyn tried to reply, but he had already lingered far longer than he should. The vision ended almost as abruptly as his last visit to Fabian and he could tell it would be several days at least before he had the strength to come back to him again.

Chapter Six

Even though he couldn't go into the past, Delwyn had plenty to occupy his time the following day.

His paid an early visit to Justin, son of King Nereus and heir to the throne. Justin had been raised on land by Cari and her brother and was familiar with all things human.

"The date?" Justin asked.

"Yes, humans mark time by dates, don't they?"

"Yes, but the mer don't, so what difference does it make what date it is?"

"I just wondered." Delwyn didn't want to get sidetracked by talking about Fabian and his trips to visit the Atlantean in the past.

Justin made a sound of annoyance. *"You know, I'm not sure of the exact date now. I know what it was when I left England, but the days here do sort of blur together."*

"Can you guess?"

"Well, we've just had the December solstice, so we're in the winter."

"I know that. But what year is it?"

"Um, the end of 2016 or the start of 2017. Like I said, I lose track of the days now."

The numbers meant little to Delwyn and he hoped they made more sense to Fabian. He thanked Justin for his help and went to search for the temple of the Goddess of Sea Creatures.

Although he had been in the temple before, he had taken little notice of the furniture where the crystal used to transport people to the Isle of the Gods had been. He had preferred to study the paintings and carvings on the walls, reading the stories of the ancient Atlanteans.

Only later had he discovered that his innate knowledge of the ancient language of the Atlanteans was a sign that he would one day be an Oracle. He had merely thought it his special gift. He realized now that without his linguistic talents, he would have been unable to understand anything Fabian said to him.

He went to the temple alone. Kai would help him search for the crystal if he asked him, but he wanted to try to find it by himself first.

He fumbled about the temple while his guard waited outside. The servant wouldn't question what he did.

It took him quite a while, but eventually he found the smooth stone of the crystal and pressed his thumb to it.

At first, he thought it no longer worked. He certainly wasn't whisked away to the beautiful paradise island as he had been before.

He was about to give up when he fell to the ground in a heap.

"Yeah, that was graceful," Delwyn muttered as he waited for his tail to dry and his legs to appear.

The world shimmered into focus when his vision returned. The room he found himself in was barely recognizable as the same place he had visited while following Fabian and Isander. A thick layer of dust covered everything and weeds had crept through the cracks in the stones. The place seemed neglected, much like the sunken city itself.

Delwyn headed outside to see how the rest of the isle had fared.

Tears welled in his eyes as he saw the devastation around him.

The beautiful gardens had gone, replaced by weeds and tall grass. No one seemed to have been here in centuries. Nature had begun to reclaim the buildings around them, swallowing them up until, in a few more centuries, nothing would remain at all.

He wondered if he had made a mistake in coming here.

Still, he *was* here now and he might never have another chance to see if his present from Fabian had survived. He tried not to dwell on the thought that if the flower had died, it meant Fabian had, too.

He hurried through the overgrowth, taking a few wrong turns in the changed surroundings.

The place was completely deserted. Even the birds had flown away. When he arrived at Cari's temple, right on the edge of where the two parts of the isle joined, Delwyn could see from the outside that hers was one of the better kept buildings, though it still had a slight air of abandonment about it.

Delwyn found Fabian's quarters and slipped inside. The room hadn't changed much, though the dust had gathered here as well. Delwyn climbed onto the bed and settled into the same spot Fabian had been in while they had talked. Had it really only been yesterday?

The shelf built into the wall opposite still held the small carved ornaments Delwyn had glanced over during his visit. And there, right in the center, were the bright rainbow petals of the flower Fabian had picked for him.

Delwyn's eyes watered with tears of relief. The bloom still lived, which meant Fabian did, too. All Delwyn had to do was find him.

Somewhere, out there in the vast expanse of the world, Fabian carried on with his life, with no idea Delwyn was now alive and eager to find him.

He closed his eyes and smiled as he drifted off to sleep.

* * * *

He woke to the sound of a female voice and a nudge on his shoulder. When he opened his eyes, Cari stood beside the bed.

The sky outside had darkened and he wondered how much time had passed.

"It's nearly dawn," Cari said in answer to his unspoken

question.

"You do know it's annoying when you read my thoughts." Delwyn rubbed sleep out of his eyes.

"Yes," Cari replied with a smile that told Delwyn she clearly wasn't bothered. "Do you have any idea how much worry you've caused Ula and Kai?"

"I fell asleep," Delwyn said. "I didn't mean to be gone so long. Besides, Kai can use his powers to see I'm okay."

"Oh, he did use his powers," Cari informed him. "He saw you sleeping in an unfamiliar human building which he had no idea existed. With no clue how to find his way to you, he thought maybe you'd left the city."

"Oh dear."

"Yes, quite. His panic was strong enough to summon me to him. I searched for you myself and recognized Fabian's rooms."

Delwyn rolled over and swung his legs onto the floor. "I'll go back right away and assure them I'm well."

Cari raised a hand. "Not yet. We need to talk."

He supposed he should have expected this. "You said I could talk to him," he reminded the goddess.

"Yes, I know."

"Am I in trouble for doing so, now you've changed your mind?"

"Who says I've changed my mind?"

"You mean I can carry on talking to him?"

"Of course."

"How much can I tell him? What if we change the future somehow?"

Cari sat beside him. "You may tell him whatever you wish. The future, that is Fabian's future, cannot be changed so easily. He's Atlantean and his people were banished from the city long ago. There is nothing you can say or do to change that. It's out of your hands, just as it was out of mine."

"Where did the Atlanteans go?"

"They were scattered all over the world," Cari replied.

"They retained no memories of the city, the mer or the gods."

"And Fabian?"

"You know I can't tell you anything specific about him, not when your life has already touched his."

"Why not?" Delwyn whined. "You obviously know something about him I don't."

"I know many things about him that you are unaware of. It doesn't mean I can tell you."

Cari wrapped her arm around his shoulders and gave him a quick hug. "Fabian was one of my most devoted Oracles. When he pledged his life to me, I took a peek into his future and saw you there."

"Is that why you chose me as an Oracle?" Delwyn had never understood why he had been picked above all others.

"It was your destiny, but yes, as soon as I saw you swimming through my temple with Prince Finn, I recognized you as my future Oracle."

"Because you'd seen me with Fabian?"

"Yes."

"You see so much."

"My visions show me nearly everything," Cari said. She didn't sound happy about it.

"Nearly?"

"There are some things even a Goddess of Prophecy doesn't see coming, not until it's too late, anyway."

Delwyn wondered what, but something about the goddess's demeanor kept him from asking.

"I want to visit him again," Delwyn whispered. "I don't know why, but something draws me to him."

Cari smiled and it was as though her sadness evaporated in a moment. "Of course you do. He's very handsome, isn't he?"

"Um…" It was awkward talking about Fabian in such a way with the goddess. Cari had been almost a second mother to him.

Cari chuckled and nudged him on the arm with her elbow.

"I'll stop embarrassing you. Besides, you should go back to the city now. There are a couple of Oracles there who you should probably apologize to."

"I will. There's one more question I want to ask, though."

"About your blindness?"

"Yes."

Cari sighed. "I'm afraid only true Atlanteans can become Oracles and retain their sight. Mer, and even humans of other races, lose their vision when they are bound to me."

"Then it's not because the mer are being punished."

"No, my darling boy. I would never do such a thing."

Delwyn understood. He reached up to the shelf and stroked one of the petals of his flower. "The dust settled on everything except this."

"That's because it has been preserved by the power of the gods."

"Fabian is only a demi-god, though."

"Nevertheless, his powers are strong enough to work this piece of magic."

"Will it survive if I take it back to the sunken city?" Delwyn asked.

"Yes, of course."

Delwyn picked it up and sniffed the pollen. "It smells as though it's just been plucked."

"And it will forever, though you might find the scent somewhat dulled when underwater. You can leave it here if you wish. I won't stop you visiting the isle."

Delwyn studied the room for a moment before shaking his head. "I don't think I'll come back here again, not in the present, anyway."

"It's too empty," Cari agreed as she stood and walked to the door. "This place once teemed with life. Now, only the ghosts remain."

"Don't the other gods visit here?" Delwyn asked.

"Medina has been back a few times, but most of the others stay away. This place is a reminder of what we used to have, when most of my kind would rather forget. Come, you can return to the city through my temple. You'll find it easier and quicker than using Mariana's. Although the stones in any god's temple will work for anyone who is bound to any immortal, the ones belonging to the goddess you are bound to will always work best for you."

They continued in silence until Cari showed Delwyn where to find the crystal that would take him back to the sunken city. He thanked Cari and touched his thumb to the stone. His vision blurred as he found himself underwater. He caught a quick glimpse of Kai and Ula before his legs became fins and he was blind once more.

"Where have you been all night?" Kai shouted into his mind. *"We've been going out of our minds with worry."*

"I'm sorry," Delwyn replied. *"I fell asleep."*

"Well, it's nice to hear someone got to sleep last night," Ula said. *"Some of us spent the night swimming all over the city trying to find a missing merman."*

"I didn't mean to fall asleep."

"Where were you?" Kai asked. Delwyn knew Kai's anger stemmed from worry, and now Delwyn was safe, curiosity was at the forefront of his thoughts. *"I saw you in some sort of human building on land. Yet Cari told us to wait for you here."*

"I was on the Isle of the Gods," Delwyn explained. *"Those who are bound to the gods, like we are, can travel there by placing our thumbs to the crystals."*

"You mean you've had a way to travel to land all this time?" Ula asked. Delwyn could hear the fury in her voice. *"We could have gone there at any time during the mating seasons."*

"If I'd known about it then, I supposed we could have," Delwyn admitted. *"But I only found out about it myself recently."*

"How did you find out?" Kai asked. *"In a vision?"*

"Yes. I saw a couple of Atlantean men using it in the past. I wanted to see if it still worked."

"Well, now you know it does," Ula snapped, and Delwyn could practically see her tapping her fingers and shaking her fins in frustration.

Thankfully, Kai calmed down and Delwyn felt his fellow

merman wrap his arms around him in a tight embrace. *"Leave him alone, Ula. He's home now, and that's all that matters."*

"You were even more worried than me," Ula reminded him.

"I know, but I don't want us to argue."

Delwyn hugged Kai back. He had always appreciated his ability to smooth things over and act as peacemaker between him and Ula. Even though they weren't related by blood, Ula was very much a sister to the both of them, but unfortunately she and Delwyn fought like siblings, too.

Ula sighed and muttered something rather uncomplimentary about idiotic mermen, which Delwyn pretended not to hear.

* * * *

Kai didn't leave Delwyn's side for the rest of the day. Every time the merman moved, he seemed to bang into Kai.

"I'm not going to disappear again," Delwyn assured him. *"I just thought I'd go take a swim through the market."*

"I'll come with you," Kai said.

Delwyn didn't bother to argue with him. He liked Kai's company more than anyone else's in the sunken city.

"Are you going to tell me his name?" Kai asked as soon as they swam out in the open.

"What?"

"I thought perhaps you didn't want to say anything in front of Ula, but I think it's pretty obvious you've been daydreaming about some merman for most of the day."

Delwyn laughed. *"There's no merman for me to be dreaming over."*

For some reason, Delwyn was reluctant to talk about Fabian with Kai. He wanted to keep the Atlantean to himself for a little while longer.

"I don't believe you," Kai said. *"I can always tell when you're lying. You blush so prettily."*

"I do not!"

"Yes, you do," Kai teased. *"But if you insist on keeping your secrets, I suppose I have no choice. I'll be watching to see which mermen are favoring you these days. I'll figure it out eventually. After all, your soulmate is just around the corner."*

"What do you mean?" Delwyn asked.

"Don't you remember what Medina told me before I left on my journey with Dax? The merman for you is already here in the city."

Delwyn frowned as he recalled the conversation. If Medina had been correct, that meant Fabian wasn't the one for him. There were no Atlanteans left in the sunken city. It was impossible for one to have hidden here for all these centuries without being seen.

"What's wrong?" Kai asked. *"You look deep in thought."*

"Nothing." Delwyn shook his head and forced a smile to his face.

Kai let it go and they wandered through the market stalls, sampling food and chatting with the vendors.

He's a demi-god! Delwyn smacked his forehead with the palm of his hand. *How could I have missed it?*

The gods and goddesses of the Atlanteans slept, or at least most of them did. Fabian, a half-god himself, had to be sleeping with the rest of them. That would explain why Medina had said he was in the sunken city, a place where no humans now lived. Now that the immortals were waking, it meant sooner or later Fabian would rise and Delwyn could meet him in the flesh.

Delwyn recalled how summoning a god through their given name gave them the strength needed to waken. He knew Fabian's name already. He just had to find out where to call for him. The two obvious places were Fabian's mother's temple and that of the Goddess of Prophecy. He resolved to call out for him in both before he had another vision of the past. Seeing Fabian in the present was far preferable to watching him centuries ago. Even though he had enjoyed talking to him, he found the idea of touching him far more enticing.

Chapter Seven

Fabian kneeled before the goddess' throne. His fellow Oracles sat to his right, Hiron beside him and Astrid at Hiron's other side. Behind them, the rest of Cari's priests and priestesses lined up on their knees, heads bowed in supplication. At the back of the room, a crowd of Atlanteans formed the rest of the congregation. It wasn't often any of the immortals chose to show themselves to humans who had not bound themselves to the gods, but this was a special occasion. Today, Cari would be choosing a new priest to replace one who had passed away a few days before. The Atlanteans were curious to know which of them would be chosen for the honor.

Only two beings knew the identity of the new priest — Hiron, as the Oracle with the power to see the future, and Cari herself. Fabian had asked Hiron to tell him who would be chosen, but he had refused to reveal what he had seen. Fabian had not pressed him. Hiron had always kept his own counsel when it came to such things. Fabian simply lived in hope that one day he might let something slip.

Astrid, the Oracle of the Past, tried to stifle a yawn as they waited for their goddess to appear. Fabian hoped it would be soon, because his knees were starting to ache from his position on the cold stone floor. He idly wondered if he might be getting old, before dismissing the thought with a rueful smile. He hadn't aged a day in decades.

Finally, the gasp of the crowd behind him signaled the arrival of the goddess. She appeared in a flash of light, seated on her throne, her shimmering white gown flowing to the floor.

"Thank you for coming to witness the birth of my new priest," Cari announced. Her voice rang clear in the minds of everyone in the underwater city. She always referred to the anointing of her priests as a birth, saying they had left their old lives behind to begin anew.

Fabian had certainly begun a new life the day he had sworn his oath to the goddess. There had been no turning back, even if his mother still tried to convince him to forsake his vow and swear loyalty to her instead.

The priest who had died had not been the only one to lose his life in the shark attack. Two regular Atlanteans had also been killed, as well as one of his mother's priests.

Fabian had already received a summons from Mariana and he couldn't put off visiting her much longer. As soon as Cari's ceremony ended, his mother would be expecting him. The pain in his legs from kneeling so long would be preferable to yet another argument with the Goddess of Sea Creatures.

* * * *

Fabian walked to his mother's palace on the Isle of the Gods. He set a leisurely pace, putting off the confrontation for as long as he could. As he wandered through the gardens he spied the familiar rainbow flowers. He smiled when he recalled the merman he had impulsively picked one for. Even now, more than a season later, the bloom remained fresh. Although he rarely used his powers, he didn't regret magically preserving the flower. It had been worth it to see Delwyn's smile.

He wondered if he would see the merman again. At first he had expected him to appear at any given moment, but when the days passed without any sign of him, Fabian wondered if perhaps the novelty of talking to someone from the past had worn off.

As he approached his mother's home, Fabian pushed all thoughts of Delwyn from his mind. His mother had never been shy about prying into his private thoughts and the forthcoming discussion would be difficult enough, without bringing her prejudices against the mer into it, as well.

Fabian bowed in the archway to Mariana's pool. "It's about time," Mariana complained. "I expected you to come immediately I sent for you."

"I had duties to attend to first," Fabian replied. "I came as soon as I could afterwards."

"Duties to *her*, I suppose."

Fabian didn't bother to answer. He had no intention of being goaded into a fight.

Mariana rose from her chaise and glided across the room. Her red hair shimmered when it caught the sunlight through the windows. "You will know I lost one of my priests in the shark attack."

"I'm aware of that and am sorry for your loss."

"His death leaves an opening for a new priest to join my ranks."

"Or a priestess," Fabian said, knowing his mother would never raise a female so high. Despite being a woman herself, she was remarkably prejudiced toward her own gender. Or, Fabian admitted, it was more likely she preferred to have male priests so she had fewer rivals on the isle for their attention.

"You know I prefer to be served by men."

Fabian nodded and held his tongue.

Mariana picked up two flutes of wine and handed one to him. "Are you ready to take your rightful place yet? Can we finally drink a toast to your new appointment and have done with this?"

"I'm already bound to a goddess," Fabian told her — not that she needed the reminder. The whole isle had shaken with her anger when she had found out what he had done.

"You are *my* son, not hers."

"Nevertheless, I have sworn my life to her."

"Were you mortal, your life would have been snuffed out long ago. You're my only child — you should be my second-in-command."

Fabian had always suspected his birth had been some kind of slip-up. How he didn't have dozens of half-siblings had been a mystery he had often pondered on when growing up. His mother didn't have a maternal bone in her body.

"Fabian, darling," his mother wheedled. "Were you to pledge your loyalty to me, I would reward you with more power than you could ever imagine. Anything you desire would be within your grasp. Think about it. And all you have to do is take your rightful place at my side."

At your feet is more like it. Not that Fabian had any problem bowing to the gods — he often kneeled in the temples of not only Cari, but many of the other immortals, too. His mother didn't just want his loyalty, though. She wanted to be able to control him.

Fabian put his glass down without taking a drink. "Choose your new priest from amongst your followers."

"I *could* appoint you without your permission," Mariana commented with a sly glance from the corner of her eye.

"Not without bringing the wrath of Cari and her family down on you," Fabian reminded her. "I don't think you're rash enough to invoke their fury, not for this."

Mariana flung her glass across the room, shattering it to pieces as it hit the wall. "What will it take to make you see sense?"

Fabian didn't cringe at her shout or bother to answer her question.

"Whatever you want, it's yours for the taking," Mariana said. "Let me see…"

Fabian, as a demi-god, could tell when an immortal pried into his thoughts, even if he could do nothing about it. He tried to put up walls to keep his private thoughts to himself, but he could tell it was too late when his mother let loose a scream of pure rage.

"You want to bed a fish?"

"A merman," Fabian snapped. "They are wholly human on land, as well you know."

"You could have any man or woman you want. Even immortals would fall into your bed at the snap of your fingers."

"I'm not going to have this discussion with you." Fabian turned to leave.

"You *will* take your place at my side," Mariana shouted. "It's only a matter of time."

"Don't you understand yet? I don't *want* to be at your side. I wish to walk my own path. And, yes, I want to be with the merman you saw when you intruded in my private thoughts. And take that sour expression off your face. You're the Goddess of Sea Creatures, and in case you've forgotten, the mer are creatures of the sea. You should be embracing them instead of looking down on them as you do."

"If they remembered their place, I wouldn't look down on them."

"Their place is Atlantis. It was their waters before you and the rest of the gods sank the city beneath the waves. They've been nothing but welcoming to the Atlanteans. Why do you hate them so much?"

"I don't hate them at all, but they need to remember their place. The mer should never presume to share their bodies with a god."

"I'm only a demi-god, and if I choose to bed a merman, that's my decision. He would be far more welcome in my bed than most of the gods."

Mariana swept away and vanished into thin air as she strode across the room.

Fabian guessed his visit was over, and with a sigh of relief he hurried from the palace.

Once outside, he took several deep breaths to calm down. He and his mother had never seen eye to eye over the mer, but today she had spewed even more venom than usual. He wondered whether it was simply because of what she had seen in his head, or whether something else had happened.

He pondered on the mystery for only a short while. He

had long since ceased to care why his mother did or said anything.

Fabian made his way back to his quarters across the other side of the isle and when he arrived he was delighted to see a familiar set of silver fins near his bed.

"Delwyn?"

The merman turned and smiled at him. "Do you know any other mermen who float around as I do?"

Fabian laughed. "I was beginning to think I'd never see you again. It's been so long since you were last here."

"Nine days isn't so long," Delwyn replied.

"It may have been nine days for you, but it's been somewhat longer for me."

Delwyn frowned. "I guess the accuracy of my visions isn't as good as it could be."

"Most likely you're too tired," Fabian said. "You look as if you're not getting enough sleep."

"Oh, don't you start," Delwyn muttered. "My fellow Oracles have been nagging me about spending too much time, too far in the past. I'm perfectly well."

Fabian raised his hands in surrender. "I'm not going to argue with you. I'm just happy to see you again."

Delwyn smiled brightly and pointed to the flower on the shelf. "It's survived all the way to my time. I found it sitting right there where it is now."

"Really?" Although Fabian had hoped for that, he was quite surprised. Surely someone would have moved it at some point during the centuries that had passed.

Delwyn nodded. "It smells as gorgeous in the twenty-first century as I'm sure it does here."

Fabian's legs buckled as he stumbled to the bed. "What century?" he asked.

"It's the year 2017 now, at least according to human calendars."

Fabian recovered from his shock long enough to realize what Delwyn had said. "So many years I'm going to have to wait before I come to find you."

"I don't think you'll need to," Delwyn replied. "The Goddess of Love says my soulmate is already in the sunken city. I just need to find *you*."

"You think I'm your soulmate?" Fabian asked. He gave a small chuckle that he quickly tried to hide on seeing Delwyn's crestfallen expression.

Delwyn flicked at his fins with his fingers in an obvious nervous gesture.

Fabian was immediately contrite for his thoughtless reaction. His first instinct was to take the merman into his arms and give him a hug. Unfortunately that was impossible, at least for the moment.

"I'm sorry," he offered instead. "I didn't mean to laugh."

Delwyn accepted his apology, but he didn't seem his usual bright self. Fabian tried again.

"I'm afraid I just don't believe in such things," Fabian admitted. "I've lived a lot longer than you, and I suppose I'm rather jaded."

"It doesn't matter," Delwyn replied. "It's a foolish notion. I understand that. I just thought…"

"It's not foolish," Fabian said. "Aunt Medi has always told me I'm far too cynical for my own good. She believes in soulmates. I nearly bound myself to her rather than Cari, when I was young and idealistic."

Delwyn arched an eyebrow. "Really?"

"Yes, *really*. Is it so hard to believe?" Fabian laughed. "I liked the idea of uniting lovers and my aunt was eager to try to teach me how to spot souls who were destined to be together. Unfortunately, I was a poor student."

"How did you end up becoming an Oracle?" Delwyn asked. "I just got chosen by Cari. Was it the same for you?"

"Not exactly. Although most are chosen by the goddess, as a demi-god, I chose my calling for myself. I always liked Cari, and the way she welcomes both the Atlanteans and the merpeople into her temple. Not all the gods are so accommodating. My mother would be furious if a mer dared to poke a fin into her temple. If she had known you were in Isander's quarters I shudder to think what she would have done."

"What can she do when I'm not really here?" Delwyn asked.

"She's a goddess, and immortals have infinite patience when it comes to their vengeance. All she would have to do is wait until your twenty-first century and find you there."

"Cari won't let her hurt me," Delwyn replied. "Besides, she'll probably have forgotten about me by then."

"Let's hope so," Fabian said. "Now, how are you planning on finding me in your time?"

Delwyn brightened and grinned. "I think you must be sleeping with the rest of the Atlantean immortals, most of them at least."

Fabian recalled what Delwyn had told him during their last day together, about how the gods and goddesses were now waking from what seemed to be centuries of sleeping. He had no idea what had happened to cause them to sleep in such a way. As a demi-god he supposed it was possible he might be in a similar sort of stasis, even if he had never truly embraced his god side.

"I need to find a way to wake you," Delwyn said. "I already tried calling you by name in Cari's temple and the one belonging to your mother, but nothing happened."

Fabian found himself rather grateful nothing had occurred when Delwyn had entered his mother's temple. The shocking idea of a merman in her sanctuary apparently wasn't enough to wake her from her slumber.

"Do you have loyalties to any other gods, or your own temple?" Delwyn asked.

"I don't have any worshippers. While my birth means I have divided loyalties, my primary bond is with Cari."

Delwyn frowned. "Cari never went to sleep, so I wonder why you did."

"She didn't?"

Delwyn shook his head. "Some of the immortals stayed in the world, but from what I've seen, they were only minor ones."

"Aunt Medi wouldn't agree with being called minor," Fabian told him.

"She's only recently awoken," Delwyn replied.

Fabian didn't know what to suggest. If he was sleeping somewhere within Atlantis, he had no idea where that might be, or how Delwyn could go about the task of finding him.

A cough from the doorway drew Fabian's attention away from the merman.

"Isander," Fabian greeted his lover with a smile.

"Oh, you do remember my name at least," Isander teased. "Did you forget our plans to meet for the midday meal?"

Fabian cringed. It had completely slipped his mind. "I'm sorry."

Isander laughed and flopped down onto the bed. "I can see how staring into space might be preferable to being with me. No, wait, I can't see that at all."

Fabian glanced at Delwyn.

"I should go," Delwyn said.

"No!" Fabian shook his head and ignored the curious expression on Isander's face. "You don't have to leave."

"I wasn't planning on going anywhere," Isander replied.

Fabian rolled his eyes at Isander. "I wasn't talking to you."

Isander stared about the room deliberately. "Then who *are* you talking to?"

Delwyn raised an eyebrow and folded his arms across his chest.

Fabian shrugged and faced Isander again. "I have a visitor, an Oracle of the past, who is visiting me from the distant future."

Isander howled with laughter. "Of course you do."

"I'm perfectly serious," Fabian insisted. "His name is Delwyn and he's a merman. He's standing — er, make that floating — right here beside me."

Isander continued to chuckle. "You're not going to fool me into believing such a fanciful tale."

"It's the truth. He's visited here twice before. The first time, he watched us having sex."

Delwyn flushed and glared at Fabian.

"Well, you did!" Fabian reminded him. "There's no use denying it."

"I didn't expect you tell your lover I'd been watching the two of you," Delwyn complained. "It's embarrassing."

"Isander won't mind," Fabian assured him. "It's a rare occasion when I'm the only man in his bed. He's insatiable."

Isander choked as his mirth came to an abrupt halt.

"You aren't going to deny it, are you?" Fabian asked.

Delwyn smiled at Isander even though the priest couldn't see him. "Tell him I'm sorry for spying on you."

"There's no need to be sorry," Fabian said. "I didn't mind and I'm sure Isander doesn't, either."

"That's not the point," Delwyn replied. "I shouldn't have done such a thing without your permission. Kai always scolds me for being a voyeur."

Isander sat up and peered toward Delwyn, squinting and scowling. "There really *is* a merman in here with us?"

"Yes," Fabian answered. "Just as I've been telling you. Delwyn, this is Isander. Isander, say good day to Delwyn."

The two men offered awkward greetings to each other.

"What does he look like?" Isander asked. "You said he's floating."

"He is. He's in his mer form right now. He has short brown hair floating around his face, as though he were still underwater."

"I am underwater," Delwyn reminded him. "At least my physical body is."

Fabian nodded to indicate he had heard him. "He has silver fins and the eyes to match."

"Is he handsome?" Isander asked.

"He is most pleasing to the eye," Fabian replied with a wink at Delwyn. "I intend to search for him in his own time when I catch up with him."

Isander snorted. "He must be gorgeous if you intend to

go to such lengths to see him again."

"He is."

"Typical," Isander muttered. "I'll be long dead before I ever have the chance to see him."

Fabian smiled to himself. He was uncharacteristically pleased at the idea of keeping Delwyn for his own.

Isander clapped his hands together. "Not that I truly want to change the subject from that of a handsome merman, but I wanted to ask you what you'd done to upset your mother this time."

"What makes you think *I'm* the cause of her anger?" Fabian asked.

"Are you denying it?"

"No, but the smallest thing seems to send her into a fury these days."

"Her temper tantrums are always far worse when it's *you* who has caused them." Isander gave a rueful shake of his head. "Today is one of the worst for a long while."

Fabian sighed. "I refused her offer to take a position as one of her priests."

"Is that all? You've had the same argument with her how many times before?"

"Too many to count."

"I thought perhaps something else might have happened."

"She poked into my thoughts—again—and didn't like what she saw." Fabian gave a subtle nod toward Delwyn.

"Ah." Isander grinned. "I guess some of those thoughts you've been having about this merman involve him being in his human form."

"Oh, yes."

Fabian could tell the moment Delwyn understood what they were speaking about. The merman's face and neck reddened once more. If they embarrassed him any further, Fabian suspected he might blush all the way down to his fins.

At the merman's reaction, the most unexpected thought popped into Fabian's mind. Delwyn seemed so innocent.

He believed in soulmates, he spied on other men when they made love — *could he still be untouched?*

He wanted to ask, but they had already embarrassed the poor merman enough for one day.

"I should go home," Delwyn said.

"Will you come back again soon?" Fabian asked.

"He's not leaving, is he?" Isander interrupted. "I don't mind him staying with us."

"I'm tired," Delwyn explained. "I've been here too long already. Seeing so far into the past for so long takes a lot out of me."

Fabian understood that problem, though from his perspective it was distance that made the visions tiring. Seeing something nearby took relatively little effort, yet to see the other side of the world was exhausting.

"Come back soon," he said.

"I promise," Delwyn assured him before he faded out of sight.

"Is he gone?" Isander asked.

"Yes, but I'm sure he'll be back before too long."

Isander pulled Fabian down onto the bed and took him into his arms. "Maybe next time we can give him a show, a preview of what he can expect when you find him in his own time."

Fabian nipped on Isander's ear. "We already did, remember?" he teased.

Isander laughed and rolled Fabian onto his back. "I can't believe you didn't tell me we had a voyeur at the time."

"And distract you from your task of pleasuring me?" Fabian laughed and untied the belt of his robes, pushing the material aside.

Isander did the same with his own clothing and they were soon flesh to flesh, moving together with a well-practiced rhythm.

Fabian tried not to think about Delwyn, but it was remarkably hard to push him from his mind. Those shining silver eyes already burned in his memory.

He knew Isander could tell he was distracted, but he didn't say anything to him about it. He simply made love to him the way he had always done.

Chapter Eight

Delwyn knew exactly why Kai had practically dragged him up to the island the mer used during the mating season. It was because he didn't want him disappearing into a vision of the past in an attempt to avoid the conversation Delwyn knew was coming.

Kai paced the beach as Delwyn waited for his fins to dry off so he could stand eye to eye with Kai.

"We're worried about you," Kai began.

"There's no need to be." Delwyn tried to cut him off before he started, but Kai wasn't having any of it.

"I know you enjoy looking into the past, but you've not usually gone back this far, or this frequently. You're tiring yourself out too much."

"I don't go back so far again until I've fully rested," Delwyn argued.

"Only because you can't," Kai said. "You wait until the moment you've recovered and go back again immediately. And you're not going back for short periods, either. We've all noticed how long you've been lost in your visions."

Delwyn tried to brush off his concerns again, but Kai didn't want to listen.

"What's so fascinating to you in the past?" Kai asked.

"I've always liked seeing the past, you know that."

"Yes, but this is different. I don't know why, but it doesn't seem right. Are you traveling too far back in time?"

Delwyn shook his head. "I've been back farther than this before. I'm not even going back as far as the time when Atlantis was still an island."

"You aren't?" Kai's eyes widened in surprise. "I thought

perhaps you were, because you've been so tired recently."

"No, the city has sunk in the time I've been going back to."

Kai studied him closely. "It's the same time you're going back to each time you have a vision?"

Delwyn nodded. "Roughly, yes."

"Why?" Kai seemed to want to genuinely understand, but Delwyn wasn't sure anyone would, if he told them the truth. "What's drawing you back to that particular time period? Or should I say who?"

Delwyn flushed and immediately cursed his face for betraying him.

Kai pointed at him and grinned. "I *knew* it. You're going back to watch a particular merman, aren't you?"

"No." It wasn't a lie, because Fabian wasn't one of the mer.

Kai didn't believe him and Delwyn knew he would have to confess and tell him the whole truth.

"He's an Atlantean, not a merman," Delwyn admitted. "I like him and I think maybe he likes me a little, too."

Kai gaped at him. "How can he like you?"

"I'm not completely hideous, you know," Delwyn replied. "You never had any complaints about kissing me before you met Dax."

"That's not what I meant, and you know it. How can you know if he likes you when all you can do is watch him live a life that is long since over?"

Delwyn had to tell Kai the truth. He hoped he believed him. "Fabian can see me when I'm in his presence."

"What? How?"

"He's an Oracle of the present, just like you. He's also a half-god. His combined powers mean he can see and hear me."

"But you have no substance in the past. You can only observe. That's always been the case, otherwise you might be able to change the course of history."

"That was true until now. But Fabian is special."

"Does Cari know about what you're doing?" Kai asked. "I don't think she would be happy to hear about you messing things up in the past. You could alter the entire course of history."

Delwyn scowled at Kai's assumption that he would do such a thing. "Cari is well aware of my visits with Fabian. In fact, *she* introduced us after she realized Fabian could see me. She trusts I won't do anything to change history."

"And she has no problem with you tiring yourself out to visit this Fabian?"

"No."

"Are you sure about that?" Kai asked. "Does she even know how much you're exhausting yourself?"

"She's the Goddess of Prophecy. She sees everything in the past, present and future. I'm quite sure that if she had a problem with anything I've done, she'd tell me about it."

Kai continued to grumble. "Maybe she hasn't yet seen how your visions of the past are affecting you."

"I'm fine and you need to stop worrying about me. I enjoy going into the past and talking with Fabian."

"You're falling in love with him, aren't you?" Kai asked. He didn't sound happy about the idea.

"What if I am? He's strong, kind, amusing, and he's gorgeous, and he thinks I'm handsome, too."

"He's something else, too," Kai said. "Dead!"

"No, he isn't."

"He's an Atlantean who lived so far in the past it's exhausting you to visit him. Here, in your actual life, he's dead."

"He's a demi-god and he's alive today. I just need to find him."

Kai stared at him in confusion. "What do you mean?"

Delwyn flushed. "He gave me a flower in the past and he used his powers to preserve it for me. It will remain just as it was when he picked it so long as he lives."

"And where's this miracle flower?"

"It's in my chambers. When we go back to the city, you

can see it for yourself. It's as fresh as it was the day he picked it, which means he still lives."

"If that's the case, where is he?"

"I've no idea. I'm still working on that."

"Medina said your soulmate was here in the sunken city," Kai reminded him. "You know as well as I do there are no Atlanteans left here. They vanished long ago."

"I think Fabian must be sleeping with the rest of the gods."

"And how do you plan on waking him?"

"I don't know. I've tried calling him in our temple and also his mother's, but he hasn't answered yet."

"You aren't going to forget about him, are you?"

Delwyn shook his head. "I want to find him. I need to prove to him we *are* soulmates."

"He needs convincing, does he?"

"He doesn't believe in such things, but I'm going to persuade him otherwise."

Kai sat on the beach and patted the sand beside him. Delwyn took a seat.

"Do you *really* believe Fabian is the one for you?"

Delwyn nodded immediately. "I can't explain it, but something sparked in me the first moment I saw him. I haven't felt this way for a long time, not since Finn."

Kai sighed. "I guess we'd better find a way of tracking down your Atlantean, then. Have you had any other ideas about how to wake him?"

"No. I don't even know for sure if he's sleeping. I hope he is, because otherwise it means he left the city with the other Atlanteans."

"If he left, he might come back," Kai pointed out.

"He could, but it would also mean he isn't the one for me, because my soulmate is here in the city. And I *really* want it to be him."

Kai wrapped an arm around Delwyn's shoulder. "Sometimes having that belief is enough. I hope in your case it is."

Although he didn't admit it out loud, Delwyn worried

that it wasn't.

* * * *

When calling for Fabian in every temple in the sunken city had failed, Delwyn knew he was out of options. There was no other choice — he had to call in the goddess herself.

He summoned Cari in the audience chamber of her temple and was relieved when she announced her presence a few moments later.

"Delwyn, what's the matter?"

"I wanted to talk to you about Fabian," Delwyn replied. *"I've been trying to wake him in the various temples, but he's not answering my call. Is Fabian his true name?"*

"Yes, it is, but Fabian won't be able to answer you."

"Why not? He is sleeping, isn't he?"

Cari remained silent and Delwyn wished he could see her expression. He resolved to look over their meeting again when it was a part of the past. Sometimes he could tell a lot more from a person's face than from their words.

"Are you still here?" he eventually asked. He hoped the goddess hadn't chosen to vanish in the middle of their conversation. If she had, he had no doubt she wouldn't be returning if he tried calling her again.

"I'm here," Cari replied. *"I'm just wondering how much I can tell you without angering certain other gods."*

Delwyn waited patiently while Cari thought things over. Finally she spoke again.

"Fabian is no longer bound to me," Cari explained. *"He chose to sever ties with me, gave up his Oracle powers, and swore loyalty to his mother."*

"Why would he do that?" Delwyn asked. *"I thought he didn't want to be bound to his mother."*

"He didn't."

"Then why?"

"You would have to ask him," Cari said.

"It's a shame I can't find him and do that," Delwyn reminded

the goddess.

"*Sarcasm won't help you,*" Cari chided. "*Fabian still lives, as you know, but he is out of your reach and likely to remain so.*"

"*What do you mean? Where is he?*"

"*The only way for you to be with your Atlantean is for you to wake his mother, but heed my warning… Mariana never had much love for the merpeople, and her hatred of them grew with time. If you wake her, you may not survive her fury long enough to capture the heart of her son.*"

"*I have to try. I can't give up on him. I…*"

"*Love him?*" Cari finished his sentence for him. "*I know you do. It was inevitable from the moment your vision took you to him. Soulmates always find one another. No power on Earth can stop them.*"

"*Then Fabian is my soulmate?*" Delwyn asked. Even though he knew the answer already, he wanted to hear it from the goddess herself.

"*Of course he is. But you already knew that, didn't you?*"

Delwyn smiled.

"*Oh, my sweet young merman, I hope you find a way to be with Fabian. Of all my Oracles, Fabian has always been one of my favorites. He has been lonely for such a long time. He needs you in his life as much as you need him.*"

"*He didn't seem very lonely when I visited him. He has Isander.*"

"*He does, but Isander isn't the other half of his soul. They are friends and lovers, much as you and Kai would have been if you had taken him up on his offer during the solstice.*"

"*Then Fabian has room for me in his life?*" Delwyn asked.

"*Of course he does, and he always will. Now, I must go, but not before I give you one more gift.*"

Delwyn wondered what she meant. He felt the palm of her hand on his chest and a burning sensation that wasn't entirely unpleasant.

"*Just a little boost to your own powers,*" Cari explained. "*You will no longer become quite so tired when you visit the past. You should still be careful not to stay too long, though.*"

"*Thank you.*"

"One final thing before I go," Cari said. *"I haven't the power to hide you from Mariana when your visions take you into her presence. I wish I did, but unfortunately, her powers were greater than my own back then. Try to stay out of her way."*

"She can't hurt me in the past, can she?"

"No, but in this time she only sleeps, and she has been known to hold grudges for centuries. Try not to invoke her anger."

Delwyn promised to stay out of her way. When Cari didn't reply, he guessed she had left and he went back to his rooms.

He had a lot to think about, but the one question playing on his mind was why Fabian had chosen to bind himself to his mother. He had no idea why a man who was so adamant he didn't share his mother's views would turn away from Cari, give up his powers, and choose to serve another instead.

* * * *

Knowing Fabian wouldn't have his Oracle powers forever, Delwyn tried to ensure little time had passed when he next triggered a vision. He didn't want to risk Fabian being unable to see him when he visited.

Fabian's bright smile made it obvious he was still an Oracle when Delwyn arrived in his presence.

"Have you missed me?" Delwyn asked.

Fabian grinned. "Of course I have. Now come and watch the sunset with me."

"That sounds quite romantic," Delwyn teased as he positioned himself on the beach beside him.

"It does, doesn't it?" Fabian replied. "I guess your talk of soulmates must be having an effect on me."

"Or you were already that way inclined," Delwyn said. "After all, you did pick me a flower."

"You're never going to forget that, are you?"

"No," Delwyn replied with a grin. "I love it."

They sat quietly as the sun dipped below the horizon. The

waves licked at Fabian's toes.

"Have you found me in the future yet?" Fabian asked.

"No, not yet."

Delwyn wondered whether he should say anything about what Cari had told him about Fabian giving up his powers and swearing loyalty to his mother. He didn't know why he held his tongue, but something kept him from telling Fabian what the goddess had said.

Would it make any difference if Fabian knew what he was going to do in the future?

Could knowing what would happen to him cause him to change his course?

Delwyn didn't know, and while a part of him contemplated throwing caution to the wind and telling Fabian everything he knew, a tiny voice in his head reminded him Cari had told him he had no power to change the course of history. Whatever he told Fabian would make no difference to what happened. All it was likely to do was give him cause to worry.

So he remained silent on the subject and enjoyed the pleasant company of his handsome Atlantean.

"Do you know what happened to my people?" Fabian asked. "You said they no longer live in Atlantis, but I can't help wondering why."

"I don't know," Delwyn admitted. "I've often wondered myself. I've seen the city before it sank below the ocean and I've watched my people welcome the humans to the underwater world we live in. Your gods and my people ensured the Atlanteans survived under the water, but then suddenly they were gone."

"The gods or the Atlanteans?"

"Both."

"Maybe that's the answer," Fabian suggested. "You said it yourself, the gods helped my people survive under the ocean. When they went to sleep, perhaps they inadvertently destroyed the Atlanteans, too. Perhaps the power that allowed them to live underwater was lost with the disappearance of the gods."

"I don't think so."

"Why not? It's as good a theory as any."

"According to Cari, your people were sent away, with no memories of the city," Delwyn said. "I don't think they lost the power to survive here, they just forgot they could."

Fabian paled slightly.

Delwyn sought for something to reassure him and remembered Jake. "One of Medina's descendants lives on land with two mermen and he has the power to survive underwater, just as the Atlanteans did. If he can do it, so can other lost Atlanteans."

"Are you sure?"

"Yes."

"Perhaps he has the power because Medina gave it to him?"

Delwyn had no idea. For all their speculating about what had happened, Delwyn wanted to know why the Atlanteans had been banished, and whether it had something to do with why Fabian had turned away from Cari and sworn loyalty to his mother.

Fabian saw Isander's shadow before he heard him. He was sure the man must be part cat, the way he crept about.

"Won't you join us?" Fabian said as he checked over his shoulder.

"Us?" Isander asked. "Oh, I take it your merman is here?"

"Yes," Fabian clarified. "He's just beside me."

"I suppose that means you won't be inviting me to your bed tonight."

Fabian ducked his head. He had already been neglecting his lover in favor of what Isander referred to as mooning over his merman.

He wasn't sure what had come over him. He had taken many lovers during his long life. He had never wanted for company in his bed. Yet now, for the first time he could recall, he was turning down the offer of a skilled lover—for what? A merman who he could only gaze upon and never actually touch.

"You can be together if you want," Delwyn said. "I won't mind. I think I might enjoy watching you again."

Fabian's cock rose at Delwyn's words, which Isander quickly commented upon.

"What did he say to you?" Isander asked with a grin.

"He likes the idea of watching us," Fabian admitted.

"I'm beginning to like your merman." Isander gave an exaggerated leer in Delwyn's general direction.

"Behave yourself," Fabian warned, but it was already too late.

Isander slipped his hand into Fabian's robes. Already hard, thanks to Delwyn's admission, Fabian groaned when Isander took him in his hand, stroking him expertly.

Delwyn gave a whimper beside them.

Fabian leaned back on his elbows and closed his eyes.

"You can call out his name, if you want," Isander whispered into his ear. "I won't mind."

Fabian shivered and his breathing quickened.

"Do you want him to do this to you?" Isander asked between licking Fabian's neck. "His hand around your shaft?"

"Yes!" Fabian cried out as Isander moved down to his nipples, biting and sucking them until they peaked into hard buds.

"Oooh." Delwyn made delighted sounds of pleasure.

Fabian opened his eyes and stared at Delwyn.

The merman's face had flushed and his breathing came raggedly.

"Is he hard for you?" Isander asked.

"He's in mer form," Fabian reminded him.

"Maybe he should visit you some time when he's all human."

"I can't," Delwyn said. "I can only have visions in my mer form."

Fabian relayed his words to Isander, who appeared

mildly disappointed.

"Taste him," Delwyn whispered, even though Isander couldn't hear him.

Fabian nodded and stroked Isander's hair, drawing him back from his chest. "He wants you to taste me."

Isander stared at him with wide-eyed surprise. "Oh, my goddess."

"Please," Delwyn asked. "Isander, please."

"He's begging," Fabian said.

Isander didn't need any more encouragement. He dove on Fabian's cock, taking it into his mouth, just as he had so many times before.

Fabian fell back onto the sand and closed his eyes. "Delwyn," he gasped.

Isander didn't lose his rhythm at the sound of another man's name on his lover's lips. He continued to pleasure him, licking and sucking at the hot, hard flesh.

Fabian soon forgot who kneeled between his legs. In his mind's eye, it was a silver-finned merman who had his lips wrapped around his shaft. They could even do this while Delwyn was in his mer form. He didn't need his legs and dick to pleasure him.

For a few blissful minutes Fabian lost himself in the fantasy.

It was Delwyn sucking him. Delwyn's tongue teasing his length. Delwyn tasting him as he licked at his seed.

For the first time in his life, he was being pleasured by a merman. Those beautiful, sexual creatures who had welcomed his people with open arms.

When he came, Fabian screamed Delwyn's name out into the night.

Beside him, Delwyn whimpered and moaned. "Kiss him."

Even though Isander couldn't have heard him, he did as Delwyn asked.

Fabian kept his eyes closed as he kissed his lover, holding on to the fantasy for a few moments longer.

When they parted, he finally opened his eyes.

Isander stared at him with an expression on his face Fabian had never seen before.

"What is it?" he asked.

Isander smiled and stroked Fabian's cheek with his hand. "You've never kissed me that way before. Not in all the years we've been lovers."

"We've kissed many times."

"Not like that. But then again, it wasn't me you were with just then, was it?"

Fabian ducked his head, only for Isander to lift his chin so he looked him in the eye once more.

"I didn't say I minded," Isander said. "I've never been in love before, not completely, yet now I know what it feels like to be loved."

"I'm sorry."

"There's no need for apologies." Isander turned in Delwyn's direction and smiled. "You're a very lucky merman. I hope you know that."

"I do," Delwyn replied.

Fabian raised his hand to Delwyn's face, wishing he could touch him, just once. "One day, Delwyn."

Delwyn nodded. "We'll find each other, I promise."

Fabian didn't notice when Isander slipped away from them, disappearing into the night.

Delwyn stayed with him until he fell asleep on the sand.

Chapter Nine

The first sign something unusual might be happening in the world of the Atlantean Pantheon was when Fabian found Isander and two of the priest's other lovers talking in Fabian's rooms. Although Isander visited him frequently, he had never brought other guests with him.

"We're hiding out for a while," Isander explained with a sheepish grin. "Your mother's in a foul temper."

"What have you done this time?" Fabian asked as he joined the trio.

Isander gave him an affronted look. "Nothing."

"Do you know why she's angry?" Fabian hoped it had nothing to do with anything he had done.

Something of his concern must have shown on his face, because Isander waved his friends from the room and patted Fabian's arm. "Don't worry. It isn't you this time, which makes a pleasant change. She's angry because one of the gods has petitioned the Pantheon to make his lover immortal."

Fabian frowned. For a god to request immortality for someone was unusual, but not unheard of. The other gods watched the human in question and judged whether he or she was worthy of such a gift. They then voted on whether the human would be allowed to drink of the cup of immortality.

He couldn't understand why his mother was so angry about the latest petition. If she had a problem with the mortal in question, all she had to do was say no when she cast her vote. If she was outnumbered by the other gods, so be it.

"Do you know which god has made the request?" Fabian asked, wondering if perhaps the god might be one his mother already despised.

"Caspian," Isander replied.

Fabian whistled and shook his head. The God of Justice was well known and, for the most part, well liked amongst both the other gods and the humans. He was also one of the most promiscuous of the gods, taking new lovers frequently. Had he finally fallen in love? Fabian hoped so. Although he didn't know Caspian particularly well, as the brother of the Goddess of Prophecy he visited Cari's temple on special occasions, and from what Fabian had seen of him, the easy-going god, with a smile for everyone, deserved someone in his life to love him.

Still, he wasn't sure why Caspian's request would anger his mother. As far as he had seen, Mariana and Caspian had always been relatively friendly. He hadn't heard of any problems between them.

"There has to be more to this than what you've told me," Fabian said. "What are you leaving out?"

Isander drew in a deep breath. "The mortal who is the subject of the petition is mer."

Fabian gaped at Isander, not sure if he had heard him correctly. "Mer?"

Isander grinned. "Yes. Caspian has fallen in love with a merman."

Fabian didn't know what to say. That was the last thing he had expected to hear.

"Your mother nearly brought down the temple roof with her screeching when she heard about the request," Isander said. "We slipped away at the first opportunity."

Fabian well understood their need to escape. "You can stay here as long as you wish."

"I'm thinking a century or two should be sufficient," Isander replied. "I've never seen her so furious. You'd better make sure she doesn't find out about your own merman obsession."

"The more Delwyn is in my thoughts, the less I want to be in her company," Fabian said. "I don't need her poking into my head and learning any more about him than she already does."

"Are you sure it's a good idea to become involved with him?" Isander asked.

"Are my mother's prejudices rubbing off on you?"

Isander glared at him. "No, I don't mean because he's mer. I mean because he lives so far in the future. Even if he were to visit you at various points between now and then, you still have an awfully long time to wait before you can truly be together."

"He can't seem to visit me much farther ahead than this time now," Fabian admitted. "He's already tried."

"You don't find that a little strange?"

"Yes, but what can I do about it?"

"Find someone to love here in your own century."

"I want him, and one day we'll be able to touch, just like you and I do now."

"You really think you can wait that long?"

"I know I can."

Isander gave him a doubtful look.

Fabian smiled back at him. "You're mortal, you don't know what it's like to live longer than the brief lifespan you have. I've already lived far longer than you have. I've watched my lovers grow old and pass from the mortal realm time and again. I've held them in my arms and wept for their loss. Now I have something to look ahead to."

Isander frowned. "Centuries of waiting for him, just for a few brief years of pleasure, before he, too, leaves the mortal world. Then what will happen to you?"

"I'll mourn him and carry on, just as I always have. Or maybe, if the gods are good to me, my life may even come to its natural end shortly after his does. I'm not immortal, remember."

"You could be if you joined us in serving your mother," Isander reminded him.

His mother's offer to petition for Fabian to join the immortals in truth came with too many strings for Fabian's liking. The price was too high for him to pay. Besides, even though the offer had been tempting when he had been younger, he found as he grew older that the idea of living forever didn't sit well with him.

No, immortality wasn't for him. It was hard enough living as long as he did.

Fabian shook his head. "I don't want immortality."

"What if the reason Delwyn can't visit you in times between now and his century, is because you die?" Isander asked quietly. "Would immortality be worth the price then?"

The thought of not living long enough to see Delwyn in the flesh had already occurred to Fabian. He didn't want to dwell on the idea, even if it would explain Delwyn's inability to find him in other eras. Instead, he chose to focus on the flower, which Delwyn had assured him still bloomed in the distant future. He *would* live long enough to touch Delwyn. The alternative didn't bear contemplating.

"I have to believe I'll be with him," Fabian said. "I think I'm in love with him."

"Of course you are," Isander replied. "I've been telling you so for ages. But love doesn't always have a happy ending."

Fabian knew that, but again, he didn't want to consider the idea of not getting what he most desired.

"You could always visit Medina," Isander suggested. "She would be happy to work a little magic to help her favorite nephew. You just have to ask her."

Fabian grinned and wondered why he hadn't thought of it himself. "You're right. I'll go see her immediately."

Isander shooed him from the room. "You go do that. And if you happen to see two naked men out there, send them back to me. All this talk of love is making me hard."

Fabian laughed and promised he would send them in if he saw them.

* * * *

Fabian found Medina wandering in the gardens with one of her many lovers.

"Fabian, my darling." Medina greeted him with a smile and kiss to his cheek.

The glare her lover gave Fabian made him step back a pace at the venom. Medina caught the look and rolled her eyes.

"Fabian is my nephew," Medina told him. "Now, run along while I talk to him."

Although the man's sour expression vanished when he discovered Fabian wasn't a rival for Medina's affections, he made it obvious he didn't like being dismissed.

Medina sighed as she hooked her arm through Fabian's. "He really is the most jealous of men."

"Then why do you keep him?" Fabian asked. "I thought you only took lovers who understood they had to share you with others."

"Usually I do, but he is quite talented. He can do the most wonderful things with his tongue, but I'm sure you didn't come to talk to me about him. So, tell me what I can do for my favorite nephew on this beautiful day?"

Fabian wondered for a brief moment whether his aunt shared her sister's prejudices against the mer. He tried to recall whether she had taken any mermen as lovers.

"Of course I have," Medina said. "They're most energetic, especially during their mating seasons. Before you were born, I ruled the sunken city with two lovers, one of whom was a merman."

Fabian frowned at her. "You know I don't like it when you read my thoughts."

"When you're thinking about lovers, it can't be helped. I'm the Goddess of Love. You might call it an occupational hazard. I take it you've heard about Caspian and his merman lover?"

"Yes. Mother's apparently furious."

Medina gave a most unladylike snort. "She'll get over it."

They wound their way through the flowerbeds as Fabian attempted to put his jumbled thoughts into words. He could tell that Medina was trying hard not to invade his privacy by reading his mind. She waited patiently for him to speak.

"There's this merman," Fabian began. "He's an Oracle of the past."

"Would this be the silver-tailed beauty I saw floating through the gardens with you some time ago?"

"You remember that?" Fabian asked.

Medina gave a light airy laugh. "I remember *him*. Seeing mermen floating over land is quite unusual, and he was such a fine specimen. I was quite disappointed you didn't bring him over to introduce me."

"I'm sorry."

"It's no matter. I trust next time he visits you'll rectify that. Such a handsome young merman."

"He is indeed," Fabian agreed. "He hasn't been born yet."

"I would imagine that would be the case if he's an Oracle. As you know, I've already met the current ones."

"And slept with two of them," Fabian teased. His aunt appreciated beauty in all forms.

Medina laughed. "And if you would just retire from your position so Cari can choose a replacement, I might be able to make it all three."

Fabian chuckled along with her. "I'm quite happy in my post for the moment."

Medina gave a dramatic sigh. "You do make your poor aunt suffer. Now, what about your pretty young merman?"

"I wondered whether you might be able to see him in my future," Fabian asked.

"He's already in your present. I'm sure he's in your future, too."

"I mean in truth, not simply because of his visions of the past. I want to be with him properly."

"You should learn to say what you mean," Medina scolded. "You want to have sex with him."

"Yes. Can you see if that might come about?"

Medina stopped walking and closed her eyes. "Delwyn is the other half of your soul," she said. "Soulmates always find each other, one way or another."

"He's already found me, but that doesn't mean we have a future together."

Medina opened her eyes and gave him an appraising look. "You're far too cynical for one so young."

"Aunt Medi!"

Medina laughed again. "Come, nephew, let us talk about your merman."

Fabian told Medina everything. From seeing Delwyn for the first time, talking to him, his desire to wait out the centuries for him and, most importantly, his growing feelings for the merman.

Medina listened patiently. "You missed something out," she said when he had finished.

He frowned as he tried to think what she might mean.

"The beach," the goddess clarified.

"Oh." Fabian blushed. He had deliberately kept from telling her about what he considered to be the most erotic experience of his life.

Medina smacked him lightly on the arm. "You always did leave out the best parts."

Fabian rubbed his arm. "You're my *aunt*," he reminded her. "I wouldn't talk to you about that any more than I would my own mother."

The truth was that Medina had been a better mother to him than Mariana ever had.

"If you told your mother about your desire for a merman it would no doubt be the last thing you ever did," Medina said. "Especially right now. But you should know you can talk to me about anything. I'm not only your aunt, I'm the Goddess of Love, Lust and Carnal Desire. Who else can you discuss your sexual fantasies with, without being judged?"

Medina was right, but even after all these years, Fabian still felt awkward. He suspected he always would.

Medina, who Fabian knew wasn't quite as oblivious as some people believed, patted his arm and smiled. "I'll stop teasing you now. So, you've fallen in love with a merman and he desires you, too. It seems as if you've already managed the hard part."

"I want to spend my life with him," Fabian said. "Can you help me?"

Medina shook her head. "You don't need my help. What good is a love spell when the one you desire is already enamored with you? All I can do is give you my blessing, but I'm sure you already know you have that."

"Then you can't tell me for sure whether I'll be with him in his time?"

"You chart your own course. It may take you away from your merman for a while, but as long as you have faith in your love for each other, all will be well."

"Do you really think so?" Fabian asked.

"Of course I do. I'm the Goddess of Love. I *have* to believe that, else what am I even here for?"

Fabian could tell that was as much as he would get out of his aunt. He had hoped she could tell him for certain that he would live long enough to be able to catch up to Delwyn's time, but he supposed even a goddess had her limits.

Chapter Ten

Delwyn rested on his sleeping sponge and smiled at the thoughts of his recent meeting with Fabian. He knew he was falling hopelessly in love with him and he was helpless to stop his growing feelings.

The sponge dipped beside him. *"Kai?"*

"Who else?" Kai replied. *"You're not going into the past again, are you?"*

"I thought I might try another time," Delwyn said.

"Good. I think you've been spending too long in Fabian's era."

"What's that supposed to mean?" Delwyn snapped. *"Cari gave my powers a boost so I don't get tired as quickly when I visit him."*

"I wish she hadn't done that," Kai said. *"You were already spending way too much time with him. Now you're barely here at all. It's like you're hardly in your own body these days because you're too busy spying on him."*

"You're exaggerating. And I don't spy on him. He always knows when I'm there."

"I don't think you should see him again," Kai whispered.

Delwyn pulled away from the merman and smacked him in the chest. *"How can you say that? You left the sunken city with Dax so you could find your love. That's far more dangerous than anything I'm doing."*

"It's not the same thing. Dax is here in this time, flesh and blood."

"Fabian is, too," Delwyn argued. *"I just haven't found him yet."*

"Do you honestly think you will?" Kai asked. *"You told him what era we live in, even the exact year as the humans mark time."*

Don't you think that if he were still a part of this world, he would be here with you already?"

"Cari said I needed to wake his mother before I find him again."

"This would be the goddess who hates the merpeople, right?"

"Yes."

"Tell me you aren't going to try and wake her."

"It's the only way I can be with him, but it doesn't matter because she isn't answering me, anyway."

"Well, that at least is something to be thankful for," Kai muttered. *"I know you don't want to hear it, but you have to face facts. You've called for him in every temple in the city, sometimes more than once. You've called for his mother and she isn't answering, either. He isn't coming to you."*

"He is!"

"You don't know that. It's been hundreds and hundreds of years since the time you saw him in the past. He probably won't even remember who you are."

Delwyn swam off the sponge and nearly barreled into one of the columns in his anger. It had been ages since he had been so disoriented in his own chambers.

"You don't have to believe me," Kai said. *"But at least consider the possibility you might never see him outside of your visions."*

"I'm prepared to find him, whatever it takes," Delwyn insisted. *"He loves me. I know he does. And we're going to be together one day. We just have to be patient."*

Delwyn didn't give Kai the opportunity to say anything else. He swam from the chamber, too frustrated to try to trigger a vision. He would return later, when he had calmed down a little.

As he swam aimlessly through the city, his guard at his side, Delwyn realized he had no idea where he was.

"Guard?" he asked tentatively. He wasn't even certain which one was with him right now. Normally, he made sure to speak to the guards as they changed their shifts, so he knew who was around.

"Yes?" the merman replied.

Delwyn recognized Marin's voice. He was one of Delwyn's

favorite guards. The young recruit had a reputation as one of the worst guards the sunken city had ever seen, but he was kind and enthusiastic. He also didn't mind what some of the guards referred to as the 'babysitting duties', that being guarding the Oracles.

"Where are we?" Delwyn asked.

"You must be really mad at Kai if you don't know where you are."

Delwyn sighed. *"He's my best friend, but sometimes he just doesn't understand me."*

"He's just watching out for you."

"I know, but he doesn't need to. I can take care of myself."

"He loves you. He'll never stop worrying about you. You've seen the way Calder fusses over me. Sometimes it frustrates me, but I know it's because he cares."

Delwyn didn't doubt Calder's feelings for Marin, or Kai's love for himself. That wasn't the issue.

"Do you think I'm foolish to want to find Fabian?" Delwyn didn't have to ask if Marin was aware of Fabian. Very little slipped past their guards, especially when the Oracles argued, and were less likely to shield their conversations from the minds of others in their presence.

"If you love him, and you believe he returns your love, then yes, you should continue to believe you'll be together."

"Would you wait for him?"

"I don't know. I think I enjoy sex too much to be celibate while I'm waiting around."

Delwyn laughed. *"Maybe I should try calling him again."*

"Okay. Where do you want to try this time?"

"Where are we right now?" Delwyn asked.

"Just outside Medina's temple, across from the market place."

Delwyn had already called for Fabian from the temple of the Goddess of Love more than any of the others.

"Maybe you could try calling for Medina?" Marin suggested.

Delwyn nodded and, after Marin guided him in the right direction, they swam into the temple.

The Goddess of Love appeared immediately, almost as if

she had been waiting for his call.

"Hello, Delwyn. It's nice to see you. I think I can guess why you are here. Fabian is very handsome, isn't he?"

"He is. Do you know where to find him?"

"Of course."

Delwyn hadn't expected the reply she gave him and something of his surprise must have shown on his face.

"Fabian is my nephew," Medina explained. *"Though I believe you already know that, don't you? I've always watched over him, ever since he was a baby. I want nothing more than for him to be happy and reunited with his soulmate."*

"Can you tell me where to find him?"

"You'll see him here soon," Medina promised. *"Now, why don't you go and visit him in the past? I know he's anxious to see you again."*

"He is? How can you tell?"

Medina laughed. *"Because he loves you, you silly merman. He's never happier than when you come to see him. He's* always *anxious to see you. Now run along and make my nephew's day."*

Delwyn left the temple feeling more at ease than he had all day. Medina's assurance that he would be with Fabian was enough to reinforce his own belief once more.

* * * *

Delwyn found Fabian in his vision with little effort. It was almost as if he was so attuned to him, he could find him without even trying. He just wished he could find him in the present, or any time between now and then, so easily.

The Atlantean stretched out on his bed. He was alone and naked with his eyes closed. He stroked his hard length with his right hand, while using his left to fondle his testicles.

Fabian hadn't noticed Delwyn's arrival and so the merman looked his fill for several minutes, enjoying the view.

Delwyn licked his lips as he watched Fabian pleasure himself. He wanted to make his presence known, but he couldn't seem to summon up a single word. His voice had deserted him completely.

When Fabian opened his eyes, clearly startled, Delwyn realized he must have made some sort of sound to give himself away. Fabian relaxed and smiled.

"You made me jump," he accused.

"I'm sorry. I didn't mean to disturb you."

Fabian grinned widely. "You didn't. I was just thinking about you."

Delwyn stared straight at Fabian's hands, still now, but right where they had been when he'd entered. His face heated.

"You blush so easily," Fabian teased. "Have you never touched yourself before?"

Despite the number of occasions Delwyn had visited Fabian, they had never discussed Delwyn's experience, or more accurately, his lack of it.

"Not often," Delwyn admitted. "I've rarely gone to land since I hit puberty."

He didn't want to admit that even after the law forbidding the Oracles from going to land had been lifted, his obsession with Fabian had kept him below the waves.

Fabian beckoned him closer. "One question, my merman, and I want you to answer honestly. I'll know if you lie."

"I don't lie," Delwyn said. "What's the question?"

"Are you untouched?" Fabian asked.

Delwyn gulped and gave a small nod. "Do you mind?"

Fabian shook his head immediately. "Of course not. I just wanted to know for certain. I suspected as much."

Delwyn drew closer to the side of the bed. "I want to touch you, and I want you to be my first. I'll wait for you, however long it takes."

"I know you will." Fabian sighed and moved across the bed to make room for Delwyn to hover beside him.

Delwyn joined him and rested his head on his arms. "His name was Finn," he said. He knew he didn't need to explain anything to Fabian, but it felt right to talk to him about those he had loved, and Finn had been the first.

"You loved him?"

"Very much. We grew up together in the sunken city. He was a prince and I was the son of one of the palace workers. We were close in age and our parents let us play together. We explored every inch of the city, getting into mischief and trouble at every turn."

"I'd like to meet this Finn."

"He's gone now. He left the city with the merman he loved to seek a new life on land. We were both confined to the city during the years when we might have become lovers. Prince Finn because of his parents, and me because I became an Oracle. It's only recently the law has been changed to allow Oracles to visit land and have sex. For years it was forbidden, because the Oracle powers were inherited by our descendants. I loved him a great deal, but we missed our chance."

"Has there been no one else?"

"Not like Finn," Delwyn said. "Kai, my fellow Oracle, is my best friend now, but I don't love him the same way."

"He's more of a brother to you?"

Delwyn laughed. "Not exactly. I would never have kissed a sibling the way I used to him. But he isn't what you would call the love of my life. He's not you."

Fabian rolled onto his side and rested his head on his arm. "I eagerly anticipate the day when we can be together in the flesh."

"Me, too." Delwyn liked that Fabian had mirrored his pose. He glanced at Fabian's groin. He was still swollen and hard. "Aren't you going to finish?" he asked.

"Do you want me to?" Fabian replied.

Delwyn nodded. "I like watching you."

"Have you watched others in their pleasure?" Fabian asked as he took himself in hand.

"Yes."

"Who?"

Delwyn grinned. "Many people, strangers mostly. I watched Finn a time or two, but it was too hard seeing him so happy with someone else."

"You liked watching me and Isander?"

"Yes."

"Were you jealous?"

Delwyn lowered his gaze. "A little, but only the first time. I wanted what you two had together."

"One day you *will* have it for yourself," Fabian promised. His breathing became labored as he continued to pump his shaft.

Delwyn found it hard to catch his own breath and he raised his hand to his chest, touching his nipples with the tips of his fingers, squeezing and pinching them. He could never climax in his mer form, but he could come close.

Fabian closed his eyes and pushed himself closer to the brink. He moaned quietly and every word from his lips was Delwyn's name, repeated over and over in synchronization with his strokes of his cock.

When he came, he screamed out "Delwyn!" one final time. Delwyn suspected his cry had been loud enough for everyone on the isle to hear.

Fabian closed his eyes and Delwyn leaned in toward him. He puckered his lips as if to brush them across Fabian's, before drawing back. Fabian would have no idea he had done anything so sappy and foolish.

When Fabian smiled knowingly at him, Delwyn knew he had been wrong. He flushed again, but he wasn't sorry for his action.

"I love you," Fabian said. "I need you to know that."

"I love you, too," Delwyn replied. "Remember that, always, and don't forget me."

"Never."

Chapter Eleven

Mariana's bursts of temper were becoming most tiresome. Even her own priests stayed out of her way as much as possible. Fabian, who had never made a habit of visiting her, now actively avoided her temple and anywhere else she was known to frequent.

When his mother summoned him to her temple, however, he had no choice except to obey.

"Mother." He gave a small bow of respect and waited for her to tell him why she had called him to her.

Mariana sat on her throne in the temple audience chamber. The room was entirely empty save for the two of them.

"You have no doubt heard about Caspian and his request to make one of those mer creatures immortal," the goddess said.

"I have."

Mariana nodded. "The gods have decided to allow this travesty to take place."

Fabian ducked his head to hide his smile. Caspian would no doubt be delighted.

"You needn't try to hide your pleasure," Mariana snapped. "Do you think I'm unaware of your own dalliances with the mer?"

Fabian met his mother's glare with one of his own.

"Oh, yes, I've seen you and that unnatural creature together," Mariana continued. "I've marked the way you simper over him. Even the loosest robes can't hide how much you want him."

"I don't deny it," Fabian stated. "He's the other half of my soul."

"You've been spending too much time with my dear sister."

Fabian had never cowed before his mother and he didn't intend to start now. "Was there something you wanted from me?" he asked.

Mariana rose and glided down to stand in front of him. "What does that fish have that's so special?"

"He has a human form and a human heart," Fabian told her. "You'd know nothing about the latter, though, would you? If you ever possessed such a thing I'm sure it turned to stone long ago."

"You dare to speak to me in such a manner?" Mariana snarled. "I'm a goddess and your mother."

"You've never been a real mother to me. As for your powers, you can threaten me all you want. It makes no difference. I'm not bound to you and I have the protection of both Cari and Medina. You cannot harm me."

Mariana snapped her fingers and a sharp burst of pain shot down Fabian's spine. He fell to his knees with a cry.

"You forget your place," Mariana said. "For too long, I've allowed you to speak your mind. It ends now."

Fabian gasped as the pain finally began to recede. He kneeled on the stone floor as he blinked back tears.

"You will end all ties with that creature or I will destroy you. I will not sit by idly while my own flesh and blood beds one of those abominations."

"Leave him alone." Medina arrived in a flash of light and a waft of flowery perfume.

"Stay out this, sister," Mariana warned. "This has nothing to do with you."

Medina ignored her as she helped Fabian to his feet. "Are you all right?"

Fabian couldn't yet speak, but he managed a shaky nod.

"You should return to Cari," Medina advised. "While you are bound to her, she can command the greatest power to protect you."

Fabian glanced at his mother.

Mariana glared back at him. "You *will* swear loyalty to me, Fabian. It's only a matter of time."

"Never."

Medina shook her head. "Never say never, my darling nephew. To do so only tempts fate. Now go to your goddess and let her restore your strength."

Fabian did as she suggested and escaped his mother's presence with great relief.

* * * *

Fabian was sitting in the bathing pool when Delwyn found him. He had an expression of discomfort on his face that Delwyn had not seen before.

"Are you well?" Delwyn asked. "You look pale."

Fabian gave him a shadow of a smile. "I just had a minor argument with my mother."

Delwyn's stomach lurched and he felt slightly queasy. "Was it about me?" he asked.

Fabian shook his head. "If it hadn't been about you, it would have been about something else. We've never seen eye to eye on anything of importance."

"I don't like to think of you arguing about me."

"Then don't dwell on it," Fabian said. "Now, come and sit with me while I recover."

"What did she do to you?" Delwyn asked as he gave the appearance of lowering himself into the water.

"It doesn't matter," Fabian said. "Talk to me about something else, please. Tell me about the future."

"What do you want to know about it?" Delwyn asked. "I've told you all about the city and what it's like in my time."

"Tell me about the rest of the world," Fabian suggested. "Distract me with tales of the mortal men."

Delwyn obliged as best he could, talking of the strange inventions humans had produced over the years, machines that flew through the air or traveled across country without the assistance of animals to pull them. He told him of buildings stretching up into the clouds, and tunnels built under great bodies of water. He attempted to describe modern music, but with limited success. He tried to sing some of the songs he had heard in his visions, but he couldn't carry a tune.

Long into the night, Delwyn stayed at Fabian's side. Various visitors wandered into the bathing chamber, sometimes joining Fabian in the water, sometimes merely passing through to another part of the building. None of them seemed to think it strange that Fabian was spending so long in the water, or that he appeared to be talking to himself much of the time.

When Cari hurried into the chamber Delwyn could tell something was wrong. He had never seen her so distressed. Tears ran down her face and her eyes were red and puffy.

"Everyone gather in my audience chamber, immediately," she called.

Delwyn wondered what had happened. He had no intention of leaving Fabian's side while he was in pain, so he followed him from the pool, not caring whether the summons was meant to include him or not. As one of her Oracles, albeit one who hadn't yet been appointed, Delwyn didn't believe she would send him away. If she even noticed him there. She was so upset, he would not have been surprised if she had overlooked him entirely.

Fabian quickly tugged on a robe and followed the others.

The three Oracles and the twelve priests and priestesses congregated in the audience chamber. Every single one of them appeared to be confused. It seemed that no one knew what had happened or why they had been summoned.

Cari walked to her throne and took a seat. "Thank you for coming and for all you have done in my service. The time has now come for us to part ways."

Delwyn watched the men and women as they exchanged glances. None of them apparently knew what the goddess meant.

Cari drew in a deep breath. "The Atlanteans are being banished from Atlantis even as we speak. They are all condemned to walk amongst humans and their memories are being wiped. Even though you are bound to a goddess, I haven't the power to stop this. I'm sorry I did not see this coming and could not warn you. You are protected within the confines of my temple, but as soon as you leave the building Atlantis and this isle will be closed to you forever."

"But why?" Hiron asked.

"There's no time to explain fully," Cari replied. "Do not blame yourself for not seeing this, either. You could not have known. No one could."

"How —?"

"I know you feel guilt for the same reason I do. No Oracle of the future, not you, nor even I, can ever see events which will happen in the temple of another god or goddess. Only Oracles of the past have that ability, because they cannot change what has already come to pass. These are the rules we are bound by and I have never regretted that as much as I do today."

"Where are we being sent?" one of the priests asked. "Will we be together?"

"I don't know," Cari replied. "But it makes no difference. You will have no memory of your time here, or of each other. It will be as though this place was nothing more than a dream."

"What of the Oracles?" Hiron asked. "You have always appointed three beings to see as we do."

"And I will appoint three more, but they cannot be Atlantean."

Delwyn knew she would look to the mer. He tried to gauge Fabian's reaction to the news, but his expression was carefully guarded.

"Can we stay here?" someone asked.

Cari shook her head. "Those who seek to avoid their fate will be hunted down after everyone else has been banished."

Delwyn shivered. This was *that* day. The day Cari and

her mother had talked about. When the Atlanteans had vanished forever from the sunken city.

One by one the Atlanteans said their goodbyes, many with sobs and tears, before they made their way to the door. Even though Delwyn could see them as they walked through, they each disappeared the moment they left the temple, vanishing into thin air as whatever power was at work sent them to their new lives.

"Fabian, a moment, before you go out there," Cari said.

Fabian nodded and stepped aside from the remaining people. Hiron pulled him into a hug and Delwyn could see that the loss of his friend was a huge blow to him.

When the room was empty of everyone else, Cari approached Fabian and Delwyn.

Delwyn shifted uncomfortably, wondering if he should leave.

Cari spoke to Delwyn first. "You should stay. No, you *need* to be here. Stay by Fabian's side until you have seen what you have to."

"Will he see where I'm sent to?" Fabian asked.

"You're half-god," Cari replied. "There's another option for you."

"What option?"

"I cannot save you from banishment," Cari said. "But your mother could. If you go to her, swear loyalty to her alone, you may be in with a chance."

"What of my aunt Medina?" Fabian asked. "She's powerful and likely to be sympathetic to my plight."

Cari shook her head. "Medina's priests are being sent away, too."

"Are you saying my mother's aren't?"

Cari bit her lower lip and sighed deeply. "I've seen some of your mother's priests in Atlantis, with their memories intact. I don't know how or when, but I know what I saw."

"Is this what I'm destined to do?" Fabian asked. "Have you seen me with them?"

"Yes," Cari admitted. "But you know that's only a *possible* future. You chart your own course. You can still walk out that door and let my father banish you with the others. You always have a choice, and only you can make the final decision."

Fabian looked at Delwyn.

"There's one more thing you should know before you decide." Cari gestured to Delwyn. "It is the combination of your half-god status and my Oracle gifts that enable you to see and hear Delwyn. If you swear loyalty to your mother, you must renounce me."

"I'll lose my Oracle powers?" Fabian asked.

"Yes."

Fabian shook his head. "I won't give up Delwyn."

Cari sighed. "I thought you might say that. But if you want to keep him, you may have no choice. If you're banished, your memory will be erased, just like the other Atlanteans. You will have no recollection of Delwyn or any of the mer. I don't even know if you'll remember your demi-god status."

Fabian pointed at the door. "How would I even get to my mother's temple? It will mean stepping out the door, just as the others did."

"Don't you have the power to transport yourself?" Delwyn asked.

Fabian chuckled. "No, I'm afraid not."

"Actually, you do," Cari informed him. "But it would take more time than we have to teach you how to wield powers you've spent your entire life ignoring. Thankfully, I have enough power to send you both there."

"Are you sure that's wise?" Fabian asked with a nod to Delwyn. "My mother isn't exactly enamored of the mer at the best of times."

"She cannot harm Delwyn while he's merely having a vision."

"I'll be fine," Delwyn assured him. "Cari's right. I have to see what happened to you. It may be the only way for me to find you again."

Fabian nodded. "Send me to my mother," he said to Cari.

The goddess swept him into her arms and hugged him tightly. "Be safe, my dear."

A flash of light blinded Delwyn for a few seconds. He could hear angry voices all around him, and when he could see again he realized he was in the temple of the Goddess of Sea Creatures. He recognized Isander and a few of the others who he had seen in passing during his visits.

"Fabian," the goddess at the center of the crowd of men exclaimed. "You dare to bring one of those creatures into my temple?"

"Delwyn is an Oracle, having a vision, and not truly here. I have no control over where he goes."

Mariana snorted as if she didn't believe him. "What are you doing here? Why aren't you cowering away in your precious Cari's temple?"

Isander stepped closer to Fabian and linked their hands together. "You came to check on me, didn't you?"

Fabian gave Isander's fingers a squeeze. "Not this time. I'm here to swear loyalty to my mother."

Delwyn was hard pressed to decide who was the most shocked, Isander or the goddess.

"A fine time for you to decide to switch sides," Mariana snapped.

"I can always leave again," Fabian said. He took a step toward the door, as if to walk out.

Mariana vanished from her spot and appeared in his path. "Don't be hasty. You might have been the most disloyal son ever to walk the earth, but you *are* my son. You should be here, as well. I presume Cari has explained the situation to you and the rest of her followers."

"She has. The rest of her Oracles and her priests have been banished already."

"They have?" Mariana appeared surprised at Fabian's words. "Then it seems time is of the essence."

The goddess stalked to her throne and took her place. "Kneel before me, Fabian."

Fabian did as she asked without hesitation. Delwyn

hovered at his side.

"Do you swear loyalty to me?" Mariana asked. "Or do I send you from my temple right now?"

"I swear loyalty," Fabian replied.

"And you renounce all other gods and goddesses?" Mariana pressed on.

Fabian glanced at Delwyn.

"I love you," Delwyn said quickly. "Never forget me."

Fabian nodded. Delwyn knew he did not dare say the words in the front of his mother, but he heard them all the same.

"I renounce all others," Fabian said.

A flash of lightning lit the room and Delwyn wondered whether it was done.

When Fabian looked up he seemed to stare right through Delwyn.

"He can no longer see you," Mariana said with an unpleasant smile at Delwyn. "You are nothing to him. No more than a memory he will soon forget. You should leave now."

Delwyn knew her words for the lies they were. Fabian would not forget him, he was sure of this fact. He remained in his place, his arms folded across his chest. "I think I'd rather stay and see what happens next," he stated.

"If you must," Mariana replied. "I'm sure you'll soon grow bored and leave."

The goddess clapped her hands and her priests lined up before her. "The God of War seeks to banish you all to the land of humans. He will remove your memories of Atlantis and of your lives in it. I offer an alternative."

Delwyn wondered what she had in mind. Was it possible to avoid the banishment, and if so, why didn't Cari do the same thing for her loyal followers?

Mariana rose to her feet and raised her hands above her head. Lightning seemed to jump from one of her palms to the other and back again. Her red hair flew around her face as the wind in the temple picked up.

"Come, my followers," the goddess said. "We return to Atlantis."

One by one the priests walked forward and touched their thumbs to the crystal that would transport them to the sunken city. Delwyn hitched along with one of the priests and waited for everyone to arrive.

The goddess herself appeared last of all. When she spoke her voice echoed through Delwyn's mind, just as it did the others.

"The gods seek to send you out into the world of man once more. They are taking back the gift they once bestowed upon you. We sank the city below the waves to protect you from the wars of men. Now they send you back into danger. I may not be able to stop them from sending the rest of the Atlanteans away, but I can save you, my most loyal followers, and you, my son."

Mariana nodded to Fabian and gave him the first genuine smile Delwyn had ever seen from her.

"How do you plan to do this?" one of the priests asked. From his elaborate robes he appeared to be the most senior of the group. Delwyn was relieved they projected their voices for all to hear. He had always been frustrated with those visions where he could see that people were communicating privately and not hear a word of what they said.

Mariana smiled. *"As humans, you are vulnerable. But I am not the Goddess of Humans, I am the Goddess of Sea Creatures. I give you one final gift to save you from banishment."*

She conjured a plate in her hands and said words in a language Delwyn didn't understand. As she spoke, strange items appeared on the plate. They seemed to be fruits, but not any he recognized.

"Eat one of these delicacies and witness my power for yourself."

None of the men seemed particularly eager to take her up on her offer. Delwyn didn't blame them. Goodness only knew what mischief her magic had conjured.

"Fabian," Mariana said. *"You first."*

Delwyn could tell he was nervous about what would happen, but he swam forward.

He took one of the fruits from his mother's plate and bit into the treat. It was gone in a couple of bites.

Nothing happened. Delwyn wondered how long it would be before the magic had any effect on the eater.

The goddess pointed at the door leading out into the city. *"Go forth, my son. Show me that my faith in you has not been wasted."*

Fabian nodded and swam out of the archway. Delwyn stayed at his side, needing to be close in case Fabian vanished, despite whatever his mother had planned. He hoped that if that happened he would be taken along with him to wherever he ended up.

Thankfully, Fabian didn't disappear the moment he left the temple. Instead, he seemed to shimmer and grow right before Delwyn's eyes.

Lightning surrounded him and he let out a scream of pain that Delwyn cringed to hear. Then the cry became a roar and Delwyn clapped his hands over his ears to try to dim the noise.

He watched Fabian change, his hair receding into his increasing body. His robes stretched and tore as he transformed.

When it was finally over, Delwyn could do nothing but stare for several long minutes.

Fabian *was* in the sunken city, where he had been for centuries, waiting for Delwyn to find him. Delwyn had even seen him, without ever knowing it.

The orange sea dragon hadn't tried to kill him. When Fabian had swooped down during the earthquake, he had been saving his life, letting the falling stones hit him instead of Delwyn.

One by one the priests left the temple and transformed. The Goddess of Sea Creatures was the last to emerge.

"What is the meaning of this?" an unfamiliar voice roared. *"You dare to defy my edict?"*

"Ah, Cynbel, you're too late, as usual." Mariana waved her hand toward her new sea dragons. *"You cannot send my*

priests to land like this." Delwyn could hear the gloating in her voice. *"They are creatures of the sea. To send them to land would be to murder them. They will remain here."*

"I can undo whatever magic you have wrought," Cynbel said.

Delwyn didn't know how powerful he was, but he was clearly furious at the way Mariana had undermined his authority.

"Do feel free to try," Mariana said.

Cynbel sent what appeared to be a bolt of power toward the nearest dragon, but it bounced off the creature, which didn't even flinch.

"The sea dragons are creatures of my domain," Mariana said. *"For as long as I wish my priests to retain this form, they will."*

"They must be destroyed."

"You wouldn't dare."

Delwyn nearly cried out *no,* before he recalled that the sea dragons were alive and well in his own time, and hadn't been killed.

"To murder the priests of another is a crime even you dare not commit," Mariana said.

Cynbel lowered his trident, apparently agreeing with her.

Mariana waved her hand toward the sea dragons. *"Come, mer, look upon your new neighbors. They will be with you for a very long time."*

Cynbel pointed his trident at the goddess. *"What do you mean by that?"*

"Why, only that they will be living very long lives."

"You've made them immortal?"

"No, but they will not age a day until I decree it. One day, when the time is right, they will reclaim our city from these interlopers. The mer will regret they didn't leave these waters as soon as we arrived."

Cynbel didn't lower his weapon. *"The Atlanteans will never again call Atlantis home. Undo this magic or face the consequences."*

"You wouldn't dare strike at me," Mariana yelled.

The god replied with a bolt of blue sea-fire right at the

goddess. She raised some sort of shield that appeared to absorb the blast, but as it continued to come at her she visibly struggled to maintain her position.

She eventually ran out of strength and vanished from the area.

"*Sleep now,*" the god said. "*You will need to regain your strength if you intend to take me on again.*"

Delwyn didn't think the god looked so good himself. His battle with the goddess had worn him out.

Other immortals appeared beside him, each god and goddess as stunned by the new additions to the city as the last.

"*What are we going to do with them?*" Cari asked.

Delwyn knew they couldn't be allowed to roam the city freely. Several were already trying to attack some of the mer who had swum too close, and others bared their teeth at the arriving gods.

Cynbel came up with the solution. "*They will be collared and held by the mer until such time as their goddess awakens and returns them to their human forms.*"

Delwyn didn't have time to wonder how he intended to capture the sea dragons. In the blink of an eye, collars appeared round the necks of each of the beasts, including Fabian.

"*The collars will also prevent them from hiding from the mer who inhabit the city,*" the god explained.

"*Hide?*" one of the nearby mermaids asked. "*How can creatures that size hope to hide from anyone?*"

Cynbel turned to smile at the mermaid who had spoken. "*Sea dragons, like their counterparts on land, have existed as long as they have because they have the power to become invisible. Men cannot kill what they cannot see. To those within the boundaries of Atlantis, they cannot hide themselves, though if they value their lives they will keep themselves and the city hidden from humans and other predators in these waters.*"

"*Can they be destroyed?*" Cari asked.

Delwyn glared at the goddess, believing she thought to

kill Fabian after all, before he realized she simply wanted to know the answer to the question.

The god shook his head. *"Mariana is right on one point. To murder the priests of another god is a great crime, and one I do not wish to commit."*

The god stumbled and seemed to flicker out of sight for a moment.

"You've done too much, Father," Cari said.

The god nodded and offered her a shaky smile. *"You're right, daughter. I must sleep, too. Pray I wake before Mariana does."*

"You have always been more powerful than her," Cari said.

"I know, but today I have used my powers more than at any other time in my existence. Do what you can to protect the mer."

"I will."

"And take care of your brother. He needs you."

Cari nodded, and a moment later, her father vanished in the same way Mariana had.

One by one the other gods herded the sea dragons away from the main city. Delwyn was torn between following Fabian and staying with Cari.

In the end, he watched Fabian leave and turned to the Goddess he served so many years in the future.

"Did you know what Mariana had planned?" Delwyn asked. *"Did you see that, too?"*

Cari shook her head. *"I only suspected. Fear not, my Oracle. Fabian has never been far from your side."*

"What happens now?"

"You will return to your own time," Cari replied. *"You've seen all there is to see here."*

Delwyn knew his time in this era was over, so he ended his vision and returned to the present.

Chapter Twelve

Fabian watched his guards with disinterest. The mermen who had the duty of keeping the city safe from his kind had become lax in recent years. They had no idea of the danger they were in.

He tilted his head toward the surface of the ocean. Isander swam above him, his guards nudging him in the direction they wanted him to go.

The dragons rotated around Atlantis, sometimes guarding the perimeter on the ground, at other times circling above the city. It had been a monotonous and boring existence for so many centuries that Fabian had long since lost count.

Isander's black scales disappeared into the darkness and his mother's high priest, Urion, swam into view.

When the priest spotted Fabian watching him, he snarled. "*Useless Oracles*," he called down.

Fabian supposed he couldn't blame him for his anger. The Oracles had failed to see the fate of the Atlanteans and now this was what they had become. Their people had been scattered around the world, lost amongst other races, their identity as Atlanteans forgotten. Only Mariana's priests remained, along with Fabian.

Urion disappeared on his way and Fabian returned to his contemplation of the city.

So many years had passed since their imprisonment by the God of War. As sea dragons they had no real way of marking the passage of time. At first Fabian had tried to count the days and the seasons, but there had been so many he had soon lost track. It didn't matter anymore.

Instead he'd noted what he could and waited, mostly

patiently, for the sight of a set of familiar silver fins.

There had been others over the years, youngsters with fins that glowed with the light of the moon. Fabian had watched them grow up into young mermen, but none had borne any resemblance to Delwyn.

As the years had passed, he had listened intently. The guards, often bored with watching the sea dragons, had gossiped constantly. They had talked of their families, their lovers, their children and their jobs. Most of all they had chatted about the royal family, and for that Fabian had been grateful beyond words.

The day he had heard one of the guards talk about the new-born prince, who the king and queen had named Finn, had been one he would never forget. In all the years, there had never been a royal named Finn.

After so many centuries of imprisonment, finally Fabian had let himself hope again. He had watched the palace whenever he'd been able, waiting for the sight of the prince and his young friend, Delwyn.

The first time he had seen Delwyn with the prince, he'd appeared to be around six years of age. The boys had slipped away from their minder, ducking into one of the ruined buildings.

Afterward, Fabian had spotted them many times, though only from a distance. Even boisterous boys knew not to approach the sea dragons.

Delwyn grew up into a handsome youth and there had been whispers amongst the guards that Prince Finn kept company with him a little too often, and that maybe the Prince was a lover of men.

Fabian knew this to be the truth, and that at some time since his imprisonment, laws had been imposed upon the mer, forbidding sexual relations between two mer of the same gender. Prince Finn and Delwyn were playing with fire.

Then more gossip had reached his ears, this time about Delwyn, and his new position as an Oracle of the past.

Fabian smiled to himself, knowing the time would soon come when Delwyn would know of his existence.

It didn't take long for Isander to notice Fabian's gaze wandering to a particular merman on a frequent basis.

"You're mooning, Fabian," Isander teased as he passed overhead again.

"I don't moon," Fabian replied. *"I'm merely thinking quite hard."*

"About a certain merman, I presume?"

"Of course." There was little point in denying it. It had taken all of a few days for Isander to figure out when Fabian had first spotted Delwyn.

"I thought I saw him enter the barracks on my last pass over there," Isander said.

"Much good that does me over here on the opposite side of the city."

Isander's laughter lingered in Fabian's mind long after his friend and former lover had swum out of sight.

Fabian could sense the time was close when Delwyn would discover the truth of what had happened. The merman appeared exactly the same now as he had the last time Fabian had seen him, right before he'd renounced his commitment to Cari and sworn loyalty to his mother. Even after all this time, he wondered whether he had made the right decision.

* * * *

"You've lost your mind," Marin said. He sounded half-asleep. *"That or I'm dreaming right now."*

"That was my reaction, too," Kai muttered.

Delwyn glared in what he hoped was Kai's direction. Sometimes it could be a little difficult to tell, not that Kai necessarily knew he was scowling at him, anyway.

They had sneaked out of the temple after requesting their guards leave the room to give them some privacy. The guards had been reluctant to do so, until Dax had intervened and cleared the room with a few threats and the jab of his spear. They wouldn't have been able to get away with such a thing not so long ago, but the abolishing of the law relating to the Oracles and the ban on sexual relations meant they had a lot more freedom now. These days, their guards were mostly to help them get around the city — something Kai had never really needed, since he frequently used his powers to see where he was.

Delwyn had thought that slipping past the guards and Dax would be the hard part. He hadn't banked on the opposition of Kai and Marin to his plans.

"*I'm not insane,*" Delwyn insisted. "*I have to go talk to one of the sea dragons, but you know the guards won't let me near them.*"

"*With good reason,*" Kai said. "*They're dangerous monsters and would eat you just as soon as look at you.*"

"*Have you been listening to what I've told you at all?*" Delwyn asked.

"*Yes, I heard every word, but don't you think we'd know if the sea dragons were actually human? Wouldn't there be records of such things or stories about their transformation on the walls of those temples you're so fond of exploring?*"

"*The stories on the walls of the temple were written by the Atlanteans. All the Atlanteans were banished the day the Goddess of Sea Creatures transformed all her priests into sea dragons. There was no one left to write the story.*"

"*If they were really people, why do they always get so violent towards the mer?*" Marin asked. "*You know how dangerous they are. I'm not even allowed to guard them myself because of how vicious they can be.*"

"*They're prisoners of the mer,*" Delwyn reminded him. "*After all these centuries, of course they're angry.*"

"*All the more reason to stay out of their way,*" Kai insisted. "*Even if this dragon is the man you met in your visions, he's been trapped in the body of a sea dragon for hundreds of years. He might not be the same man you knew back then. Do you really want to risk this?*"

"I'm going to see Fabian, with or without your help," Delwyn said. "But it would be a lot easier with, since, in case you've both forgotten, I'm completely blind."

"Calder will be furious," Marin said. "Are you sure you want to do this?"

"How many times do I have to say it?" Delwyn snapped.

Marin patted him on the arm. "I guess we're off to poke a dragon."

Delwyn threw his arms around Marin, knocking Kai in the process. "Thank you. I won't forget this."

"How are we going to do this?" Kai asked. "As Marin has already pointed out, he's not allowed to guard the dragons himself and they always have two mermen guarding each of the beasts. They aren't going to let any of us near them."

"I'll distract the guards," Marin said. "Maybe I can convince one of them Calder is giving me a chance to guard one of them for the rest of the shift. Then I can distract the second guard while you get Delwyn close enough to... What do you intend to do when you get close?"

Delwyn had a feeling this was where his plan might fall apart. "I don't know. Talk to him, I guess."

Kai spotted the flaw in his plan immediately. "Delwyn, don't you think if the sea dragons could communicate with us, they would have done so at some point already?"

Delwyn huffed and scowled. "I'll figure it out when I get there."

"I don't like the sound of this," Kai said, not for the first time.

"You don't have to like it," Delwyn replied. "I didn't stop you from traveling to the land of humans when your chance for love came, so don't stop me now."

"There's a big difference between swimming to land and getting up close and personal with a sea dragon. I'd rather take on a shiver of sharks single-handed."

"And I wouldn't stop you if you wanted to," Delwyn said. "Now, are you going to help me, or are you going to hover there and tell me what a fool I am?"

Kai sighed audibly. "Of course I'll help you, but don't blame *me if you get yourself eaten."*

* * * *

"Which one is he?" Marin asked. *"The last thing we need to do is find the wrong one."*

"He's orange with a golden streak down his belly."

"There's only one orange dragon," Marin said. *"Thank goodness for that. If you'd said black we might be in trouble."*

"The color of the dragons matches their hair color," Delwyn explained. *"Fabian was the only red-haired man there. He inherited his mother's hair, but most of her priests were blond or black-haired."*

"Let's go find him then," Marin said.

Delwyn gave him credit for trying to sound enthusiastic. He almost believed him.

Fabian was on the perimeter of the city, apparently sleeping while his guards sparred with each other to pass the time.

"Well, there he is," Marin said. *"This is your last chance to back out."*

Delwyn shook his head. *"You go distract the guards and Kai will steer me closer to him."*

Marin snorted. *"You owe me for this, Delwyn."*

Delwyn waited until Kai confirmed Marin had drawn the guards' attention away from the dragon.

"I don't think they believe he's allowed to take on dragon-guarding duties," Kai said. *"Neither of them are leaving."*

"What are they doing?"

"Marin is joining in their fighting. It looks as if one of them is giving him some pointers."

"Are they looking this way?"

"No, I think we're in the clear. It's now or never. Come on."

Delwyn let Kai guide him closer to Fabian. He could feel Kai shaking as they approached. He gave his hand a reassuring squeeze. *"I promise he won't hurt you."*

"Let's just get this madness over with."

They swam to Fabian on the opposite side to where the guards were.

"Here we are," Kai said. *"Now what?"*

Delwyn reached out and found the hard scales of the sea dragon under his hand. *"Fabian?"*

He sent his thoughts out to the sea dragon alone, hoping to hear a familiar voice respond.

"Can you hear me?" Delwyn tried again when the only response was a deafening silence.

"Can we go back home now?" Kai asked. *"Clearly, he doesn't want to talk."*

"I don't believe that. Whatever magic turned him into this must be stopping him communicating with us."

"Maybe you're right, but since we have no way of undoing this magic, why don't we leave it for now and come back when we've figured something out?"

"I'm not leaving him," Delwyn insisted. He had no idea what to do, but he had no intention of leaving. Who knew if he would have another opportunity to get this close to Fabian? If they were caught, the guards would never be so lax again.

"Wait a moment," Kai said. *"I think he's trying to do something."*

"What?" Delwyn asked. It was so frustrating not to be able to see what Kai could. He cursed his blindness again.

"He's clawing at his collar."

"Maybe if we take it off, he'll be able to speak with us."

Kai made an uncomplimentary noise. *"First, you want to come pet a dragon, now you want to take his collar off."*

"Please try."

Delwyn waited impatiently while Kai studied the collar.

"I can't see where there's a catch on it," Kai said. *"It's solid all the way round."*

"They were collared by one of the gods," Delwyn explained. *"I doubt they wanted them to get free any time soon."*

"Sounds like a good idea to me."

Delwyn fumbled his way to Fabian's collar and felt

around the edge. The metal was one smooth, solid ring.

"*Maybe we can blast it off with sea-fire?*" Delwyn suggested. "*The gods were the ones who first wielded sea-fire, so maybe it'll break the collars.*"

"*Delwyn, will you listen to yourself? We don't have any tridents with us, and even if we did, we don't know how to conjure sea-fire. Calder told me they took the tridents off the guards because they were so volatile.*"

"*But you've been studying the tridents for him,*" Delwyn pointed out. "*Surely, if anyone can work it, you can.*"

"*Do you see a trident here?*" Kai asked sarcastically.

"*I don't see anything, remember?*" Delwyn snapped back.

Kai sighed. "*I'm sorry, I don't mean to shatter your dreams here, but I don't think this is a good idea.*"

"*Can you at least fetch a trident from the barracks so we can try?*"

"*You aren't going to give up, are you?*"

"*Never.*"

"*I'll be back as quick as I can,*" Kai promised. "*Just try not to get caught by the guards while I'm gone.*"

"*Is Marin still distracting them?*"

"*Yes, he's letting them best him over and over again. They won't send him on his way while they're gloating over their victories.*"

Kai made sure Delwyn was hidden out of sight, round the back of Fabian, just in case the guards actually remembered what their duties were supposed to be and checked on the sea dragon.

Delwyn nestled down beside Fabian and stroked his scales, impatiently waiting for the time when they could talk again. It struck him as rather amusing that previously he had only been able to speak with Fabian and could not touch him. Now he could touch him, but Fabian had no way of communicating with him. Soon they would have it all — he just knew it.

Kai returned with a trident and a lot of mumbled complaints about lax security in the barracks and idiotic mermen.

Delwyn moved out of the way of Fabian's long neck so Kai could take aim. *"Try to hit the collar, not him,"* he warned.

"You can aim it yourself, if you like," Kai replied.

Knowing his own aim would be dreadful, Delwyn kept quiet and left Kai to it.

Although he couldn't see the sea-fire, he felt the heat of the flame as it shot through the water. His fear that Kai wouldn't be able to conjure the sea-fire at all was unfounded.

"It's put a hole in it," Kai said. *"I think one more blast should do it."*

The second shot heated the water even more than the first.

"What in the world is going on here?"

Delwyn cringed as Calder's voice resounded through his mind.

"Fuck." Kai's expletive summed up Delwyn's thoughts perfectly.

"Marin, what are you doing out here? Why aren't you in the barracks?"

"Did you miss me?" Marin asked. *"I couldn't sleep, so I thought I'd take a swim and get a bit of extra practice in. I'd have been back to share your sponge before your shift finished."*

Delwyn covered his mouth to hide his grin. Only Marin would ever dare speak to Calder in such a way. And only he could get away with it.

He wondered if Calder had spotted him and Kai, before realizing what a foolish thought that was. Of course he would have seen them. The sea-fire could be seen from a mile away, and even if it couldn't, nothing slipped past the leader of the guards.

"And why do we have two Oracles tormenting one of the dragons?" Calder asked. He sounded furious.

"We're not tormenting him," Delwyn said. *"We're trying to get his collar off."*

"It seems to me you already managed that," Calder replied. *"Would you care to explain why? Guards, keep your tridents on the beast. Just don't hit either of the Oracles. King Nereus will have your heads if you harm either of them."*

Delwyn hadn't realized Kai had succeeded in breaking the collar. *"Fabian?"* he asked.

"Of course," Fabian replied. *"I'm delighted you understood what I was trying to say to you. I've missed you."*

Delwyn grinned and swam back to Fabian, wrapping his arms around the thick neck of the dragon. They wouldn't reach all the way around, but it would have to do. *"Can you transform back into human?"* he asked.

"No, I'm afraid I can't. I don't know what magic my mother used to transform us, but I'm sure only her rising from her slumber will allow us to revert to human form."

"Delwyn, step back from the dragon," Calder ordered. *"You have no idea how dangerous these beasts are."*

Delwyn guessed Fabian's words had only been for him and Calder still believed him to be in danger.

"Guards, drive it back from the Oracles," Calder shouted. *"Kill it if you have to."*

"No!" Delwyn screamed. *"He won't hurt anyone."*

Delwyn couldn't tell where the guards were, but he could feel the water moving at the back of him, as Fabian shifted his huge body.

"Delwyn, come to me," Calder said. *"Just swim straight ahead."*

"He's not dangerous," Delwyn shouted. He didn't move from his position, which he hoped was between Fabian and the guards. *"Kai, Marin, stop them, please."*

Delwyn felt Fabian nudge him in the back and he reached out blindly, seeking reassurance.

"That's my nose you're about to shove your hand up," Fabian warned him with a very un-dragon-like snicker.

"Can't you talk to Calder, make him understand you?"

"I'm trying, but he's too busy shouting at everyone to hear me."

"You need to be loud. You're a dragon. Roar."

Fabian laughed. *"Calder!"* he shouted at the top of his extremely large lungs.

Everyone went instantly silent.

Delwyn wasn't surprised to note that Calder was the first

to find his voice again.

"Did that sea dragon just speak?"

"I believe he did," Kai replied. *"Fabian, I assume?"*

"Indeed," Fabian confirmed. *"And you would be Kai?"*

"Yes."

"I thought so. Delwyn has told me a lot about you."

"Likewise," Kai said.

Calder coughed deliberately. *"Can someone please explain to me what's going on?"*

Delwyn patted Fabian on his neck and left his hand to rest there. *"This is Fabian, he's… er…"* How did he describe him? An Atlantean? A demi-god? A former Oracle? *"He's mine."*

Fabian nuzzled him with his snout. *"Yes, I am."*

"I don't understand," Calder said.

Delwyn didn't know where to start, but Fabian had obviously had plenty of time to think about what he would say when this moment arrived.

"My name is Fabian. Many centuries ago, I was an Oracle of the present, bound to Cari, the Goddess of Prophecy. My mother is the Goddess of Sea Creatures. The powers I have from those two goddesses enabled me to see and speak with Delwyn when he had visions of me in the past."

"But you're a sea dragon," Calder pointed out.

"I was human when we first met. The sea dragons are my mother's priests. She transformed us to save us from banishment when another god drove the Atlanteans from the city. We were collared and imprisoned by the gods and set to the task of hiding this city and protecting the mer."

Calder snorted in disbelief. *"Forgive me, but I don't see a lot of protection happening from the sea dragons. It takes two guards, sometimes more, to keep each of you under control. I haven't forgotten the way one of you swooped in to attack Delwyn himself, not so long ago."*

"That was me," Fabian interrupted. *"But you didn't see what you think you did. I would never seek to attack any of the mer, least of all Delwyn. The columns were falling down on him and there were too many for his guard to shield him from. I placed*

my body between the stones and him. They bounced off of me like pebbles, while they would have surely killed him."

"It's the truth," Delwyn added. "Fabian would never harm me."

Fabian nuzzled him again. "Unfortunately, the same can't be said for most of the other sea dragons."

"What do you mean?" Calder asked.

"My mother had no love for the mer and most of her priests were equally prejudiced."

"Not all of them," Delwyn said. "Isander doesn't hate us."

"No," Fabian agreed. "Isander is a gentle soul, who hates no one. The others are not so pleasant. They are biding their time until the day they are freed from their collars, when they intend to drive the mer from the city and reclaim it for my mother and the other immortals who want Atlantis to be for the Atlanteans alone."

"Then I suggest we don't go around removing the collars of any other dragons," Calder said.

"Except Isander," Delwyn said. "I would like to speak to him again."

Calder huffed and sighed. "Which one is he?"

"He's the smallest of the sea dragons," Fabian confirmed. "He's circling above the city tonight."

"I can't believe I'm even considering this," Calder complained. "Or that I'm actually talking with a dragon. Can you turn back into your human form? It would make this a lot easier."

"It would make a great many things a lot easier," Fabian agreed. "But I don't have the power to change back. I suspect only the waking of my mother will give us the ability to transform back into what we once were."

"And your mother intends to drive us out of the city?"

"Yes."

"Then I guess we're going to be stuck with two talking dragons," Calder said. "King Nereus will probably wish to speak with you."

"He can if he wishes. I'll answer his questions as best I can, though, I suspect most of what he wants to know is outside of my knowledge."

"I'll speak to him in the morning. In the meantime, I think our Oracles should return to their temple. Marin, you can escort them back. If you don't mind, Fabian, I'd rather the two guards remain with you."

"You don't trust him?" Delwyn asked.

"I don't know him," Calder replied.

"He's quite right," Fabian said. "Calder is a good leader and a merman of great wisdom. The guards have nothing to fear from me, but they cannot know that yet. Trust must be earned."

"Yes, it must." Calder patted Delwyn on the shoulder. "Come on, let's get you back to the temple."

"I'd rather stay here, if you don't mind?" Delwyn said. "Fabian and I have a lot to talk about. I'll be perfectly safe with him."

Kai chuckled. "I wouldn't bother arguing if I were you. I've not won an argument with him yet. Marin, go get some rest. I can find my own way back to the palace."

Delwyn said goodnight to Marin and Kai and felt his way to a comfortable spot in between Fabian's front legs. "Do you mind if I rest my head on your leg?"

"Of course not. I've waited a long time to feel you in my arms."

"You are talking to me privately now, aren't you?" Delwyn asked.

"Yes, why would you think otherwise?"

"I don't know. Maybe because it's been so long since you could speak."

"I've been able to talk to the other sea dragons without any problem. Though I've had difficulty communicating with other sea creatures, and the mer, of course."

"You can speak to other species of the sea?" Delwyn couldn't believe he hadn't known that.

"A gift inherited from my mother. I don't use it often."

Delwyn snuggled down in Fabian's embrace. "Finally, we get to touch, and we can't even do anything. I didn't like what I saw of your mother, but I want her to wake up, just so I can be with you properly."

"Me, too, Delwyn. Me, too."

"Talk to me," Delwyn asked. "Tell me you love me."

"I gave up my Oracle powers only so I could be certain I would remember you," Fabian said. "Nothing else other than my love for you would have convinced me to swear loyalty to my mother."

"Was it worth it?"

"We're finally living in the same time. We can touch each other, and somehow we will find a way to be together."

"Even if it means waking your mother?"

Fabian remained silent for a long while.

"Fabian?"

"Yes, Delwyn. Even if it means waking her up. I know I shouldn't say it, because when she wakes she will command her priests to take over the city, but I've waited so long for you, I have to believe somehow things will resolve themselves."

They continued to talk for a long while, until eventually Delwyn closed his eyes and let the soothing sound of Fabian's voice lull him to sleep.

He had no idea how they would find a way to turn Fabian back into a human without destroying their city, but he hoped they figured it out soon.

Chapter Thirteen

Fabian nuzzled Delwyn as the merman slept in his arms, or as near enough to arms as he had right now.

Isander, much to Calder's annoyance, rushed over to see Fabian immediately he was released from his collar. *"So this is the little merman you fell in love with?"*

"Yes. This is Delwyn. He's sleeping right now."

"I can see that."

"I'll introduce you when he wakes up."

"I can't wait," Isander replied. *"He's most handsome, isn't he?"*

Fabian growled deep in his stomach. While he and Isander had shared lovers before, he had no intention of sharing Delwyn with anyone. He didn't need to say a word to get his point across.

"You weren't always so selfish with your lovers," Isander teased. *"When did you become the possessive type?"*

Fabian couldn't smile in his dragon form, but inside he was. *"The day I met him."*

"What are you going to do about him? You can't be together without waking your mother."

"I know. I keep trying to come up with another solution, but I have no idea what to do. Even when all the gods walked, no one would have had the power to undo my mother's magic."

"You want to wake her, don't you?"

Fabian honestly didn't know the answer to Isander's question. The thought of the battle that would come to the city if his mother should wake wasn't one he wanted to dwell upon. The mer had no idea what would be coming.

Unfortunately, no matter what Fabian chose to do

regarding his mother, she *would* wake up, and when she did, all hell would break loose. It was simply a matter of when.

"Fabian," Isander continued. *"Please don't make any rash decisions."*

"I don't intend to. If I was going to do that, I'd already be swimming into her temple and shouting for her."

Delwyn stirred in his arms. Fabian nudged him with his snout and Delwyn made a delightful snuffling noise. He rolled over and nestled closer.

"He is a sweet-looking merman," Isander said. *"I can see why you're attracted to him."*

Fabian shielded Delwyn a little more, causing Isander to chuckle at his protectiveness.

"You know my mother will wake soon, regardless," he said. *"Other immortals are already walking among us once more. Were it not for the last magic my mother worked, she would already be here."*

"I know. But I'd rather she slumbers away a little longer, if you don't mind."

Fabian agreed. *"How did you ever end up in my mother's service? You don't share her ideals or beliefs. I never understood why you chose to swear loyalty to her."*

Isander sighed. *"I love the sea and everything in it. I was always happier in the water than on the land. I thought the Goddess of Sea Creatures loved and embraced all those who reside in the oceans of the world. I'm afraid I was rather idealistic."*

"There's nothing wrong with that."

"I seem to be in the minority," Isander pointed out. *"Almost all of Mariana's priests share her views when it comes to the mer. They are the most intelligent and beautiful beings of the sea, yet she spurns them at every turn."*

"You would have been a wonderful High Priest," Fabian said.

"Don't let Urion hear you say that."

Urion's anger at their situation had festered over the centuries, and for the most part it was directed at Fabian.

Fabian tried to stay out of his way as much as possible,

but in the confines of the city it was difficult.

Delwyn stirred again, waking this time. *"Fabian?"*

"I'm right here with you," Fabian assured him. *"I have someone here who would like to meet you, too."*

"You do?"

"Yes. Technically, you've already seen him, though he wasn't able to see you."

"Isander?" Delwyn sat and turned his head this way and that, as though trying to see him.

"It's a pleasure to meet you, Delwyn," Isander said.

He always had been a charmer. Fabian squirmed with pride that the sexy young merman had chosen him.

Delwyn blushed and Fabian had a feeling he recalled the last time he had *met* Isander.

Suddenly Delwyn grinned widely.

"And what are you so happy about?" Fabian asked.

"I just realized all my worrying about you forgetting me over the centuries was a little pointless. All this time you've been stuck in these sea dragon forms."

"And not getting any sex," Isander finished for him. *"Believe me, we know. I'm pretty sure that's why most of the priests are so bad-tempered."*

"Maybe they're angry about being imprisoned," Delwyn suggested. *"I know my confinement to the city wasn't exactly fun, but at least I had a few freedoms."*

"You don't like being an Oracle, do you?" Fabian asked.

"I hate being blind and dependent on others to get around the city. I feel such a burden."

"You'd never be that to me," Fabian assured him. *"I rather like the idea of being needed by someone again."*

"I'd rather we had an equal partnership."

"I know you would, and it will be, as much as it can. But you must know I'll be here whenever you need me."

Delwyn frowned. *"Except for what I need from you the most."*

Fabian didn't have to ask him what he meant. He wanted Delwyn just as badly now as he had all those centuries ago. The touch of the merman's hand on his scales reminded him what it was like to crave the touch of another man. For so long, even before his final day as a human, he had desired only Delwyn.

"*Are you sure you can't become human again?*" Delwyn asked.

"*We were just talking about that,*" Isander said. "*There's only one being who can transform us back to human, and that's the Goddess of Sea Creatures, who turned us into sea dragons in the first place.*"

"*She's still asleep, though.*"

Fabian nodded. "*But not for long. The immortals are waking and it's simply a matter of time before she joins us.*"

"*Can we wake her sooner?*" Delwyn asked.

"*We were just debating whether that was a good idea or not,*" Isander admitted.

"*And what did you decide?*"

"*We hadn't,*" Fabian said. "*But while we're discussing the situation she may wake, anyway.*"

"*Cari woke her mother, at least partially, by getting us to call her by her given name from her temple. It gave her strength. Would that work for your mother?*"

Fabian gave another nod. "*Even if it didn't work right away, eventually, it would be enough to wake her. Calling any god or goddess by their name, from one of their temples, gives them a power boost. My mother is no exception.*"

"*Then I should go to her temple as soon as possible,*" Delwyn stated in a firm tone that caused Fabian's arguments to die on his tongue.

Isander, who had not been rendered mute, said what Fabian was thinking. "*Even if you wake her, she may not turn us back. She made us dragons so we could become her warriors and reclaim the city for the Atlanteans. If we become human again, we would be little use in the coming battle.*"

"*You wouldn't fight the mer, would you?*" Delwyn asked.

"*No, we wouldn't,*" Fabian said. "*When the time comes, I swear, I will do everything in my power to protect you.*"

"*Can you really protect me from a goddess intent on war?*"

"You forget, I'm half god myself, and I have powers of my own. We'll also have Cari on our side. You are one of her Oracles and I used to be. She won't let any harm come to you."

Delwyn patted Fabian on the front paw and stretched. *"I think I should go and see if I can rouse your mother."*

"She won't thank you for it," Isander warned.

"Maybe she will. She's had plenty of time to calm down, and maybe she'll be thankful to the mer if one of us were to wake her."

Fabian snorted and bubbles shot from his snout. *"You're an eternal optimist."*

Delwyn leaned in and gave Fabian a quick peck on the side of his face. *"I have to try. And who knows, it may be that nothing happens when I call her anyway."*

A part of Fabian hoped that was the case, while another felt ridiculously pleased at the small kiss of affection Delwyn had given him. He wanted that again, and even more besides.

* * * *

It took several minutes of arguing with Fabian before Delwyn convinced him he didn't need a sea dragon escorting him to the temple. He could manage with his regular guard.

Fabian hadn't liked the idea, until Delwyn had pointed out to him that in his current form he wouldn't even be able to fit through the entrance.

In the end, they settled for a compromise. Fabian and Isander would circle above the temple, just in case they were needed. Calder wasn't too pleased about changing the rotation of the sea dragons, but soon saw the wisdom of ensuring the protection of one of the Oracles.

Delwyn knew from his previous explorations that the temple was structurally sound, even if it had seen better days.

The statue of the goddess stood in the center of the room. Delwyn swam toward it and settled himself on the floor at the foot of the statue.

"Mariana?" he called out telepathically to anyone in the vicinity who could hear him.

Nothing happened, at least that he could hear. For all he knew, the goddess had appeared and was glaring straight at him. He wouldn't be able to see her.

"Do you see anything happening?" he asked his guard.

"Like what?"

"I don't know, someone appearing or anything unusual."

"Not a thing."

Delwyn sighed, but he didn't want to give up so soon. *"Mariana? Goddess of Sea Creatures, I call to you. Mariana."*

Still nothing stirred.

For nearly an hour, Delwyn called out for the goddess. All he could hear in response was the increasing mumbling and muttering in his head from his guard.

"I don't think it's working," his escort said during one of Delwyn's brief breaks from trying to summon Mariana.

"Me, neither."

Delwyn's stomach growled and he recalled that he hadn't eaten anything since the previous day. Perhaps he should come back later. His guard liked the suggestion and swam toward the door.

"Or you could exercise a little patience."

Delwyn froze as the voice of the goddess rang loud and clear through his mind. *"Goddess?"*

"I am not your *goddess,"* Mariana replied. *"I'm the Goddess of Sea Creatures."*

"I'm a sea creature," Delwyn said.

"You're an abomination."

Delwyn cringed. It seemed the goddess wasn't exactly thankful to be woken by a mer.

"I'm not awake yet," Mariana said. *"Though I'm able to speak with you, since you shouted for me so annoyingly persistently."*

Delwyn realized Mariana must be on the verge of waking, just as Cari's mother was.

"That's correct. Now, why don't you explain to me what you

thought you were doing by calling me? Be careful when you answer. It might make all the difference when I wake."

"What do you mean?"

"Why, whether I kill you instantly or make you suffer first. Did you think I would have forgotten you?"

Delwyn had hoped she had.

"The presumptuous merman who dared to desire my son."

Perhaps telling her he wanted her to return Fabian to his human form so they could be together wasn't the best idea.

"No, it wouldn't be," Mariana agreed.

Delwyn wished the goddess would stop reading his mind, but saying so probably wouldn't improve her temper.

"Understand this, merman," Mariana said. "I never allowed the mer to enter my temple before you. I did not seek you as worshippers, and I neither want nor need you now. It is because of you and your kind that I'm reduced to this. An echo of what I once was."

"You still have powers in your present form," Delwyn reminded her.

"Not as strong as they will be soon," Mariana replied. "And nowhere near powerful enough to undo the spell my priests and son are under."

"Then Fabian is stuck in sea dragon form?"

"Isn't that what I just said?"

Delwyn wondered how long it might be before the goddess was able to work her magic.

"Soon," Mariana answered his thought before he had even completed it. "While they are collared I cannot siphon power from my priests. Now they are free, Fabian and Isander are helping me emerge from stasis, merely by existing. If you were to uncollar more of my priests, it would hasten my return."

"And you'd turn Fabian back into a human?"

"Perhaps."

It wasn't an outright refusal, and Delwyn clung to the slim hope that maybe the goddess had a soft spot for her son and would want him to be happy. When she didn't instantly shatter his dreams, Delwyn hoped he was right.

"Or, if you don't free my priests, you can always wait for my strength to be restored."

"How long will it be if I can't free them?"

"A year, a century, who knows? But it doesn't matter to Fabian, does it? He is half god and even though he will one day die a mortal death, it will be many more years before that happens. As long as he remains in dragon form, it may never come to pass."

"What do you mean?"

"My sea dragons have not aged a single day in all the time since they have transformed. I made sure of that. As they were all men, they could not breed amongst themselves. I couldn't have them all dying of old age within a few short years. My spell ensures they will still be here to serve me when I wake, whenever that might be. Then they will serve me, for as long as I need them to."

Delwyn didn't even realize the goddess had vanished until his guard spoke.

"Are you sure you want to wake her?"

Delwyn didn't know anymore. He wanted Fabian restored to his human form, but at what price? It was obvious from what she had said that Mariana's contempt for the mer was as strong as ever.

Either way, he knew they could not release any of the other sea dragons without Calder's permission. He had to talk to Fabian and Isander. Maybe some of the other priests would agree to help them protect the mer from the goddess's wrath.

* * * *

Delwyn let his guard lead him to Fabian, who waited above the temple. *"You can go get something to eat,"* he said.

"So should you," his guard pointed out.

"Bring something back for me?" Delwyn asked.

"You know I'm not supposed to leave you alone."

"I'm not alone," Delwyn said. *"I have Fabian with me."*

"He'll be perfectly safe with me," Fabian assured the guard. *"And I'll ensure he eats soon."*

The guard reluctantly went off in search of food.

"*Your mother can't undo the spell yet,*" Delwyn said. "*She's not strong enough.*"

Delwyn told Fabian what his mother had said. When he was done, Fabian immediately shook his head.

"*She deceived you,*" Fabian said. "*She needs her priests freed to wake, and is using your feelings for me to bring that about.*"

"*You don't think she'll make you human again?*"

"*No. She knows how much you and I both want that. For that reason alone she'll leave me in this form.*"

Delwyn sighed and curled into Fabian's side. There *had* to be a way, if only they could find it.

Chapter Fourteen

To free any more of the sea dragons would require the approval of Calder, and it was clear from the start he wasn't going to give it.

"You do realize the sea dragons will attack us as soon as they get the chance?" he asked.

"Fabian and Isander didn't," Delwyn reminded him.

"That doesn't mean the rest of them won't. Do you know how many of the mer have been attacked and injured by getting too close to these beasts?"

"They're not animals. They were people, Atlanteans. They're just trapped in the bodies of dragons."

"Yes, I know that, but do you see that makes it even worse? It means they're not just dumb animals. They're as smart, perhaps even smarter, than we are. They can coordinate their attack and know exactly how to inflict the most damage. They won't be frightened off by anything we do to try to contain them, because they know they have the advantage. Now, don't let me hear another word about this. The sea dragons were collared for a reason and they're going to stay that way."

Delwyn could have screamed in frustration. *"I know why they were collared. I was there and I saw it happen. If you would just consider the fact that some or all of them could become our allies if you'd just give them a chance."*

"A chance to kill us?" Calder asked. *"Delwyn, I know you think the sea dragons are all like your Fabian, but you haven't worked with them like I have."*

Fabian nudged Delwyn with his snout. *"Don't try to talk him round. He's probably right. My mother's priests are unlikely to be sympathetic to the plight of the mer. They're far more likely* to bring about the destruction of your people in my mother's name."

"See," Calder said. "Even he knows it's a bad idea."

"But it's the only way we can even hope to be together."

"A slim chance is all it is. My mother is unlikely to restore me to human form."

"You can give up if you want, but I'm not going to admit defeat just yet."

"Delwyn, you don't understand."

"I understand enough. You could at least have helped me convince Calder."

"Delwyn!"

Delwyn cursed under his breath and swam back toward the temple of the Oracles. He ignored Fabian's voice in his head, calling him to return to him.

He had thought at least Fabian would be on his side. After all he had said, didn't he want them to be together?

When he arrived home he nearly swam right into Kai, he was so distracted. Normally he could sense when other mer were in his direct path, whether by the change in heat in the water, or simply by instinct.

"Calder didn't like the idea, I take it?" Kai said.

"He wouldn't even listen to me."

"I'm sure that's not true. Calder has always been fair. What did he say?"

"That they're too dangerous to be freed."

"He has a point."

"He won't even give them a chance."

"Delwyn, you have to remember that they're angry with the mer. We've been holding them prisoner for centuries. Look at how much we hated being confined to the city. And we weren't held here anywhere near as long as the dragons have been."

Delwyn sighed. "I know, but I want to be with Fabian, and while he's stuck as a dragon, that's impossible."

Kai struck him on the arm, hard.

"What was that for?"

"You're being an idiot," Kai replied. "You're sulking about

not being with Fabian when he's right here with you."

"You know what I mean."

"Yes, of course I do. You're talking about sex, but that's not the beginning and the end of everything."

"Says the merman who gets plenty of it whenever he wants," Delwyn muttered.

"You've had how many years of celibacy?" Kai asked. *"Ten years, or thereabouts?"*

"Something like that."

"And Fabian, how long has he had to wait? Oh, yeah, hundreds upon hundreds of years. Try putting yourself in his position."

Shame at his selfish desires washed over Delwyn.

"Is that all you want Fabian for? Someone to have sex with?"

"No, of course not."

"Good. Because if it was, there are plenty of mermen who would be happy to fulfil your curiosity."

"I don't want anyone else. I love him."

Kai wrapped his arms around Delwyn and rested his chin on his shoulder.

"I know you do, so you just have to have a little faith that everything will work out."

"I don't see how it can," Delwyn replied.

Kai chuckled in his ear. *"Neither did I when I went to Medina's temple and she told me I would have to leave the city to win my love. But look at how that turned out."*

"At least you and Dax are the same species."

Kai smacked him again, lightly this time. *"Stop that. If you love him as much as you say you do, then you'll take what you have."*

Kai was right. He just had to remember what was important. He didn't just want Fabian for his body and sex. He loved him completely. He wasn't sure exactly when it had happened, but now he had fallen he couldn't imagine a life without him in it.

He thought of his first love, Prince Finn, and found he could think about those days without the stabbing pain of loss.

Then he considered what it would be like if he lost Fabian. The thought didn't sit easy with him. He couldn't lose him.

His mind made up, he swam right back out of the temple, causing his guard to curse with annoyance at their swift arrival and departure. He set a course for the temple of the Goddess of Love. She had answered Kai's plea — surely she wouldn't ignore his own.

Medina's temple was the best-restored of all the buildings in the city. When the heir to the throne and his partner had sworn vows to each other in her presence, the goddess' powers had been given such a boost they had returned her temple to its former glory in a matter of moments.

Unlike when he had called for Mariana, Medina appeared far more promptly.

"Delwyn, my dear young merman, it's lovely to see you again. What brings you here?"

"I wanted to talk to you about Fabian."

"My darling nephew. I take it that means you've found him again. How is he?"

"He's trapped in the body of a sea dragon."

"Yes, I know." Medina giggled. *"My sister always did have a flair for the dramatic."*

"Can you help him?"

"He seems to be doing quite well on his own."

"But he's stuck as a dragon. Can you make him human again?"

"I'm sorry, but even when she is sleeping, my sister's powers far exceed my own."

"Then he's going to be stuck as a dragon forever?"

"Oh, I doubt that. I'm sure you'll find a way to get over such a minor obstacle."

"I don't know how."

Medina's laughter echoed through his mind. *"When my sister wakes, she will restore him to human form."*

"Fabian thinks she will keep him as he is just to spite him."

"Why would she do that? As a sea dragon, my nephew is an equal match for her. A demi-god in dragon form versus a full goddess in human form. The battle would be short and I'm willing

to wager on who would win it. If my sister values her existence, she will make him human again."

Delwyn drew hope from Medina's conviction. He hadn't considered the possibility that Fabian would be too powerful in his current form, and his mother would have to return him to his human form to ensure her own survival.

"Go to him," Medina said. "My nephew is no doubt missing you greatly."

Delwyn took her advice and, to the consternation of his guard, he decided to head back to where he had started and join Fabian.

"Back so soon?" Fabian asked as Delwyn curled up beside him.

"I'm sorry," Delwyn offered. "I don't mean to take my temper out on you."

"Don't worry yourself about it. I understand."

"You do?"

"You're a merman. I've been around the species long enough to know how sexually frustrated you all become at certain times of the year."

"It's not the mating season at the moment."

"I know, but you've never had the chance to experience one properly. The longer you go without having sex, the more difficult it is to shake off the feelings you're having at the moment."

"What do you mean? Are you saying I'm still in the mating season because I didn't break my fever?"

"Yes, exactly. I've seen so many of the Oracles go through what you're experiencing and the same thing happens to all of them. The older they get, the worse it becomes."

"I don't like the sound of that."

"Me, neither. I'm hoping by the time you next go into heat, I'll be able to come to the island with you and help you with the problem."

"Me, too, though, I think perhaps I'd like to visit your isle instead. It's a bit more private than the island the mer use."

Fabian chuckled. "Did I manage to find the only shy merman in all the oceans of the world?"

"I guess you did."

Delwyn felt the waters move about him and Fabian stiffened at his back. *"What is it?"*

"Urion," Fabian whispered. *"Keep quiet and don't respond to his taunts."*

"I don't hear him saying anything."

"Sorry, I forgot. While he's collared only the other sea dragons can communicate with him. In his case, I think that's probably for the best."

Fabian curled his long tail around Delwyn, shielding him from the high priest, even though he had no doubt already spied the merman.

"Your merman seems to be a little nervous," Urion said.

Fabian made sure Delwyn couldn't hear what he was saying and sent his words privately to Urion. He didn't want Delwyn getting the wrong idea after hearing half of what would no doubt be an unpleasant conversation. *"He's fine. Why don't you carry on with your swim round the city and leave him be?"*

The mermen guarding the dragon did their best to keep Urion moving, but he was too big to be bossed about. Most of the time, Urion and the other sea dragons did what the mer wanted them to do just because it was less trouble. They were all biding their time until their goddess set them free. None of them wanted to aggravate the mer to such an extent they were killed.

It was remarkably hard to kill a sea dragon, as had been proved over the centuries when, now and again, one ruler of the city or another had decided the dragons were too dangerous to be allowed to live. One king, about three hundred years before, had come close to killing one of them. How the priest had survived was something of a mystery. Any other sea creature would have succumbed to their injuries.

The incident served as a reminder they weren't immortal, and if the mer tried to wipe them out, they could succeed in their efforts.

Urion had perfected the art of swimming the fine line they had all crossed from time to time in their early days in their new bodies. He knew when to back down and do as the mer wanted, and when he could push against his boundaries a little.

Right now, he was pushing more than he had in a long time.

"You want him quite badly," Urion commented. *"He's untouched, isn't he?"*

"That's none of your concern," Fabian replied.

"Your mother would be furious if she knew you were bedding a merman."

"My mother is well aware of my feelings for Delwyn. What you don't seem to understand is that I don't care what she thinks."

Urion let loose a roar that momentarily scattered his guards. *"I eagerly await the day my goddess walks the earth once more."*

Fabian knew better than to make snide remarks, but the temptation was too much to resist. *"You might have to get in line for her attention. You were getting quite old before the day she transformed us."*

Urion snarled back at him. Fabian knew he had hit a sore spot. Urion had always worried about Mariana losing interest in him, a concern that wasn't entirely groundless.

"When she wakes, she will destroy you and your merman."

"My merman will be long since dead already by the time she walks among us."

"You think it will take that long before she rises? Look around you, fool! Her brethren are already waking."

"But she isn't," Fabian replied. *"Only the release of her priests, and probably you specifically, can give her enough power to rise. Unfortunately, Calder has no intention of releasing any more of you from your collars. So as long as you remain your usual disagreeable self, you have no chance of walking free and therefore there is no possibility of my mother waking."*

* * * *

"Good morning, Fabian."

Fabian glanced up at Urion as he swam overhead. *"It's evening,"* he replied as he closed his eyes, wishing the priest to the other side of the city.

"Is Delwyn not with you?" Urion asked.

Fabian's first instinct was to wonder whether Urion had done something to Delwyn, then he realized that Urion had referred to him by his name, rather than sneering about the merman, or worse, the fish.

"He has duties in the temple," Fabian told him, thinking that would be an end to the conversation. *"I expect he'll be here soon."*

Delwyn had formed the habit of coming to find Fabian each night and sleeping while curled up in the sea dragon's protective embrace.

Fabian wasn't sleeping much at all these days. He spent most of his time reaching out telepathically to see which of the immortals stirred. Far too many of his mother's friends, those who shared her opinions, were beginning to rise. And, unfortunately, too few of the allies of the mer were waking.

It didn't bode well for the survival of the merpeople.

Urion swam off on his circuit of the city and Fabian put the conversation from his mind, at least until the next time the high priest stopped by in his swim to ask about Delwyn.

Fabian gave him his usual polite but brief answer and left it at that.

Slowly, though, he began to wonder what exactly Urion was trying to achieve with his unusually friendly attitude, after centuries of veiled and open threats.

"Maybe he realizes it doesn't pay to be so grouchy all the time," Delwyn suggested.

"More like he wants to be freed and is trying to convince us he's changed," Isander replied.

Fabian was far more inclined to believe Isander than

Delwyn. His merman was still quite naïve.

"Well, he's not going to be uncollared, anyway," Fabian said. *"Calder will never allow it."*

Still, Urion became increasingly polite and even friendlier, asking after Delwyn and making what would appear to be a real effort to get to know him. Fabian didn't believe a word of it.

Fabian didn't know when Urion would strike, but he knew it would come. It was just a matter of time. He kept a close watch on him, waiting for the attack.

Eventually, Urion seemed to tire of his efforts to get along with Fabian, Isander and Delwyn. Instead, he ignored them entirely, which Fabian considered was at least an improvement over making snide comments.

As the days passed, Fabian found himself guarded less stringently. Instead of two mermen watching his every move, he often found only one at his side. On rare occasions, he was even left completely alone. He hadn't been able to enjoy a moment of total solitude since the day he had been transformed. He hadn't realized how much he had missed the simple pleasure of being alone with his own thoughts.

Of course, he didn't stay isolated for long. Delwyn spent time with him every day as well as all night.

Fabian soon discovered the guards were happy to let him go where he pleased within the boundaries of the city. He wasn't confined to one spot all day or prodded into swimming in circles while searching for predators.

He still did his share of protecting the city and keeping it hidden from the world.

Like all of the sea dragons, Fabian had, within a few days of transformation, mastered the power to become invisible, as well as hide his surroundings. For centuries, they had been keeping the city and the merpeople from being discovered, particularly in the years since human technology had enabled mankind to venture into the deep.

The only drawback to his powers had been that within the boundaries of what had once been the island of Atlantis, he was perfectly visible.

Strangers in the area had to get past them before they could see them, and the only way they could do so was with a merman escort.

His mother had ensured her dragons would protect the city until she awoke, but the God of War had ensured they couldn't hide from their jailers.

Now that his collar had been removed, Fabian realized he could hide from the mer within the city. He hadn't told Isander yet, but he needed to mention this to Calder, especially in light of what he intended to do.

"You don't trust Urion's apparent change of heart?" Calder asked.

"No. Do you?"

"Absolutely not."

"I intend to keep a close eye on him, but without him being aware of my presence. I want to know what his plans are and this is my best chance of finding out."

Calder agreed. *"Let me know if you discover anything I need to know."*

Fabian nodded and summoned the power to shield himself from sight. He hoped the other sea dragons couldn't see him, but he didn't know for sure. With their powers partially bound while collared, he hadn't had a chance to test it. Deciding there was no time like the present, Fabian swam to the other side of the city, where Isander currently patrolled. If he was seen, his plan would fail, and he would rather find out from a friend than a foe.

When he found him, Isander was seeing off a giant squid who lingered a little too close to the harvest stores. Calder had always ensured that at least one sea dragon remained in the area, because even though they could make the building invisible, other sea creatures could tell there was food nearby and often tried to access it.

Fabian swam right up to Isander. He wanted to be sure he was invisible and not that Isander was simply distracted.

He didn't bother with telepathy, since he didn't want to

distract Isander from his task.

When the squid had been sent on its way, Isander swam over to sit on a large flat rock, the same one most dragons guarding the food store chose to sit on.

Fabian sat beside him and waited for Isander to acknowledge his presence. He remained oblivious.

The sensible thing to do would be to speak to him, but Fabian hadn't had a lot of fun in his centuries as a dragon and the impulse to tease his old lover was too strong to ignore.

He kept it simple at first, poking him with his tail and waiting for Isander's reaction.

The sea dragon jumped and stared about him, searching for whatever had touched him. In the ocean, it could be any number of smaller fish that had inadvertently swum too close.

Fabian waited for him to settle down again, then ran his clawed paw along Isander's tail, flicking a couple of the spines on the way.

Isander growled as he spun round. *"Who's there?"*

Fabian could barely contain his mirth, but he managed to keep quiet long enough give Isander a bump on the snout with his own.

Isander shot back, his rear legs stumbling off the rock as he scrambled with his front paws to remain up.

Fabian couldn't hold in his laughter any longer. He roared while Isander, who looked as affronted as a dragon possibly could, glared round in every direction.

"Fabian, I know you're here. I can hear you giggling."

"I don't giggle," Fabian replied, mildly insulted at the suggestion. *"I would never do something so unmanly."*

"You're not a man at the moment," Isander reminded him. *"You're a sea dragon, and you definitely giggled."*

Isander, despite being a little slow on the uptake, soon figured out what Fabian had done and in the blink of an eye, he too vanished.

Fabian made himself visible for a moment then vanished

again. Isander did the same. They each tried to catch the other before they vanished. For several minutes they played their childish game of tag.

Unfortunately, Isander's guards weren't quite as lax as those in charge of Fabian, not when they wanted to ensure the harvest was properly guarded.

When the two dragons realized their game wasn't being appreciated by the two mermen, Fabian made himself visible again, just in time for Isander to barrel into him with a roar of victory.

"You need to lose some weight." Fabian groaned as he staggered back to his feet.

"I'm not getting the exercise I used to," Isander replied. *"There's been a distinct lack of sex in recent centuries."*

Fabian laughed. *"And until my mother wakes up, it'll remain that way."*

Once they had assured the guards they weren't going to run amok, Fabian explained to Isander his intentions regarding Urion.

"Do you think it'll work?" Isander asked. *"I can't see Urion trusting anyone with his plans."*

"He has friends amongst the priests. If he confides in anyone, it'll be them."

Isander wasn't convinced, but he had no better ideas to offer.

Now that he had tested his invisibility powers worked as he wanted, Fabian swam round the city, unseen by the inhabitants, as he went to track down Urion.

The high priest was being guarded by three mermen, rather than two. After Fabian had told Calder who he was, the leader of the guards had decided to take extra precautions around him. Urion wasn't happy about it at all.

Unlike when Fabian had seen him in recent days, where Urion had been polite and friendly, right now he appeared to be his usual antagonistic self. Fabian was disappointed, but not surprised, to have his suspicions confirmed.

Urion snarled at the guard hovering nearest to him,

causing the merman to point his spear at him and force him back to his position.

Fabian made a mental note to speak with Calder about the spears. They would be no use whatsoever if Mariana woke. The guards would be far better off equipped with tridents. He knew why the tridents had been mostly taken out of commission. The weapons were the only ones that could conjure sea-fire, a dangerous bolt of power that could kill instantly.

As the immortals woke, more and more of the mer found they had the ability to conjure sea-fire. When one of the guards had been injured during practice, Calder had made the sensible decision to keep the tridents safely secured in the barracks.

What Calder didn't know was each of the sea dragons had the equivalent of a furnace in their belly and could breathe sea-fire from their mouths once they were uncollared. Fabian made a mental note to mention that to Calder, too.

As soon as Mariana woke and released the dragons, the mer would have no way of defending themselves against the coming attacks. Fabian had no doubt the priests would use their best weapon to defeat the mer.

Since Urion was on his own, there was nothing else Fabian could do to find out his plans. With that in mind, he returned to the barracks to speak to Calder about the tridents. Provided the mer were properly trained in how to wield them, there shouldn't be any more accidents. Fabian just hoped there was time to get the mer up to speed on how to use the tridents properly.

Calder wasn't any happier about with the idea of bringing tridents back into commission than he had been about the suggestion of uncollaring any of the dragons.

Fabian groaned in frustration. *"Don't you understand what danger you're in?"*

"I'm well aware of the danger," Calder replied. *"I just don't think it's wise to add to it with the tridents."*

Marin, who had been training nearby with a spear, swam

over. *"I think it's a good idea."*

Calder rolled his eyes. *"You can barely keep from stabbing yourself with a spear. If you think you're going to be running round the practice area with a trident, you're sadly mistaken."*

"All the guards need to learn how to use them," Fabian insisted. *"You can't fight sea-fire with spears."*

"How do I know you can even breathe sea-fire?" Calder asked. *"For all I know, this could be a ploy to see us destroy ourselves."*

Fabian privately thought Calder was taking his caution a little too far, but if he wanted proof, he would have it.

Fabian swam above the barracks and threw back his head. With an almighty roar, he let loose his first ever burst of sea-fire. The bolt of power shot up as far as the eye could see, lighting the dark waters above them. It felt good.

When he turned back to Calder, the merman looked even more pale than usual.

"Convinced?" Fabian asked. *"We might not have been able to breathe sea-fire before, but we all know we have the ability. We can taste the fire in our guts every day we remain in this form."*

Calder gave a small nod. *"If all of you can produce sea-fire like that, I'm not sure the tridents will be enough."*

"Me, neither," Fabian agreed. *"But they're all we have."*

Chapter Fifteen

One by one, the guards had training in how to handle the slightly heavier tridents, and also in how to produce sea-fire from them.

The trick to it was relatively simple. Calder, after coaching from Fabian, explained to his guards that they had to stop thinking about what they were trying to do and simply treat the tridents like extensions of their bodies. In no time at all the majority of the guards could conjure sea-fire at will.

Naturally, there were a few mishaps amongst the guards, though thankfully nothing fatal. The worst injury was to one of the guard's hands. No one had quite anticipated the long range of the sea-fire and a strong blast from the two mermen training behind him had caught him during his own practice. From that point on, only two guards trained with the tridents at a time and everyone else made sure to stay well out of the line of fire.

Calder, despite Marin's complaints, refused to let him even touch one of the tridents. Marin, along with a new recruit who had recently come to the city, who barely knew how to hold a weapon, stuck to the more conventional spears.

As the rest of the guards became used to their tridents, it wasn't unusual to see flashes of blue light around the barracks at any time of day.

After a short while Calder agreed the mermen guarding the sea dragons should be armed with tridents. After all, it would be little use having them trained with the weapons if the tridents were back in the barracks when the goddess woke.

* * * *

"I'm telling you, he's getting more aggressive by the day," Calder said.

Fabian had noticed the same thing while spying on Urion. The sea dragon stayed docile and pleasant if he saw Fabian around, but when he didn't know he was being watched it was another story entirely.

"I'd speak with him, but it won't do any good," Fabian said. "I'm not one of the priests and he has never valued my opinion."

"What about Isander? Could he see what the problem is?"

"He can try, but Urion has no liking for him, either."

"I thought Isander was one of the priests?"

"He is. But he was also my lover."

"Ah."

"I'm sure he will do his best," Fabian assured him.

Isander didn't expect his efforts to come to much and said so as he swam across the city. Fabian, invisible, followed close behind.

"Urion," Isander said. "I hear you've been giving your guards trouble again."

"What's it to you?" Urion snarled. "You and that traitor aren't even being followed around these days. Why can't the rest of us be uncollared?"

"You know why."

Urion roared and dove for Isander. The nearest guard sent him scurrying backward with a short but effective bolt from his trident.

Fabian could tell this would be a waste of time. Urion was angry and he had apparently given up on playing nice with Isander. His words also confirmed Fabian's suspicions that the high priest's overtures of friendship were duplicitous.

From the corner of his eye, Fabian caught sight of Marin, with his distinctive pale blue tail and dark blue fins. He swam with a couple of the other guards in the direction of the barracks, probably for their midday meal.

Suddenly Urion gave another loud roar. He pushed his

two guards aside with a violent sweep of his tail. One of the mermen dropped his trident, but the other fired a bolt of sea-fire at Urion. He barely seemed to feel the impact.

Fabian made himself visible and he and Isander charged at Urion, sending short bolts of sea-fire at him as they went.

"Get out of here!" Fabian shouted at the guards.

They swam swiftly out of the way and he heard one of them say he was going to fetch Calder. Fabian wasn't sure what the leader of the guards could do against Urion when he was in this sort of a temper. Still, Calder seemed to boost the morale of his men whenever he was around.

Marin and the other guards who had been passing by held back. They were all unarmed and vulnerable. Fabian considered they should be equipped with some form of weapon at all times.

The guard who had fled returned with Calder and several others. They were all wielding tridents and ready to bring Urion back under control. Fabian wasn't sure they would manage it. He knew the sea dragons let themselves be pushed around by the mer while they bided their time until Mariana returned. They wanted to be there until their goddess restored them to their former glory, and the only way to achieve that was to obey the mer who guarded them. Now that the immortals were waking, Urion and his fellow priests were taking chances they might not have done a hundred years ago.

Calder and his men lined up in formation and aimed their tridents at Urion.

Fabian suspected he and Isander were in the line of fire for some of the guards, but he had no intention of moving. If he did, there would be nothing to stop Urion charging the mer.

The first sea-fire bolt to hit Fabian nearly knocked him out. A direct blow to the head could do that, though it was unlikely to kill him.

"Aim for his head," Fabian called out to the guards.

Calder repeated his order and when the next round of

sea-fire came, two of the bolts hit Urion on the head.

Fabian suspected the guards could do with some target practice. That thought was reinforced a few minutes later when the third round of fire came. This time none of the bolts hit Urion in the head. The nearest caught him in the neck, right on the collar.

Urion gave a roar of triumph as his collar broke.

An earthquake shook the city and Fabian knew in his gut his mother was about to return. The release of the high priest *had* been enough.

A cry of alarm came from Marin and his group as the wall of the building they were next to toppled over toward them. Calder immediately left his post and swam faster than Fabian had ever seen toward his lover and the others.

Everyone managed to get out of the way of the tumbling stones, just before they crashed to the ground.

Urion continued to roar and Fabian could tell he was building up his sea-fire to the maximum volume. This wouldn't be a small demonstration for the mer to see, it would be aimed to kill as many as possible.

"Get the mer out of here!" Fabian shouted. *"We won't be able to control him for long."*

"You can't control me at all," Urion replied. *"My goddess is returning now and the mer will pay for what they've done to us. Atlantis will be ours again. Join us, Fabian, or burn and die."*

Fabian gave him his answer with a blast of sea-fire. It wasn't enough to render him unconscious. He was too weak and the angle wasn't right.

Suddenly, sea-fire shot in all directions. The guards with their tridents, Urion, Fabian, and Isander, all sent bolt after bolt through the water.

Urion, as the largest of the sea dragons, could summon the most sea-fire, and he used that to his advantage.

They fought for a long time, until Fabian realized he couldn't breathe so much as a spark of sea-fire. Isander was already drained. They would need to rest before they managed it again. Unfortunately, there was no possibility of resting right now. Urion still breathed sea-fire and didn't seem close to tiring.

Fabian didn't let his lack of sea-fire slow him down. He used his teeth, claws and tail to try to stop Urion. He and Isander alternated between shielding the mer and battling Urion.

Another earth tremor shook the city and Urion roared his victory again.

He sent another bolt of sea-fire, longer and stronger than any of his previous attempts, shooting through the water, aiming right at Marin and the unarmed mermen, who couldn't take cover due to the ground shaking the buildings around them.

The blast didn't reach them. Calder swam right into the line of fire, taking the entire bolt in the chest.

Marin screamed.

Fabian saw a flash of light beside Urion. The Goddess of Sea Creatures appeared beside him. She stroked her high priest on the chest.

"Well done, my darling. You've woken me at last. Now, it's time for us to take back our city."

Mariana raised her arms above her head. Rays of light spread out from her hands, stretching out over the city.

"Come, my priests. You are free now. Drive the mer from this land."

Fabian watched in horror as his mother freed her sea dragons from their collars. He had no hope of any of them refusing to obey her. He roared and tried to muster a little more sea-fire, but all he managed was a weak cough.

Mariana laughed. *"Ah, my loving son. Do you think to stand against me? Don't be foolish."*

"Don't do this," Fabian said. *"It doesn't have to be this way."*

"It was always *going to be this way,"* his mother replied. *"Now choose. Do you stand at my side or not?"*

"I will never fight for you."

With a wave of her hand, Mariana transformed him from his dragon form, back into his human body.

As the first to have transformed, Fabian hadn't truly comprehended how big the sea dragons were. Now he swam next to Isander and Urion, he saw how they towered over him.

Urion laughed and growled at him. Fabian tried not to flinch.

"Even as a sea dragon, you were no match for me," Urion snarled. *"As a human, you're nothing but a minnow facing off against a whale."*

Mariana raised her hand to Urion and stroked him. *"My son was never worthy of my gift. Let him fight with the mer, if he wishes. The battle won't last long."*

Isander growled at Urion, drawing the goddess's attention to him.

"And you," Mariana said. *"I had such hopes for you, until my son corrupted you. You aren't worthy of the gift I gave you, either."*

With another wave of her hand, Isander, too, became human again.

"At least I'll be able to get a bit of action now," Isander told Fabian privately. *"Well, providing we live long enough."*

Fabian wasn't sure they would.

The rest of the priests swam over, bowing their dragon heads to the goddess, earning smiles and gratitude for their patience.

The guards all flocked together around Calder.

Fabian swam to them. They had to get out of there, quickly. He looked around while he considered their options. The nearest temple was that of Medina. Even though he wasn't technically one of her followers, Fabian knew, as her nephew, he would be able to use the crystal in her temple to take them to the Isle of the Gods and temporary safety.

If Mariana followed them into her sister's temple, her powers would be severely limited. It had always been impossible for any immortal to use destructive powers while in the temple of another.

Calder appeared to be in a bad way, though he still

breathed. Marin clung to him as the others looked on.

"We need to get to the temple over there." Fabian pointed at Medina's building. *"My mother can't use her powers against us inside another immortal's temple."*

"Are you sure about that?" one of the guards asked.

Fabian nodded. *"I'm sure."*

The sea dragons didn't try to stop them.

Nor did Mariana. When she saw the direction they were heading in, she laughed. *"Go and run away to safety, like the cowards you are. And while you're hiding in there, we'll drive the mer from Atlantis."*

One or two of the guards faltered in their flight. Fabian urged them on.

"The best hope we have is to enlist the help of other immortals. Medina is the nearest, but there are others who will help the mer, too."

They entered the temple without incident and Fabian headed for the crystal. Before he even touched it, Medina appeared in front of him.

"Now, now, Fabian," she said. *"You know you can't possibly transport all of these mer to the isle."*

Fabian hadn't realized. He had assumed that as long as they were all linked together, everyone would be transported to land.

Medina didn't wait for him to answer. *"Luckily for you, I'm here and I can open the portal wider."*

The goddess clapped her hands and a moment later everyone was transported out of Atlantis and to Medina's residence on the Isle of the Gods.

The mer fell to the floor in heaps.

"Oops," Medina said. "Sorry, but you'll all get your legs back soon."

Fabian hurried to where Marin clung to Calder. Both were still in mer form, though they wouldn't be for long.

"Can you help him?" Marin asked.

Fabian wasn't sure whether Marin spoke to him, to Medina, or to the room in general. Either way, the answer was the same. It was too late.

"I'm sorry," he said, placing his hand on Marin's shoulder. "He's gone."

"No, he's just hurt," Marin argued. He brushed off Fabian's hand and tried to rouse Calder.

Fabian turned to his aunt. "Can you…?" He hadn't finished his sentence when Medina shook her head.

"I'm sorry, but you know we can't, not for any reason."

"Could Antar reverse time far enough to stop this happening?" he asked.

The God of Time and Space had the power to show a person the past, as well as rewind it, giving those lucky enough to know what had happened a second chance to put things right.

"He could, but I doubt he will. You know as well as I do, when you try to change the fate of one, in circumstances such as these, all you will ever achieve is hurt for many."

"But I love him," Marin whispered. "He's the only one I've ever wanted. He can't be gone."

Fabian didn't know what to say. Over the centuries he had lived, he had said goodbye to many loved ones, and he knew that words meant nothing in such circumstances. All he could do was try to be there for him. They weren't close friends — they barely knew each other, in fact — but Fabian would do what he could.

Marin shook his head, still refusing to believe what they told him. "Please help him. You're supposed to be the Goddess of Love, so help him, because I love him, and he loves me, and he can't be gone, he just can't."

Fabian knew that when the mer died their bodies eventually evaporated into sea foam. Calder hadn't done so yet, because they were now out of the water. A few words, together with the touch of his, or his aunt's, hand to Calder's body would send him on to whatever afterlife the mer believed in. Yet he couldn't bring himself to do it.

Even though it was too late, he couldn't bear to kill the last little bit of hope Marin blindly clung to.

Marin rested his head on Calder's shoulder and gave a single quiet sob. "Don't leave me, baby. You know I can't do this on my own."

Fabian looked round the room at the other mermen, all of whom had now found their land legs. Every single one stared at Marin and Calder. No one seemed to want to approach them.

Tears rolled down Medina's face unchecked. Fabian knew her heart was breaking along with Marin's. It had never been easy for her to witness lovers being separated by death.

"Aunt Medi," he said quietly. "Can you do something for me?"

"I can't bring him back," Medina repeated.

"That's not what I was going to ask. Can you go find Delwyn and bring him here? I don't want him in the city right now."

Medina nodded. "I understand."

She vanished instantly and returned a few minutes later with Delwyn at her side. This time, she remembered he was mer and gently lowered him to the floor.

Fabian hurried across to Delwyn and tugged him into his arms, squeezing him. For a few moments, he had been afraid he wouldn't see him again. He wouldn't have put it past his mother to deliberately target the merman he loved. "Delwyn," he whispered brokenly. His love relaxed into his embrace at Fabian's voice.

"What's happened?" Delwyn asked after his fins had changed to legs and his sight had been restored. "Why are we on the Isle of the Gods?"

"My mother has woken," Fabian explained. "She's released her sea dragons and intends to drive the mer from the city."

"Ah, that explains Cari's behavior. She came to our temple and told us we couldn't leave, but she disappeared so quickly and never told us what had happened. Kai's using his powers to view the city, to see what the trouble is, but his first vision hadn't finished when Medina arrived and brought me here."

Fabian gestured to his aunt. "I asked my aunt to bring us here. It was too dangerous for us to swim across the city while my mother wages war on Atlantis."

Delwyn nodded and turned to see who else was there. When his gaze landed on Marin and Calder his face paled. He looked at Fabian questioningly.

Fabian gave a small shake of his head. "Calder swam into the line of fire to save the others. He died a hero."

Delwyn's eyes filled with tears and he rushed to Marin's side. Fabian knew the two mermen were of a similar age and were friends. He didn't interfere when Marin collapsed into Delwyn's arms. The merman sobbed quietly as the truth finally seemed to hit him.

Fabian stood and gestured for the rest of the guards to follow him into the adjoining chambers. There was a lot to do and they didn't have much time. Delwyn and Marin were safe here in his aunt's temple. He intended to keep the two of them out of danger as much as he could.

Chapter Sixteen

Delwyn didn't say anything as he held Marin in his arms. He couldn't begin to understand what his friend was going through. Even though he had lost a love, he had always been able to take solace in the knowledge that Finn was alive, well and happy. His own small loss couldn't even compare to what Marin was going through right now and what he would have to face in the coming days.

Calder had always been a good friend to Delwyn, letting him spend time in the barracks with Marin, even though he wasn't strictly supposed to. The two of them had also offered to let Delwyn join them on the solstice, so he wouldn't have to suffer alone. Even though they loved each other more than any couple Delwyn had known, their hearts were big enough to welcome others to join them, as well.

Although it was too soon to talk about such things, Delwyn swore that when the next mating season arrived, he would return the offer to Marin. He suspected he would decline it, and choose to honor his mate's memory by staying abstinent, but Delwyn would make the offer, anyway.

As Marin clung to him, Delwyn remembered Fabian pulling him into his arms on his arrival. He had been so caught up in what was happening, he hadn't thought to savor their first opportunity to touch as two humans. The moment had passed him by and he had barely even noticed. He vowed that the next time he held Fabian, he would make the most of it. He stroked Marin's back and arms as the merman began to shiver. Delwyn couldn't seem to take his eyes off Calder. No doubt the last time Marin and his lover had touched, they hadn't had any idea their days together would be numbered. No one knew what lay in wait around the corner. The sanctuary of the sunken city had suddenly become a dangerous place.

Cari walked into the chamber and hesitated. It was clear she hadn't known who the first casualty was.

"There's nothing I can do to bring him back," she offered.

"Did you see this coming?" Delwyn snapped. "I know Ula didn't, or she would have told me. The last vision she had this morning was of the return of the Goddess of Sea Creatures, although she couldn't tell when it would happen. But did you see this?"

Cari shook her head. "Calder breathed his last here in this room, didn't he?"

"Yes," Marin confirmed with a broken sob.

"This is part of Medina's temple. My visions cannot show me what happens in the places of worship of other immortals."

"Did you see the attack?" Delwyn asked.

"I saw a battle, but I didn't see the end of it."

Delwyn glared at the goddess. "What's the use of being the Goddess of Prophecy if you can't see when something like this happens?"

"What I see in my visions can't always be changed."

"You could have warned us," Delwyn argued.

Cari kneeled at the other side of Calder. "Some things cannot be changed, no matter how much we might wish them to be."

"You could have tried!" Delwyn's voice rose along with his anger.

The appearance of another immortal stopped Cari from saying anything in response. Caspian had a scowl on his face, but this was nothing unusual. Delwyn rarely saw Cari's brother, not in visions or in person, but he never seemed particularly happy when he did.

"Calder," Caspian whispered and bowed his head, closing his eyes for several long moments.

"Caspian?" Cari asked.

Her brother held up his hand in a gesture asking her to be quiet.

When he had finished whatever he was doing, he too knelt beside Calder. "Would you like me to send him on?" he asked.

"Not yet," Marin replied. "I can't let him go yet."

"He's already gone," Caspian said.

"Not to me," Marin answered with another small sob. "I don't expect you to understand. You're immortal. You can't know what it's like to lose someone you love more than anyone else in the world. But if you have any feelings at all, please let him stay with me a little longer."

Caspian nodded. "Of course."

Delwyn mouthed *thank you* to the god.

"I think it would be best if you take Marin to land," Cari suggested.

"We're already on land," Delwyn replied, before he realized the goddess had spoken to her brother.

"Jake's?" Caspian asked.

"Yes."

"Do you think that's wise?"

Delwyn wondered what he meant. He knew Jake was one of Finn's mates, and from what he had seen, a decent human. He would have to be for Finn to give up the ocean to live with him. They lived in the faraway land of humans. Surely, it would be safer there than here or in the sunken city.

Cari gave the question some thought before eventually nodding. "Even if it's hard for Marin to be around Jake and his lovers because of what he's lost, I'm sure they'll be tactful and discreet around him. England is a long way from Atlantis and the coming war won't reach him there."

"Jake is Atlantean," Caspian pointed out.

"An Atlantean who has never been to the city."

Caspian sighed. "I don't like the idea of sending him there, but I don't have any better ideas."

Marin didn't say a word as they debated his fate. It was as

though he didn't care. Delwyn suspected that might even be the case. If their positions were reversed, he wasn't sure he would be bothered about where he went.

Gradually, Marin stopped crying, though Delwyn suspected he was going into shock.

As they sat on the cold stone floor, Fabian and some of the others who had escaped the city wandered back into the room.

"Is he still bawling?" one of the guards said with a sneer in their direction.

"Otus, shut up," Isander barked.

"Why should I? Marin is the most useless recruit in the whole city. The only reason he hasn't been relieved of his duties before now is because he's been mating with Calder. Lucky for us proper guards, he can now be sent on his way."

Otus had never been the most sociable of mermen and had craved Calder's position ever since his arrival in the city. Still, Delwyn had never thought him quite so callous.

Marin stilled in his arms and drew in a sharp breath.

"You need to shut up," Isander warned. "This isn't the time for you to begin aggravating people."

"You should mind your own damn business," Otus snarled back. "You're an Atlantean. For all we know, you're going to betray us to your goddess."

"I fought Urion when you guards were cowering halfway across the city."

Delwyn gasped as Marin wrenched himself out of his embrace and dove for one of the tridents that had been left on the floor after their arrival. He shot to his feet and aimed the trident at Otus.

"Shut up," Marin said in a quiet voice, which was somehow more frightening than if he had yelled.

"Like a pathetic excuse for a merman like *you* could ever conjure sea-fire," Otus sneered.

Marin proved him wrong in an instant. The prongs of the trident glowed blue. Only the quick intervention of Isander, in pulling Otus to the side, stopped Marin's shot from hitting Otus squarely in the chest.

Everyone in the room stared at Marin in shock. Even Delwyn was surprised, and *he* had always known Marin wasn't quite as inept as he liked to pretend.

Delwyn had asked him once why he had deliberately messed up a drill in front of Calder, when he had been executing it perfectly moments before the leader had turned his attention to him.

Marin had chuckled and nudged him. *"Isn't it ironic the only one to notice is the blind merman?"* he'd asked.

"I saw the drills in one of my visions. You were doing so well. Then Calder looks at you and it's as if you've forgotten everything you ever learned. Is it because he makes you nervous?"

Marin's mirth had escalated to full-blown gales of laughter. *"Can you keep a secret?"*

"What sort of secret?" Delwyn had asked.

Marin had been quiet for a while before the barest whisper of his voice flitted through Delwyn's mind. *"Calder doesn't scare me at all."*

"He doesn't?" Delwyn had been surprised. Calder scared most of the new recruits as well as a fair portion of the rest of the residents of the sunken city, including Delwyn.

"Calder's like me, like us."

Delwyn had known exactly what Marin referred to. *"He is?"*

"Yes, and he's mine."

Delwyn hadn't believed it at first, yet as his friendship with Marin had grown he'd begun to spot the signs, not just in his friend, but in the fearless leader of the guards, as well. He'd checked up on the couple on a regular basis, watching them in his visions, both in the water and on the island where the mer went during the mating season.

Once he had known what to look for, he had been able to tell that Calder adored Marin and that the feeling was mutual.

Marin had explained to Delwyn the reason for his deliberately messing up his drills. It was simply because it meant he could spend more time in the barracks with Calder. If he were to be promoted, he could be sent to the palace, out to guard the gatherers, maybe even one day guarding the sea dragons. Marin had decided to give up any hope of progression to be with the merman he loved.

Only two mermen in the city knew just what Marin was capable of. Delwyn glanced at Calder and corrected himself. No, there was only him now, along with Marin himself.

Otus shook off Isander's hand. "How dare you attack me?" he shouted at Marin. "You're gone from the guards as of right now. You'll never hold a trident again."

Marin aimed his weapon again. "Just try and take it off me."

Delwyn stood and walked to Marin's side. "Come on, Marin. He's not worth it."

"Stand back, Delwyn. I don't want to lose you, too."

Delwyn ignored his warning and held his ground. "Calder wouldn't want this."

"Calder hated him as much as I do," Marin replied without lowering his trident.

Delwyn looked pleadingly over toward the two immortals still kneeling beside Calder. They didn't say a word, but Cari gestured to Calder and Delwyn knew what she meant.

"Marin, come back to Calder. We have to return him to the ocean."

Marin blinked at Delwyn and his mismatched eyes watered again. "I don't want to."

"I know, but he deserves to depart this world properly, don't you agree?"

Marin finally lowered his trident and nodded. "Help me?"

"Of course."

Delwyn guided Marin back to Calder. He glanced over his shoulder at Isander and gestured for him to get Otus out of the room.

Marin brushed Calder's long auburn hair out of his face and bent to kiss him on the forehead. "Goodbye, my love," he whispered, taking Calder's hand into his own. "Go with the current, until you return to me on the next tide."

Delwyn wrapped his arm round Marin's shoulder. His friend nearly choked on the ancient words that would send Calder on his journey. "I can't," he sobbed. "Can you... please?"

"I'll say them," Caspian offered before Delwyn could reply.

"You know the custom?" Delwyn asked. The moment the words left his mouth he realized how stupid they must sound. Caspian was a god – of course he would know.

Caspian didn't answer his question. "May the seas welcome you and the oceans embrace you. Though we may not be together again, know I am with you, now and forever, in the vastness of the deep."

Marin clung to Calder's hand like a lifeline until he vanished from his grasp, gone forever.

"Give me your hand," Caspian said, and he reached out to Marin. "I'll take you to England."

Marin didn't hesitate. Delwyn sensed he needed to get out of there before he broke down again.

"I'll be back shortly," Caspian said. "We need to come up with a strategy to ensure Atlantis isn't lost to the mer."

Delwyn watched as Caspian and Marin vanished from the room.

Cari rose from her knees and approached Medina. "Do you have any ideas?"

Medina shook her head. "Do you?"

"No."

"Do you think Caspian will come up with something?"

Cari shrugged. "We'll soon find out."

Delwyn hoped Caspian had a plan, because the other immortals on their side apparently had nothing.

Chapter Seventeen

Delwyn slowly gravitated to Fabian's side. The demi-god held out his hand for Delwyn to take. Delwyn entwined their fingers and squeezed.

Fabian led him out of the room and into the empty chamber next door. Delwyn didn't let go of his hand.

Fabian gave him a tiny smile as he lifted their joined hands and kissed the back of Delwyn's. "I've wanted to be able to do this for a long time."

Delwyn snorted. "What? Kiss my hand?"

"Touch you," Fabian clarified. "Like this. In dragon form, my skin wasn't as sensitive and even though you could touch me, I couldn't really feel it."

Before Fabian had been transformed they hadn't even had that much.

"What are we going to do?" Delwyn asked. He didn't want to change the subject, but he had to know. As much as he wanted to find a soft sponge to curl up on with Fabian, to forget what had happened, now was not the time.

"I think we should go and speak with Andaman," Fabian replied.

Delwyn had never heard the name. "Who's he?"

"He's the Atlantean God of the Forge."

"Another relative of yours?"

"No, just a god who might be able to help."

"Might?"

Fabian nodded. "As you know, many of the Atlantean gods have been sleeping, just like my mother, for centuries. Others, like Cari, managed to stay awake."

"And Andaman?"

"He didn't sleep. Those immortals who had a strong following amongst the mer managed to retain their grasp on this world. Andaman had a large following amongst the guards, both Atlantean and mer. The mer kept him in this world and he has continued to make the weapons of the guards from that day to this."

"Why do you think he would help us?" Delwyn asked.

"I understand from Aunt Medi that over the centuries he's become sort of a leader to the gods who didn't go into stasis. Now that the rest of them are waking, I don't imagine he'll want to give up his position for one of them, just because they have more power than he does."

Delwyn hoped Andaman's desire to remain as leader would be strong enough. They needed all the help they could get.

"Andaman is the one who blesses the spears and tridents of the guards. It's his magic that ensures they don't rot under the water, and, in some cases, that the weapon will always meet its mark."

"In some cases?" Delwyn asked.

Fabian chuckled. "When you have two of the blessed weapons facing off against each other, you can't guarantee both will hit their target. But against sharks and other predators, they cannot lose."

"Do you know where to find him?" Delwyn asked. Even though the guards carried weapons, the rest of the inhabitants of the city were unarmed.

"He'll be here on the isle, over near the base of the volcano. He uses the heat from the magma in his forge."

"That sounds dangerous."

"Not for a god," Fabian replied. "And to forge the weapons of the gods, such a place is necessary."

"You should go to him at once."

Delwyn jumped in surprise at the voice. Caspian stood in the archway, a determined expression on his face.

Fabian nodded.

Caspian waved them back into the main room. "We're

going to use Cari's temple here on the isle as our headquarters. It's near the center of the island and Medina's will be the first place Mariana will search for us."

"We'll report back there after we've talked with Andaman," Fabian agreed. "Come on, Delwyn, let's go."

"Delwyn can come to Cari's temple with the rest of us," Caspian suggested. "From there, we'll see if any of the other immortals who are already awake intend to take sides in this battle."

"Delwyn stays with me," Fabian replied. His firm tone stopped Caspian from arguing.

Delwyn had no intention of leaving Fabian's side. Fabian found two sets of robes for them, and once they had dressed, they set out immediately for Andaman's forge.

The rest of the refugees walked with them, since Cari's temple was on the way there.

"The volcano is in this direction," Fabian said as they hurried across the grassy landscape. "You'll recall the isle is in the shape of infinity. The volcano is on the other half. The hill on this side of the isle contains the main temple where all the gods convene during times of great celebration or sadness."

Delwyn could see many buildings as they traveled across the isle. Most seemed deserted, though one or two appeared cleaner and better kept than the rest. Delwyn remembered some from his previous visits.

When they passed Cari's temple, Fabian didn't need to tell Delwyn where they were. Having already seen the inside for himself, Delwyn knew no one lived there now.

The rest of their party entered the temple, where they would hopefully come up with at least a vague plan before Fabian and Delwyn returned.

The point where the two parts of the isle joined was a beautiful golden sandy beach. Delwyn recognized it immediately as the place where he had watched Fabian and Isander come together for his enjoyment. He flushed at the memory.

Beside him, Fabian chuckled when he spotted Delwyn's embarrassment. "One day, when this is all over, I'm going to lay you down on this beach and make love to you while the sun sets."

Delwyn's face heated at Fabian's words and he looked forward to the day Fabian carried out his promise more than anything else.

Unfortunately, right now there was no time to waste, and they continued along the beach and onto the other side of the island.

The sand gave way to grass and more buildings joined by overgrown dirt paths.

As they neared the volcano, Delwyn caught a strange unpleasant smell in the air. He screwed up his nose. "What is *that*?"

"Sulfur," Fabian replied. "If you think it's vile now, you should smell it when the volcano erupts."

Delwyn hadn't thought the smell could get any worse, but he didn't doubt Fabian's word. "Does it erupt often?" he asked, hoping for a negative response.

"The volcano only ever erupts when a god dies."

"I thought the gods were immortal?"

Fabian sighed. "The gods don't age or die of natural causes. They are also remarkably hard to kill because they're able to heal their wounds with a single thought. They cannot be killed by any mortal, but they are vulnerable to other gods."

"Then Mariana can be defeated?"

"Yes, though I hope it won't come to the point where only her death can stop her. As much as I disagree with her beliefs, she *is* my mother."

Delwyn couldn't imagine ever being at odds with his own mother. He hoped she was somewhere safe and that he would see her again soon.

As they neared the volcano, vegetation became sparse and the sulfur in the air thickened. Delwyn spied a small patch of rainbow flowers and was reminded of the one Fabian had given him when he didn't have a corporeal body to take it from his hand.

Fabian seemed to remember it, too, and he bent to pick two of the blooms. "Here you go," he said as he passed him one.

"You don't have to keep giving me flowers," Delwyn said, though he took the offering with a smile. "I'm not a mermaid, you know."

Fabian laughed. "I *had* noticed. This time, however, I was thinking a little more practically. Sniff it."

Delwyn raised the flower to his face and took a small breath. The floral scent was strong enough to almost mask the stench of the sulfur. He took a deeper sniff and when he did he couldn't smell the volcano at all.

"Better?" Fabian asked.

"Definitely."

"They don't grow as much on this side of the isle, but enough patches were planted to ensure those who forget to bring one with them can make it to their destination without losing their last meal."

Delwyn was grateful that someone had had the foresight to plan ahead.

It took nearly an hour to reach the base of the volcano. They hadn't passed a building in a while. It seemed most of the gods didn't want to live this close to the smell.

"Do we need to climb it?" Delwyn asked. He couldn't see a path up the mountain, which appeared steep and treacherous.

"No." Fabian pointed to their right. "Andaman has his forge at the base on the east side."

Delwyn checked the position of the sun. He could tell they stood on the south side. At least they wouldn't have to walk all around the base.

"Come on," Fabian urged him on. "It's not far now."

Delwyn heard the sound of metal striking metal, in an endless rhythm, before the forge came into sight. He guessed the sounds to be Andaman at work.

"Who does he make all his weapons for?" Delwyn asked. "Most mortals don't know about him."

"Why don't you ask him yourself when we get there?" Fabian replied with a smile.

The forge looked nothing like the other buildings on the isle. While the temples had once been beautiful, and in some cases still were, the forge was plain and dirty. The building appeared to have been carved out of the mountain itself. Fabian confirmed this as they approached.

"This is just the entrance and the temple where his apprentices used to arrive when they traveled here by crystal from Atlantis. The forge itself is located in the caverns carved into the mountain. What you hear are the echoes of his labors."

They entered the building and Delwyn felt as though he'd walked into a wall of heat. Sweat broke out all over his body and within moments his robe had soaked through. He pulled the material away from his skin. "This is why the mer don't bother with clothes," he muttered.

"Really?" Fabian raised an eyebrow.

"All right, not really," Delwyn agreed. "But it's another good reason not to bother."

Fabian laughed. "I don't mind you running around naked, but you'd better stay clothed while we're visiting Andaman. He can be something of a prude."

Delwyn resisted the temptation to throw away his robe but promised himself it would be discarded at the first available opportunity.

"This way." Fabian lifted a torch from where it hung on the wall.

Delwyn let Fabian light the way down the passage into the mountain. The farther they walked, the louder the sound of Andaman working became.

Eventually, he saw a light ahead of them. Fabian put their torch into a nearby bracket.

"Andaman, greetings," Fabian said as they entered the god's forge.

For a moment, Delwyn wondered if he might pass out from the heat, but Fabian's hand at the base of his spine steadied him.

Steam rose from a barrel of water when Andaman dipped the weapon he was crafting into it.

"Fabian." Andaman barely glanced up from his work. "What brings you here?"

"My mother has risen."

Andaman snorted. "What of it? You won't find her in here. She isn't one for getting her hands dirty."

"You're right about that," Fabian agreed. "She intends to drive the mer from Atlantis."

"Some things never change." Andaman put aside his tools. "You would think a few centuries of reflection might have wrought a little common sense, but I guess not."

"If anything, she's even more determined now. Her priests have been freed from their collars, but they retain their sea dragon forms."

"All of them?" Andaman asked.

"Except Isander."

Andaman smiled. "I thought so. I'd always hoped that strong young man would join *my* followers, but sadly he chose another path. I'm glad to see his years in service to your mother didn't destroy his good nature."

"We're here for your help," Fabian said.

"Of course," Andaman replied. "Why else would you come to me? And who is this you bring with you?"

Fabian nudged Delwyn forward. "This is Delwyn, he's Cari's current Oracle of the past."

Andaman gave Delwyn a nod. "Greetings."

"It's nice to meet you," Delwyn said.

Andaman acknowledged his comment with another nod and turned to Fabian. "What is it you want from me?"

"Your help."

"Obviously. Do you want to be more specific?"

"Weapons for the mer."

"They already have many of my tridents and spears." He

waved his hand toward the wall behind him. "The rest are here. You're welcome to take what you wish."

"There aren't many here," Delwyn commented.

"That's because it takes time to craft perfection," Andaman explained. "A single one of these tridents takes almost fifty years to make."

"*How* long?"

"For mortals, fifty years is a long time. For the gods, such time passes in the blink of an eye."

"Whatever you can offer will help," Fabian assured him.

"What about armor?" Andaman asked. "I know the mer have an aversion to clothing—I think this the first time I have ever seen one clothed—but I make the offer anyway."

"How many pieces do you have?" Fabian asked.

Andaman pointed to a room to their left. "Go take a look."

Delwyn and Fabian went to see what was in the next chamber. They found row after row of helms, breastplates, bracers and more.

"Each item has been personally blessed by me," Andaman said from behind them. "No mortal weapon can dent or scratch them. They cannot be marred except by a direct hit from a god or a weapon blessed by one."

"What about sea-fire?" Delwyn asked. "The sea dragons breathe sea-fire and it seems to be a lot stronger than the sort from the tridents."

"Ah, sea-fire is different." Andaman grinned and left the room. He returned a moment later with a trident. "Fabian, would you care to help me demonstrate?"

"Sure," Fabian replied. He must have known Andaman's intentions, because, without being told what to do, he went over to the nearest rack of breastplates. He walked along the row until he found one in his size and put it to his chest. He shrugged his robe off his shoulders, so the material only covered him from the waist down. Then he placed the armor over his chest. The metal seemed to mold itself to his body, stretching over his shoulders and covering his back.

"No mortal armor can fit as well as mine," Andaman said.

"It feels as soft as the finest fabric against your skin and will never chafe or cut the wearer. It is also more secure than man-made armor. In such there are always gaps, weaknesses to be exploited. When you wear armor crafted in my forge, it protects you. It moves when you do, like a second skin."

Fabian turned around and Delwyn could see the armor shielded his upper body completely.

"What about his head, arms, and legs?" Delwyn asked.

"That's what the rest of the pieces are for," Andaman replied, "though the face will always remain vulnerable. Unfortunately, I have yet to discover a way to protect the eyes, nose and mouth without obstructing vision and making the wearer vulnerable in another way."

"And sea-fire?" Delwyn asked.

Andaman raised the trident to his shoulder and took aim at Fabian.

"Will that work in here?" Delwyn asked. "It's sea-fire. Shouldn't you use it in the sea?"

"It will work anywhere. Sea-fire is merely the name it was given because it is the only fire which can still burn in water. Now, watch."

The short, sharp bolt from the weapon hit Fabian squarely in the center of the breastplate. The metal absorbed the impact and the glow of the sea-fire spread out across the armor.

"What's happening?" Delwyn asked. "Is it safe?"

"The armor was forged here in the volcano, with the fire of the gods. Sea-fire was first conjured in the caverns directly below this isle. It has the same properties as the fire which helped craft the armor. It cannot destroy it, only make it stronger. Fabian, raise your right hand, palm up."

Fabian did as Andaman asked and there in the center of his palm appeared a small spark of sea-fire.

"Whatever sea-fire the armor absorbs, the wearer can summon to deliver right back to their attacker."

As Delwyn watched, the spark in Fabian's hand grew,

until it was a ball of fire about the same size as his head.

"If you don't want to use it right away, just tap your hand to the armor and it will absorb it again."

Fabian did as Andaman suggested and the sea-fire vanished.

"The sea dragons produce a lot more than a trident," Delwyn pointed out.

"It doesn't matter. Their flames will be drawn into the armor, which acts in a similar way to a lightning rod. The only difference will be that those who wear the armor will have a lot more juice to send right back at them."

Fabian took off the breastplate and set it to one side. Then he wandered along the various rows, arming himself thoroughly. By the time he had done, he had a complete set of full body armor ready to use.

"Yes, just help yourself," Andaman said with a chuckle. "Don't you want to get your merman suited up, too?"

"He won't need armor," Fabian replied distractedly. "He'll be staying here on the isle."

"What?" Delwyn couldn't believe Fabian had made such a decision without asking him about it.

"When you're in your mer form, you're blind. You are *not* going back there until it's safe."

"You can't make that choice for me," Delwyn argued. "We'll talk about this later."

Delwyn marched over to the nearest rack of armor and began browsing for something in his size. "Do you have anything to protect my fins?" he asked.

"Unfortunately not," Andaman replied. "I must admit I didn't anticipate ever needing to create such a thing. Although the mer have always been grateful for my tridents and spears, they have never taken the armor I used to leave in my temple in Atlantis for them. Since they didn't seem to want or need armor, I never bothered trying to adapt my creations for the merpeople."

Delwyn was disappointed, but there was nothing they could do about it now. The upper body armor would have to suffice. He copied Fabian's example and used his robe to cover his lower body while he tried on a couple of breastplates. He suspected armor on his tail might hamper his movements anyway.

Despite Fabian's protests, Delwyn soon had his own set of armor and took the trident Andaman offered him.

"Where do you want the rest of the armor and weapons sending?" Andaman asked Fabian.

"I'm not sure yet. We'll need to determine where the inhabitants of Atlantis are trapped and get the weapons sent to the temple of the nearest ally."

Andaman nodded. "Let me know where, when you're ready."

"I will," Fabian promised. "And thank you. I know you don't have to stand with us."

"The mer, and their use of my weapons, has kept me in this world for all these centuries. I owe them for that. Besides, if I were to turn on the mer, I would lose the last of my followers, and without those, I would have no choice but to go into stasis myself. It is those who believe in us that keep us part of this world."

"If my mother should bring the Atlanteans back to the city, they would believe in you, too," Fabian pointed out.

"They would, but I won't abandon the mer. Atlanteans and mer lived in peace once before. They can do so again."

"Were they *really* peaceful?" Delwyn asked quietly. From what he had seen in his visions, he doubted it. In Fabian's time, as well as other earlier years, Delwyn had seen the divisions between the mer and their human neighbors. They didn't appear to socialize and he had seen more than one fight between Atlantean and mer.

"Maybe not," Andaman relented. "But a fragile peace is more preferable to outright war."

Delwyn looked at all the armor around them and considered the weapons lining the walls of the other room. From the volume of items, he would have thought the god would be all for a huge battle and war.

Andaman seemed to read his thoughts on his face, or more likely had read his mind completely. "What I create can be used to fight other predators, sharks, squid and equally dangerous land animals. They do not have to be used to fight other men."

Delwyn hung his head, ashamed of his poor judgement of the God of the Forge. "I'm sorry."

"It's of no matter," Andaman assured him with a smile. "I'm glad to see the crafts of my labors put to good use."

"Come on, Delwyn," Fabian said. "Let's head back to the others."

They left Andaman working on his latest creation and headed back toward Cari's temple, each wearing their own set of armor, ready for the battle ahead.

Chapter Eighteen

When they arrived in the temple, they found everyone arguing about the best course of action. It didn't sound as if anyone had come up with a definite plan for what they should do.

No one even seemed to notice Fabian and Delwyn when they entered the room.

Delwyn, grumbling about constrictive human clothing, quickly shucked out of his upper body armor and placed it on a nearby bench. On the spur of the moment, and to Delwyn's obvious surprise, Fabian shed his own armor and placed it beside Delwyn's. He replaced it with the robe he had carried back from the forge.

Before Delwyn could take off his robe, currently being worn as a makeshift kilt, Fabian nudged him into the nearby corridor. "Come with me," he whispered.

"Where are we going?" Delwyn asked. "Your room?"

"Just for a moment," Fabian confirmed. "I need to kiss you, to touch you and feel your hands on my body. I don't want us to finally share our first real kiss with everyone else through there staring."

Delwyn gasped and raised his hand to his lips.

"Don't look so surprised," Fabian told him as they slipped into his chambers. "I've wanted this since the first time I saw you. I don't intend to go into battle without tasting your lips at least once."

Fabian took Delwyn's face between his hands and stroked his thumb over the soft skin. "I'll never tire of touching you."

Delwyn blinked at him and opened his mouth ever so

slightly. He licked his lips briefly and Fabian hardened in response to the gesture. He cursed silently that they didn't have time to play. Later, though, he would make Delwyn his and spend many lazy hours worshipping his lover's body.

He leaned down and Delwyn's eyes fluttered closed.

When he pressed his lips to Delwyn's, the merman sighed in response and opened his mouth wider, accepting Fabian's dominance without hesitation.

Fabian deepened the kiss, slipping his tongue into Delwyn's mouth, causing him to moan loudly.

He ran his fingers through Delwyn's short brown hair. Delwyn tugged his own locks in response.

Delwyn's hardness pressed Fabian's thigh. The shorter man couldn't have failed to notice Fabian's erection against his belly. Fabian guided Delwyn backward without breaking their kiss. He picked him up and held him to the wall. Their groins were pushed together now and he ground his hips against Delwyn's.

He wasn't going to last long. Even if they had all the time in the world, this first time would be quick. He had waited for centuries to know Delwyn in this way. He had yearned for him for so long, wanted him too badly. He couldn't wait another moment. His mother and the war would still be there, after the scant few minutes it would take for them to climax.

He tugged his robes out of the way and pushed Delwyn's aside. The hot flesh touching his own throbbing erection was all he needed.

With a small cry of pleasure, Fabian ended their kiss and buried his face in Delwyn's neck, breathing in the intoxicating scent of the sea. He moved his hips, thrusting once, twice. Delwyn threw back his head as he came. He was almost silent in his climax, only gasping as his hot seed spilled between them. Fabian shuddered as his own seed joined Delwyn's and he cried out again.

Delwyn clung to him as they stood there, sticky and

sweaty from their exertions.

"I'm sorry our first time had to be like this," Fabian finally said.

Delwyn tightened his embrace. "There's no need for apologies."

Fabian gave Delwyn a quick peck on the lips. "Next time, we'll have longer. When this is over, I promise to spend days worshipping your body."

"I can't wait," Delwyn replied.

Fabian used his robes to clean them both and tossed the fabric to one side. He debated whether to search for clean clothing in his cupboards, but decided against it. Clothing just got in the way when he swam and he'd be putting his armor back on, anyway.

Delwyn refused the offer to replace his own garments, just as Fabian had suspected he would. The mer had never been shy about their bodies.

Fabian walked with Delwyn back into the main chamber. Caspian smirked at him and he could tell the god had not only noticed them slip through the room, he also knew exactly what they had been doing. Fabian didn't care. With the exception of Medina, Caspian had had more lovers than most of the rest of the gods combined, and the majority of those he had taken to his bed had been men.

Delwyn, on the other hand, blushed furiously and ducked his head. Fabian nudged his chin back up and smiled. "You have nothing to be ashamed of. Now, come help me with my armor."

He didn't really need help donning his armor, but it would give Delwyn something to do while he got over his embarrassment.

"I take it from your new armor, Andaman will help us?" Isander asked.

"Yes. He has a huge store of armor as well as some surplus tridents and spears. He will send them wherever we need them to go. We just need to let him know where."

Caspian nodded and pointed to the large stone table

everyone had crowded around. "This is a map of the city. Cari, Medina, and I have been down there to each of our two temples, the ones in the city itself and the private ones in the palace. We wanted to see how things stand."

"And?" Fabian asked.

"Mariana concentrated her initial assault on the marketplace and surrounding area. Those on the outskirts of the city have fled past the boundaries in several groups. They are all heading for the cave network outside the city. They should be safe there, for the moment at least. The problem is they'll have no supplies and Mariana has set one of her priests to guard the main gathering grounds outside the city. With no food supply, they'll have to move on to more prosperous waters before much longer."

"What about those in the center of the city?" Fabian asked. The ones outside the boundaries could fend for themselves for the moment. If their small army could retake Atlantis swiftly, food supplies wouldn't be an issue.

"The priests have driven the mer to several locations where they have been contained. Here, in the barracks, there in the palace, and over here in the nursery."

"And everyone is in one of those locations?" Fabian asked.

"As far as we can tell, but there may be others hiding in private residences and temples. The priests are concentrating on keeping the mer contained in these areas, though."

Fabian nodded and pointed at the barracks. "Am I correct in assuming those held in the barracks are mainly guards?"

"That's right."

That made it a little easier. "The guards are all capable of fighting and defending themselves. We should concentrate on the civilians in the nursery and the palace, in that order." There were always guards around the palace. They could hold things until the most vulnerable had been rescued.

Fabian knew every square foot of the city of Atlantis. He contemplated the row of temples in the main thoroughfare. He judged which one would be the best location to deliver their supplies to. None seemed particularly promising, something Caspian appeared to agree with.

"I think we should split into two teams," Caspian said. "One group will go to the palace, the other to the nursery. Andaman can send the bulk of the armor and weapons to my temple in the palace. It's the most secure and the nearest to the royal family's quarters. I'll transport the first group there direct from my temple here on the isle. Once you're all suited up and armed, you can go relieve the guards in the palace so they — and anyone else who wants to fight — can get armor and weapons, too. The second group will be tasked with rescuing those trapped in the nursery. The nearest temple to the nursery is Medina's on the main street. Andaman can send enough supplies there to arm the second group as soon as they arrive."

"Why don't we just get armed here, before we go back to the city?" Otus asked.

"Because we'd be wasting time walking all the way to his forge and back again," Caspian replied. "Andaman no longer has a temple in Atlantis. The last one was destroyed many years ago. He can transport his items to any of our temples, but he can't send us there because all the crystals are broken. Cari, go to Andaman, let him know our plans, then head to the palace."

Cari obeyed her brother's orders and hurried out of the door.

"Isn't *that* a waste of time?" Otus complained. "Why don't you all just transport yourselves magically instead of running around this island?"

"We need every bit of power we have to fight Mariana and her priests," Caspian explained, a note of impatience creeping into his voice. "While it doesn't take much to move us from one place to another, that small amount can sometimes make the difference when you need just a little more power to save your own skin."

"But you're immortal, you can't die," Otus pointed out. "*We're* the ones taking the risks here."

Caspian glared at the guard with pure venom. "Even gods

can die when another god knows their weakness. However, we are in far more danger of one or more of our immortal allies being wiped out so much they go into stasis, just as Mariana and Medina have been for so many centuries."

"So you go to sleep for a few years, what's the big deal?"

Caspian sighed with annoyance. "While a god or goddess sleeps, whatever they bring to the world is dimmed. If they should be killed, their gift is lost forever."

"What do you mean?"

Caspian gestured to Medina, who was presently tidying up around the place. "While the Goddess of Love has been sleeping, fewer mortals have found their soulmates. Humans scoff at love and sneer at the idea of romance. If Medina were to die, love would disappear from the world entirely."

"And if you died?" Otus asked. "What are you the god of?"

"Justice," Caspian replied shortly. "Do you *really* want to see that gone from the world?"

Otus didn't reply.

Delwyn coughed and raised a hand nervously. "What about some of the less, er, pleasant gods, like, say, the God of War?"

Caspian's smile didn't reach his eyes. "My father is currently sleeping, not that you'd know it from the present state of the world."

"If he wakes, will there be even more wars?" Delwyn asked.

Caspian shook his head. "It doesn't work that way for the gods who bring destruction and discord in their wake. If my father were to die, it would result in a never-ending war. His sleeping makes no difference to the wars waged daily around the earth. Man will always fight man, it's human nature."

"So, there's no way to get rid of war and all the other ills in the world by killing the gods that bring them about?" Otus asked.

"That's right. They bring balance to the world. You cannot have good without evil."

"But the good, like love, can be wiped out if the Goddess of Love is defeated? That doesn't seem fair."

Caspian sighed. "Gods are nearly impossible to kill, and can only be killed by other immortals. Those who bring good to the world, like Medina, are stronger than those who don't, because they have far more followers, and more people call on them for help. This makes them much harder to destroy anyway, even if we immortals wanted to go down the route of killing each other."

"Then how do you plan on killing this Goddess of Sea Creatures?" Otus asked.

"I don't," Caspian replied. "I'm hoping we can bring her priests under control and she'll see the sense of accepting the mer rather than fighting them."

"And if she doesn't?"

"Without her priests she is far less of a threat. Once she is vulnerable, and her powers drained in fighting us, she will sleep again. Hopefully, next time she rises, she'll be more sociable."

Fabian was glad they didn't intend to kill Mariana outright. "I'll go to my mother's temple first," he said, drawing looks of surprise from round the table. "I need to try to talk to her again. Maybe she's calmed herself a little by now."

"I doubt it," Caspian replied, "but I understand. I wish you luck."

"I'll come with you," Delwyn offered.

"No." Fabian had no intention of allowing Delwyn to place himself in danger. "My mother can be difficult even at the best of times. Taking a merman into her temple, even if he's in human form, won't go down well."

Delwyn nodded and didn't try to argue.

"I think you should wait here," Fabian added. "I don't want you going to Atlantis."

Delwyn stuck out his chin and lower lip. "I won't hide

here while everyone else is fighting."

Caspian interrupted before Fabian could say anything further. "I'll make sure he goes to Cari's temple in the palace. Ula and Kai are there, with plenty of guards to keep them safe."

Fabian pointed his index finger at Delwyn. "You don't leave the temple, understand?"

Delwyn confirmed he did and Fabian let himself breathe again. He picked up his trident and, with one last peck to Delwyn's lips, he set out to face his mother once more.

* * * *

As soon as Fabian departed, Delwyn began to put on his own armor.

"What are you doing with that?" Otus asked. "Wouldn't it be more helpful to let one of the guards wear the armor, rather than *you*?"

Delwyn ignored him as he slipped on the bracers. He didn't intend to get right into the thick of the fighting, but if he found himself in danger, he wanted to be prepared. He grabbed a trident and turned back to the others.

Otus sneered. "You look ridiculous."

Again, Delwyn bit his tongue. Then his mischievous side whispered a better idea. He needed to explain to the rest of the mer how the armor worked, and to show them how to harness the sea-fire absorbed into the metal.

He tossed the trident at Otus, half hoping he would drop it, but Otus, whatever his faults, was a good guard with lightning-fast reflexes. He caught the trident in one hand.

"I already have a trident," he said, pointing to his own weapon, currently resting against the wall across the room.

Delwyn tapped the center of the breastplate. "Fire it at me."

"Have you lost your mind?" Otus replied. "King Nereus would banish me from the city if I fired a trident at one of his precious Oracles."

"He'll never know," Delwyn said. "It won't hurt me, anyway. I just need to show you how the armor works."

"I've seen armor before," Otus argued.

"Not like this. Send a bolt of sea-fire at me."

"Go ahead," Caspian told Otus, who still appeared unsure about whether he should. "Andaman's armor is most effective. Aim for the center of the breastplate."

Otus sighed and aimed the trident at Delwyn. He sent a blast from the weapon which struck Delwyn in the chest.

"Not a mark," Delwyn declared with a wide grin to mask his relief that Otus hadn't accidentally hit anything vital.

Otus appeared mildly impressed.

Delwyn grinned. "Now, for the best part."

He did what Fabian had done in the forge and drew the sea-fire from the armor and into the palm of his hand.

Otus' eyes widened.

"Do *not* throw that in Cari's temple," Caspian warned. "If you break anything, she'll be furious."

Delwyn returned the sea-fire to the armor the same way Fabian had. "You can send back at the sea dragons whatever they fire at you."

Otus nodded and passed Delwyn's trident back to him. "Good to know."

The demonstration over, Delwyn rejoined the others at the table showing the plan of the city.

"Okay," Caspian said as he rapped on the table. "As much as I hope Fabian can talk some sense into his mother, I'm not pinning all my hopes on him. So, let's decide what we're each going to do."

"King Nereus needs to be informed of our plans," Otus replied.

"Agreed," Caspian said. "Any volunteers?"

One of the guards who had arrived on the scene with Marin raised his hand. "I'll speak to him."

Caspian nodded. "Thank you, Keshet. While you speak to the king, I'll do a sweep of the rest of the palace temples. We need to know if any of the other gods are stirring, and where any newly risen stand in all this."

"I'll lead the attack on the sea dragons at the nursery," Otus said. "Who's with me?"

The guards quickly decided amongst themselves who would go where.

"How do we get to the temple from here?" Otus asked

"We'll need to go back to my home here on the isle," Medina replied. "I'll transport you all to the city from there."

"You should probably set off now," Caspian suggested. "I'll take the rest of the guards to my temple and go to the palace using my portal."

"Agreed," Medina said. "Once I've delivered everyone to the city I'll go track down my sister and nephew. If he *is* making any progress with her, I may be able to help."

"Is that everyone sorted?" Caspian asked after Medina and her group had departed.

Isander raised his hand. "Just me left, I think."

Caspian studied Isander a moment. "Can you communicate with the other sea dragons without a dragon form of your own?"

"I believe so. Once we were uncollared, we could speak to the mer while in dragon form. I see no reason to believe the remaining dragons won't be able to speak with Atlanteans. Whether they wish to is another matter entirely."

"If you can, I want you see if you can talk round any of the priests. They can't all want this fight."

"There was one priest who I'm aware had taken mermaids as lovers in the past. He kept it hidden from our goddess out of fear. He may be convinced. I just need to find out where he is."

"Can you describe him?" Caspian asked.

"Brown scales, quite small compared to the rest of them. He is generally one of the more docile ones. He spends a lot of time sleeping."

"His temperament isn't much help. Does he have any distinctive marks?"

"I'm sorry. Our scale colors reflected the color of our hair, and most of the priests had dark hair."

Caspian nodded thoughtfully. "I recall two smaller brown sea dragons during my checks on the city. One was at the palace, the other at the barracks. See if you can find him."

"I'll do my best."

"Thank you. And if he, or any of the others, chooses to join us, they must forsake Mariana."

"If they do that, they'll lose their dragon form, too. Wouldn't it be best to have a dragon on our side?"

"Perhaps, but unless they renounce their goddess, their very presence will continue to feed her powers. The weaker she becomes, the better for all of us."

Isander confirmed he understood.

Caspian finally focused his attention on Delwyn. "As one of Cari's Oracles, you have the power to travel through the crystal portal without the assistance of the gods. Can I trust you to go to her temple and wait there with Ula and Kai?"

"Yes, I gave my word I'd stay there."

Caspian shot him a doubtful frown. "I think you'd better come with the rest of us. Cari's palace temple isn't far from mine."

Delwyn would have argued, but he didn't want to linger on the isle any longer than necessary—not while Fabian was in Atlantis, facing the fury of his mother.

Caspian led them from the temple and through the overgrown grasses.

Cari, who had apparently made good time while they had been talking, met them part way to Caspian's temple and confirmed that Andaman had sent the supplies to the city. She and Caspian then led the remaining men into Atlantis once more, Caspian filling his sister in on their plans.

They found Caspian's palace temple crammed full of armor and tridents, just as Andaman had promised. Delwyn saw the supplies briefly before he transformed back into a merman and became blind once again.

Cari immediately took charge. "*Keshet, chest plates are over* here. Get one on and go speak with King Nereus. The sooner the palace guards are armored, the better. Isander, where are you going?"

"To see if we have any allies within the sea dragons."

"Not without full body armor, you're not. Suit up then head up to the main palace. I'd suggest you leave by one of the windows. The doors are sure to be guarded."

"What about you?" Isander asked.

"I intend to liberate the guards from the barracks and bring them to the palace to help defend the building. With a bit of luck, I can get them out of there without Mariana's priests even noticing their absence. Caspian, I trust you to get Delwyn to safety."

"Of course," Caspian said as Delwyn found himself ushered toward the door. Caspian guided Delwyn down a corridor and into another chamber. "Here you go, Delwyn. You'll be perfectly safe here with Ula and Kai until this is all over."

"We can help," Kai complained. "We're not completely useless, you know."

Delwyn grinned at Kai's annoyed tone. The Oracle of the Present had always longed to be a warrior, and he hated being thought of as helpless. Those who knew him well never considered him weak. He could use his power to see the present to fool even the most observant into believing he actually had his sight. Delwyn suspected he had long since grown tired of being cooped up in the temple.

"You're safer here," Caspian said. "I don't have time to argue with you. We've brought armor for everyone. I would suggest you both put some on, just in case the palace is breached."

"Ula, too?"

"Andaman's armor fits the female form as well as it does the male."

"We can help," Kai insisted.

"Kai, you're not going to win this fight." Delwyn recognized Dax's voice. Kai's lover was apparently one of their guards today, and probably as eager to fight as Kai himself.

Delwyn suspected Dax had stayed with them so he could

stop Kai doing anything rash.

Caspian left to visit the other temples and Delwyn settled himself down for a long and boring wait.

"Where have you been?" Kai asked as soon as they were thoroughly protected both with their new armor and their guards. *"When I came out of my vision to find you gone and Ula in a vision of her own I nearly panicked. When the guard told me a dark human woman had taken you, I thought the new goddess had kidnapped you. We were worried sick until I finally saw you on land in a vision. Where were you?"*

"I've been on the Isle of the Gods again. Medina took me there at Fabian's request."

"But last time you were there I could see you. Not that seeing you on a human bed was much help in finding you."

"I was in Medina's temple there, then at Andaman's forge, which I guess is kind of his temple, then at Cari's temple again. I've been all over, but you wouldn't have been able to see me in the temples of the other gods."

"And what were you doing there?"

"We've been coming up with a plan of action to stop Mariana."

"I heard a report that a couple of sea dragons turned into men," Kai said.

"That's right."

"I'm guessing one of them is Fabian."

"Yes, he and Isander were turned back by Mariana when she woke."

"I bet I know what else you've been up to." Kai added. *"While we've been worrying about you, you're finally getting some."*

"I don't know what you mean," Delwyn replied, even though he did.

Kai snickered. *"You've been on land with the man of your dreams and his former lover, and you* don't *know what I'm talking about?"*

"We weren't doing that," Delwyn muttered.

"Your face is going red," Kai crowed. *"You're a hopeless liar."*

Delwyn cursed his treacherous face. *"We kissed, all right?"*

"And?"

"And nothing much else," Delwyn said. For some reason, he didn't want to tell Kai about what the kissing had led to. He couldn't quite believe his first orgasm had been over and done with so quickly. *"There wasn't really time."*

"Everyone should make time for love," Kai teased.

Delwyn decided a change of subject was in order and he set about updating them as to what had happened and what the plans were for taking back control of the city.

When he told them about Calder, Ula burst into tears. She sobbed that she hadn't seen it coming. Delwyn did his best to console her, but there was little he could say that would help. Ula, even with her power to see the future, couldn't save everyone, and each time they lost someone, especially a friend, she took the news hard.

Delwyn held her as she cried and when she was ready, he continued to fill them all in on the rest of the recent events.

Once the others knew what was happening, Kai began to use his powers to see other parts of the city.

"What did you see?" Ula asked.

"Otus and the other guards are nearly at the nursery. They've picked up a few more mermen on the way. There are a couple of mermaids, too."

Delwyn could tell Kai was annoyed that mermaids were allowed to join in the battle while he wasn't. *"What about at the barracks?"* he asked.

Kai checked and confirmed the place seemed quiet. *"There are two sea dragons there, one in the practice yard and one on the roof."*

"Could you see the guards inside?"

"It looked empty."

"Maybe Cari got them out of there already."

Delwyn used his own powers to focus on the barracks a little earlier and confirmed that Cari had managed to spirit the trapped guards out of the building.

At least while those two sea dragons were guarding an empty building they weren't causing any trouble.

Kai checked the outside of the palace, where most of the

priests were located.

"*Are all the entrances guarded?*" Delwyn asked.

"*Yes, I think so.*"

"*Then we're trapped here even if I did approve of you leaving the temple,*" Dax said.

Delwyn knew that wasn't strictly the case. He had explored every inch of the city in his visions and had discovered numerous tunnels from the palace to other parts of the city. There weren't enough dragons to guard all the secret exits.

Of course, it was no use escaping from the palace if they didn't have a plan. As reluctant as he was to admit it, Delwyn knew his blindness would be a hindrance if he tried to fight.

Waiting here, while others put their lives on the line, was the hardest thing he had ever done.

"*Can you check on Fabian for me?*" he asked Kai. "*He was going to try to reason with his mother.*"

Kai did as Delwyn requested, or at least he tried. "*I'm sorry, I'm not seeing him at all.*"

Delwyn had suspected that might be the case. Fabian had intended to summon his mother at one of her temples, and Kai's visions could not penetrate such places. Only Delwyn had ever been able to enter another god's temple within his visions. He would just have to wait and hope Fabian stayed safe.

"*What about my parents?*" Delwyn asked. "*Do you know where they are?*"

"*They're here in the palace,*" Ula said. "*We knew you'd want to know they were safe so we ensured we kept a track of them for you.*"

"*Thank you.*" Delwyn could always count on Ula and Kai to have his best interests at heart. They were as dear to him as his parents. They were part of his extended family and nothing would ever change that.

Chapter Nineteen

Fabian found his mother's temple on the Isle of the Gods as deserted as he expected. It was the best place from which to summon the goddess, but she could choose not to answer. If that was the case, he would have to go track her down in Atlantis.

Mariana appeared on his second call, though it was clear from her sour expression she didn't want to be there.

"Mother, thank you for coming to speak with me," he offered, hoping his politeness would encourage her to be likewise.

From the roll of her eyes and purse of her lips, he had a sinking feeling that was not going to be the case.

"Mother, you don't have to fight the mer," he began. "It doesn't have to be this way."

Mariana smiled briefly. "Does this mean they agree to leave Atlantis immediately? If so, I will command my priests to refrain from attacking and merely escort the mer past the boundaries of the city."

"These waters belonged to the mer long before the gods sank the city," Fabian reminded her.

"Then they don't intend to leave."

"They want to live in peace. They don't want to fight you."

Mariana laughed. "That's because they know they cannot win. Either they leave this city voluntarily, or we will drive them out of here."

"Atlanteans and mer lived in peace once before, and they can do so again," Fabian insisted.

"Is that what you believe?" Mariana asked. "The two

societies were never entirely at peace. There was always fighting and jealousies between Atlantean and mer."

"Then we all work harder to bring everyone together," Fabian said.

"You waste your time," Mariana told him. "My loyal priests, along with yourself, were imprisoned by my brethren and held as slaves by the mer. Why do you now stand with your captors against loyal Atlanteans?"

"The mer never mistreated us," Fabian replied.

"You were their slave. Are you telling me they never once turned their weapons on you?"

"If they did, it was through fear, or in some cases, self-defense against some of your more volatile priests."

"You're a fool to defend them."

Fabian's temper rose at his mother's stubbornness. "Do you think the rest of the gods will allow you to do this to the mer? They'll imprison your priests again as soon as they're able to."

"There are few gods who have the power to contain my priests, and that mer-loving traitor Cynbel still sleeps. He won't be collaring them again."

"Mother, please. Let go of the past. You're awake now and you can make a fresh start. Get to know the mer, learn from them while at the same time teaching them about the Atlantean ways. When the Atlanteans were banished, their customs were lost, but it doesn't have to be forever."

"Those fish have nothing to teach me, and they don't deserve to learn Atlantean secrets."

Fabian could tell it was going to be no use arguing with her. He wondered why he bothered. Maybe it would be best to evacuate the mer while his mother still agreed they could leave the city alive.

He spared a brief thought for Delwyn and the possibility of getting him away from the city to begin a new life somewhere far away.

"Ah, so you're still obsessed with that creature," Mariana commented.

Fabian cursed his inability to successfully shield his thoughts from his mother. After all the centuries, he should have known better.

"Yes, you should," Mariana agreed. "You come to plead for the mer, preaching peace and understanding, when the only reason for your actions is because you want to bed one of the creatures. You disgust me."

Fabian shook his head.

"Those half-fish abominations are not fit to be our slaves," Mariana sneered. "Now I must return to my priests. If you truly care for the mer, you'll persuade them to leave the city at once."

* * * *

Delwyn hated feeling helpless. He wasn't sure what was worse. Sitting around waiting for news, or listening to Kai's updates as he used his powers to determine what was happening around the city.

Although Delwyn had always enjoyed looking into the past, he had never thought it was the most useful of powers. He said as much now.

Ula let loose a small scream of frustration. *"Curse it, Delwyn, you and Kai are the two biggest whiners I've ever met. I never had to put up with this self-pitying nonsense from either of your predecessors. Are you forgetting that without your ability to see into the past, you'd never have known Fabian existed?"*

Ula had come into her powers several years before Kai and Delwyn had. She rarely spoke about the former Oracles.

Delwyn hung his head at her reprimand and he didn't need his sight to know Kai had probably done the same.

"Right," Ula said. *"Here's how it's going to work. Kai, you keep an eye on the city, and let us know if anything changes. Delwyn, you search the past. Concentrate on the Goddess of Sea Creatures and her sea dragons. Find her weakness. I'll look to the future and see whether I can determine how we defeat them."*

Delwyn didn't argue. He slipped into the past, going

back to before the time of the sea dragons, searching for something, anything, they could use against the goddess.

He saw Mariana in her temple, welcoming her priests. He saw Fabian, still a child, peering out from behind his mother's throne as he played with a small fish who was chasing his finger.

He went back further, before Fabian's time, to when the city had thrived in the sunlight, before the gods had sunk it to save the Atlanteans from the coming wars.

He concentrated on Mariana, keeping her in his focus, watching her first in one time, then another.

It was a while before he began to spot a pattern. The goddess rarely kept company with the other immortals, but when she did, it was most often with Cynbel, the God of War, and they were always arguing. It was often about trifles, but even more frequently about the merpeople. Mariana had never liked them, wouldn't accept them and had repeatedly requested Cynbel wage war on them. He had refused, not because of any great love for the mer, but because he apparently enjoyed annoying Mariana.

The more the two immortals fought, the more Mariana grew careless. They were evenly matched with their power, but Cynbel kept his cool, while Mariana lost her temper and whatever advantage she may have had.

Her weakness was her temperament and Cynbel seemed to have perfected the art of ruffling her feathers to the point that it made her careless.

Delwyn decided he needed to take a closer look at the God of War. This was the immortal who had refused to let Mariana's priests attack the mer when they had first been transformed into sea dragons. Perhaps he could help them defeat Mariana and her men again.

Delwyn returned to the present. *"Kai? Ula?"*

"Ula's having a vision," Kai replied. *"Did you find out anything useful?"*

"I'm not sure. How are things out there?"

"Mostly the same. Isander has brought one of the priests over

197

to our side. I saw him renounce the goddess and revert back to human form. They are both fighting to free the mermaids and youngsters trapped in the nursery. The two dragons guarding the barracks have realized the building is empty now. They've joined the forces outside the palace."

Ula came out of her vision with a gasp. *"The south wing of the palace is going to collapse."*

"When?" Dax asked. *"Have we time to get everyone safe?"*

"I think so," Ula replied. *"You need to go warn them."*

"I'm on my way."

Delwyn felt Dax swim past him.

"Did you boys find out anything useful?" Ula asked.

"Delwyn thinks he might have," Kai said. *"Delwyn?"*

"I think we should try to summon Cynbel."

"Who's that?"

"He's the God of War. He's the one who collared the sea dragons in the first place. If we can wake him, he might be able to do it again."

"Won't the goddess just free them again?" Kai said.

"He was the one who caused her to drain her powers and go to sleep all those years ago. He's more powerful than she is. They've fought over and over again, even before Atlantis sank below the waves. She's never beaten him, not once."

Kai — at least Delwyn thought it was him — clapped his hands several times. *"I guess we'd better go pay him a visit then. Do you know where his temple is?"*

"Yes."

"Do you think this is a wise move?" their last remaining guard asked. *"You're supposed to stay in the temple."*

"It's not like we're going outside to face the sea dragons," Kai pointed out. *"The temple is here in the palace."*

"I'm supposed to keep you here," the guard argued.

Delwyn wished the guard appointed to them had been Ula's lover. She had him wrapped around her fins completely. Unfortunately, this one was apparently going to be stubbornly persistent about obeying his orders.

He sent a private thought to Kai. *"You think you can take*

him?"

"Are you serious?"

"Of course I am. Can you?"

Delwyn could hear the grin in Kai's voice. *"Easy."*

He wished he could see what was happening in the room, but he heard the sound of surprise and a couple of grunts from the guard as Kai overpowered him, followed by Ula's exclamation of shock. Delwyn knew he would have to look at what had happened in a vision later, just to see the expression on everyone's faces.

"Come on, then," Kai said. *"Ula, are you with us?"*

"I guess so, but it would have been nice to be included in the discussion involving deciding to attack our guard."

"You'd have tried to talk us out of it," Delwyn pointed out.

Ula responded with a hard smack of her tail in his direction. Delwyn rubbed his fins and complained. *"How is it you manage to hit me nearly every time, when you're as blind as I am?"*

"Argue later," Kai said. *"Come on. We need to hurry. Which way, Delwyn?"*

"To the left," Delwyn replied.

They hurried from the temple, trusting Kai to use his powers to ensure they weren't caught. Chances were most of the inhabitants of the palace wouldn't question them, anyway. They were no longer prisoners and could come and go as they pleased. The guards were for their protection, and to help them — Delwyn and Ula especially — get around the city.

The route between the two temples was mostly deserted. A mermaid greeted them as she passed and a couple of mermen didn't interrupt their conversation as they went by.

The God of War's temple was empty when they arrived. Delwyn knew there was a secret tunnel from the temple out of the city, but he didn't think they would need it today.

"Cynbel?" Delwyn called. *"That's his given name,"* he explained to Ula and Kai. It was little use calling a sleeping

god by his title. Only his true name would be powerful enough to wake him.

The three of them called the god over and over.

"Can you see anything?" Delwyn asked Kai. He would be the only one to know if their summons had worked.

"Not yet. No, wait, I think I see a light. Yes, I'm sure. It's working. Cynbel? Cynbel, we summon you."

Delwyn joined his plea to Kai's and Ula did the same.

"Oracles?" a gruff voice said. *"Why would my daughter's servants call me? Is Cari well?"*

"Yes, she's fine," Ula assured him. *"We seek your help with the Goddess of Sea Creatures."*

The god remained quiet for some time.

"Is he still here?" Delwyn asked Kai.

"Yes. His eyes are closed. I think he might be using his powers to assess the situation."

"You're quite right," Cynbel replied. *"I see her priests are being their usual charming selves."*

"Can you collar them again?" Delwyn asked.

"I can't," Cynbel said. *"I am not yet a part of this world, at least not entirely. I haven't the power to contain the sea dragons."*

Delwyn sighed. Their best chance and only idea wasn't going to work if the God of War hadn't completely woken. It sounded as if he hovered between his state of sleep and returning. Unfortunately, while the immortals could use their powers at such times, they were limited.

"Can you at least try?" Ula asked. *"Even if you only collar one of them, it will help."*

"Especially if you collar the high priest," Delwyn added.

"I can collar all of them, but it will drain me so much I will be forced to remain sleeping for several more centuries, and even your calls won't be able to reach me."

"Then you won't help?" Ula snapped. *"You'd rather leave us to suffer."*

"You are very brave, or very foolish," Cynbel said. *"But you do not understand. Even if I collar the sea dragons, they will not remain so. Their goddess is awake, she walks among you, and she*

can free them with barely a thought."

"Can you defeat her?" Delwyn asked. *"Like you did before?"*

"Not while I'm in this state," Cynbel replied.

"Is there anything we can do to bring you back properly?" Kai asked.

"Perhaps. If you can persuade the mer to call out for me, by my name, just as you did, it may be enough."

"We can try that," Kai said.

"Now I must go," Cynbel replied. *"If your people can wake me, I'll do what I can to bring Mariana and her priests under control."*

"He's gone," Kai said a few moments later.

"How many mer are in the palace?" Ula asked.

"I don't know, but most are gathered in and around the king's audience chamber."

"Then let's go there and get everyone calling for Cynbel. It can't hurt."

Delwyn turned to swim for the entrance and collided with a solid weight. *"Who's there?"* he asked.

"Caspian. What are you doing in my father's temple?"

"We thought he could help collar the priests, like he did before."

"Until he fully awakens, any such magic will simply be undone by Mariana, and drain Cynbel's powers, preventing him from rising."

"That's what he said."

"We thought we would try to get everyone in the palace to call his name to wake him," Ula said. *"Do you think it will work?"*

"Maybe, but there isn't time. To wake a god, to properly wake him, is a slow process. The battle will probably be over before he's fully functional."

Ula sighed. *"You were checking the other immortals. Are any of them going to help us?"*

"Unfortunately, most are still sleeping or determined to stay out of things, at least for now."

"Why won't they help?" Kai asked.

"Because they know how powerful Mariana is," Caspian replied. *"Some of them have only just woken. To take her on*

would send them right back into stasis."

"And the others?" Delwyn asked. *"You and Cari didn't sleep."*

"No, but we don't have the power to take her on. We never did because we aren't of her generation. The oldest of the gods are the most powerful – the younger generations, not so much."

"Are there any others of her generation awake?"

"Medina, her sister, of course, but between the two of them, Mariana always gained the upper hand. She can summon the most powerful creatures of the sea and command them to do her bidding. Medina's greatest power lies in love, which isn't much help in our current situation."

"Then there's no one as powerful as Mariana who can help?"

Caspian patted his shoulder. *"The only one awake right now, with the power to defeat her, is my grandfather, Antar. But I've already spoken to him, and he isn't going to interfere."*

Delwyn wanted to ask why not, but right now there wasn't time to have such discussions. They needed help and they were running out of options.

Caspian groaned loudly. *"I guess it's time I went to wake my mother."*

From the tone of his voice, Delwyn wasn't sure whether this was a good thing or a bad thing. But if she was of Mariana's generation, perhaps she would have the power to help them.

* * * *

Delwyn knew Odessa, the Goddess of Fertility's temple was close by. They had been there once before, when she had cursed the Oracles, at their request, so they didn't have to forsake love because of their powers.

As soon as they entered the temple, the goddess greeted them.

"Welcome, Oracles, and Caspian, my son, enter, enter."

"Is she here properly or is she like Cynbel?" Delwyn asked.

"She appears to be pretty solid," Kai replied.

"That's because I am," the goddess confirmed. "Now, Caspian, tell me what has happened in the world since I last walked the earth."

"A great deal," Caspian said. "The world has changed beyond recognition."

"And the Atlanteans?"

"They are long gone. When Father banished them, he scattered them around the world. Their descendants have no idea of their heritage."

"You know I didn't agree with the banishment," Odessa said. "An entire race should not be punished because of the actions of a few."

"It's too late to change the past," Caspian said. "What's done is done, and now we all need to live with the consequences."

"And how are you, my son?" Odessa asked.

"I'm well. But the mer are in trouble."

"What sort of trouble? Because of what I did?"

"No," Caspian assured her. "Their immediate problem is Mariana, who has woken."

"Oh dear."

"Her priests are in sea dragon form and have the mer trapped here in the palace and over at the old arena."

"I wasn't aware the mer used the arena. They usually avoided the games when the Atlanteans held them."

"The building is used as a nursery and education facility. The rooms around the edge are for smaller groups, while the main arena is utilized for larger demonstrations."

Delwyn heard the gasp even though he couldn't see the expression on the goddess' face.

"Preying on the weakest," Odessa spat. "Mariana always did prefer to choose such battles."

"Will you help the mer?" Caspian asked. "You're the only one who can bring her under control."

"It's heart-warming to know my son has such faith in me, but I'm not quite so confident. I am newly woken and my powers are not as they once were."

"Can you try?"

Odessa hesitated.

"Please, Mother. For me and for his people."

"Caspian..."

"If the mer are driven from the city, it's only a matter of time before they're wiped out. Their numbers are falling every generation. If they become extinct..."

Caspian didn't finish his sentence. Delwyn couldn't quite tell if he had sent the final words privately to his mother, or whether he simply could not bring himself to say them. From the choked-up tone, he suspected it might have been the latter.

"I make no promises," Odessa said. *"But I will try to reason with her."*

"Thank you."

"What now?" Kai asked after the goddess had left.

"You are to return to Cari's temple immediately," Caspian ordered. *"I seem to recall you all promising to stay safe there, rather than wandering around the palace."*

Ula huffed and Kai sighed. Delwyn, however, had no intention of going back to the temple.

"I want to find my parents," he argued. *"They're here in the palace, so I won't need to go outside. Can you take me to them?"*

"It would be safer for you in the temple."

"I don't care. I want to see them. They can come to the temple with me."

Caspian agreed to take him to his family, on the condition the others returned to Cari's temple, and stayed there this time.

Kai hugged Delwyn before they left. *"Don't do anything stupid,"* he whispered into his mind.

"I never do."

"Of course not," Kai muttered. *"Hurry back to us and try not to get snatched by any more goddesses. You might not be as lucky next time."*

Delwyn promised to join them again soon and let Caspian lead him to the main palace.

The private temples of the royal family were located

below the palace. King Nereus' audience chamber was on the ground floor, where it was easily accessible to any of the mer who wished to speak with him.

As they swam through the corridors around the audience chamber, Delwyn kept bumping into merpeople. After he had lost his sight, he had begun to avoid crowds, preferring to stick close to home and in smaller companies. He apologized repeatedly as he tried to navigate his way through the mer taking shelter in the palace.

"Mama?" he called out. *"Where are you?"*

There was such a cacophony of voices in his head he nearly missed her response.

"Delwyn, over here."

"That doesn't really help, Mama." His mother sometimes seemed to forget he could no longer see.

"Can you see them, Caspian?" he asked the god.

"It would help if I knew what they looked like."

"Sorry. My mama has silver fins, like me. My father's are green. They both have dark hair. My mama usually wears it tied up on top of her head with seaweed."

"I think they're over there on the far side of the room," Caspian said. *"Give me your hand and I'll lead you to them."*

Delwyn let Caspian take his hand and guide him across to his parents.

"Delwyn!" his mother squealed as she wrapped him in her arms. *"I'm so glad to see you. We were worried you might be out there in danger."*

"I'm fine." He hugged his mother back and held on tightly. He felt his father, a merman of few words, pat him on the shoulder. It was enough to let Delwyn know he too was pleased to see him.

"Now, Delwyn, tell me what you've been doing. I've not seen you in days. Have you found a nice merman yet?"

"Mama!" Delwyn supposed he had been neglecting his family a little. It was more than a few days since he had visited. He realized with some surprise that he hadn't been to see them since before he had found Fabian in his sea

dragon form.

"*Well, if you looked a little harder, you might have more success,*" his mother continued.

"*I don't need to find a merman, Mama. I have someone already.*"

"*Well, why didn't you say so? Is it that sweet young gatherer?*"

"*No, Mama. He's not a merman.*"

His mother went very quiet for several long seconds. "*But, Delwyn, where would you have met a human?*"

"*He's an Atlantean. He…*"

"*What is it, darling?*"

"*He was one of the sea dragons,*" Delwyn explained.

"*The sea dragons that have us trapped in here?*"

"*Yes. They are all really Atlanteans, priests of the Goddess of Sea Creatures. Well, except for Fabian. He's her son.*"

"*Are you telling me you've fallen in love with a god?*"

Delwyn couldn't tell from her voice whether she thought this was good or bad. "*Actually, he's only half a god. His father was mortal.*"

"*Oh, well, that's all right then,*" his mother said. "*As long as he's only half a god while he and his fellow dragons are terrorizing us.*"

"*What? No, Mama.*" Delwyn hastened to explain. "*Fabian isn't one of them. He's become human again because he wouldn't fight for his mother. He's trying to help us.*"

"*Are you sure you know what you're doing?*" his mother asked. "*You're a merman. You should be with one of your own kind.*"

Delwyn pulled away from his mother. "*How can you say that, Mama? Fabian's a good man and he loves me.*"

"*But he's not a merman.*"

"*I don't care about that. He's the one for me. I love him, Mama.*"

"*Are you* sure *you know what you're doing? There are so many mermen out there who could make you just as happy.*"

"*Fabian makes me happy.*"

"*I can vouch for him,*" Caspian interrupted. "*He won't let anything happen to Delwyn. He'd die defending him.*"

"*I hope it won't come to that,*" Delwyn replied. "*I'd rather have him alive."*

"If you're absolutely sure," Delwyn's mother said.

"I am, Mama."

Delwyn hoped in time his mother would come to accept Fabian. He had never thought of her as being prejudiced, and her reaction to Fabian had been entirely unexpected. As merpeople who had only ever lived in the sunken city, they had never met any humans, Atlantean or otherwise. His mother's first experience of Atlanteans had been with the sea dragons who were keeping them prisoner in the palace. He guessed he couldn't blame her for her lack of acceptance. Once she got to know Fabian, he was sure she would treat him like a second son.

The thought made him smile. Fabian hadn't exactly had the greatest of mothers. Delwyn would share his parents with Fabian, so his love could learn what it was like to have a family who loved and cared for him.

"Are you coming to the temple now?" Caspian said. *"It will be safer there if the palace is breached."*

"I think I'd rather stay here with my parents, if you don't mind."

"Kai and Ula are expecting you to join them. You can bring your parents with you."

Delwyn nodded. *"Will you come with us?"* he asked his parents.

"Of course. You can tell me how you came to meet this Fabian."

Delwyn tucked his arm through his mother's and they swam after Caspian, back to the temple below. He supposed at least bringing his parents up to date about Fabian would help pass the time, as well as take his mind off worrying about his love.

Chapter Twenty

Fabian followed his mother from her temple. She might've refused to listen to him, but he had to keep trying. He couldn't let her destroy the city or harm the mer.

He briefly considered her offer to let the mer leave, but he knew there was nowhere they could take such a large colony of mer, not without suffering severe losses, most of whom would be the young and the elderly.

Although he could see Isander had made progress in persuading one of the priests to join their side, it made no real difference. As soon as he'd renounced Mariana, he'd lost his dragon form. Despite arming himself from Andaman's supplies, he was just one more man against the might of the sea dragons and the furious goddess who commanded them.

Mariana had stopped listening to anything he said. She was too busy directing her warriors to ensure a quick victory.

Right now she focused her attention on the palace, where most of the mer who remained in the city sheltered.

"*Mother, think about what you're doing!*" Fabian screamed. "*There are innocent mer in there.*"

"*Attack the walls on the south side,*" Mariana commanded. "*There are already cracks in the structure. It won't stand for much longer.*"

"*Mariana,*" Medina said. "*You aren't seeing the possibilities here. If you can persuade the mer to worship you, your powers will grow, just as mine have. They can't boost your powers if you kill them.*"

"*Stay out of this, sister. You always did have an unnatural fondness for these wretched creatures."*

"The mer are loyal to those they love. Their devotion is as potent for us as the Atlanteans' worship was."

Mariana sneered. *"And how many of them have you invited into your bed since you woke? You've seen them during the mating seasons. They're little more than animals."*

Fabian could tell Medina wasn't having any more luck with getting through to Mariana than he'd had. They would have as much success talking to her statue.

Medina tugged Fabian aside. *"She isn't going to listen."*

"We have to keep trying."

"I know, but she's right about the building. Look at the damage they've already caused. That wing of the palace is going to come down. We need to think about those inside."

Fabian nodded. Sea-fire wasn't the greatest demolition tool, but the sea dragons weren't using it to bring down the building—they had the whole weight of their bodies to do that and it was working all too well. Unfortunately, while they were using those methods, it rendered the armor of the guards useless. There was no sea-fire for them to absorb and send back at their opponents. All they could do was watch the building take hit after hit as the sea dragons rammed the walls, the impacts increasing the cracks with each strike. Their own bolts of sea-fire bounced off the sea dragons with no effect whatsoever on the creatures.

The sound of cheers and roars echoed through the waters. Fabian looked over his shoulder to see what the commotion was.

Otus and the guards who had gone to the nursery were swimming toward them, tridents aloft.

"The nursery has been liberated," Otus announced.

Fabian grinned. *"That's excellent news. How did you do it?"*

Otus pointed his trident behind him. *"We had a little help."*

Fabian recognized Odessa, the Goddess of Fertility, Family and the Home.

"Goddess," he greeted her. *"Thank you for your help."*

Odessa nodded and smiled. *"What else could I do when*

there are families in danger? The sea dragons at the nursery are contained for the moment, but they won't be for long. My powers are not what they once were, though the gratitude of the mer for my assistance is helping to restore them."

"Any help you can give is most welcome."

Odessa gazed around her. *"There are too many for me to halt, but I can try."*

"Thank you."

Fabian turned his attention to Otus. *"The palace isn't safe. Escort the families to the temples of our allies in the city."*

"Good idea," Medina said. *"Bring them to my temple and I'll take them to the Isle of the Gods. They should be safe there, temporarily at least."*

Medina and Otus took the mer to her temple, leaving Odessa with Fabian.

When the waters were clear of innocents, the goddess raised her arms and the water around her began to shimmer.

Mariana chose that moment to notice Odessa.

"This isn't your fight, Odessa," Mariana warned. *"Get out of my way or I'll put you to sleep for another thousand years."*

Odessa ignored her and continued to whip up the waters, causing a vortex that grew larger the longer it spun.

The shark appeared out of nowhere, aiming straight for the goddess with single-minded determination. Fabian aimed his trident and sent it scurrying back where it had come from with a bolt of sea-fire.

When the second shark appeared he realized his mother had called them to attack. While her sea dragons assaulted the palace, she controlled other, equally dangerous, predators, as well.

Fabian tried to use his own powers to communicate with the sharks, but they didn't listen — his mother's influence over them was too great.

One by one he drove the beasts back, but still they kept coming. Under their own volition they would have left by now, but with the goddess manipulating them, they weren't reacting as they should. They came back at Fabian and

Odessa again and again. It was clear their primary target was Odessa, who now used her power over the water to try to force the sea dragons away from the palace. She whipped up new currents and whirlpools, driving them back, only for them to return to their attack from another point.

They were losing the fight and Fabian had no idea how they could gain the upper hand.

When Otus and the guards returned, they took over Fabian's task of fighting off the sharks so he could turn his attention back to his mother.

"Mother, please stop. You'll destroy the very city you want to claim back for the Atlanteans."

He moved forward and eased his way toward his mother.

"I warned you to stay out of this," Mariana said. *"This is your last chance to leave."*

"I'm not going anywhere."

Mariana shot a blast of power toward him. The impact reverberated through the armor. This wasn't sea-fire, it was something else.

He didn't like the sudden sensation of weakness. It was something he had never experienced before. He didn't like it.

A moment later, he breathed air as he lay on a strange hard surface, a blue sky above him instead of dark waters.

"Give yourself a few minutes to adjust."

Fabian continued to gasp. He felt sick and disoriented. Then a cool hand touched his forehead and the feeling passed.

He opened his eyes and saw Caspian crouching beside him. "What happened? Where am I?"

Caspian helped him sit. "Welcome to England."

"England? Where's that?"

Caspian conjured a globe of the world in front of him and pointed to a small island to the northeast of where Atlantis was located. "Right about here. It used to be called Albion, though you probably wouldn't know it by that name, either. You've never known anywhere except Atlantis, at least until now."

"Why am I here? I need to go back to Atlantis before my mother destroys it."

Caspian shook his head. "You can never go back there. I'm sorry."

"But the sea dragons, the mer, she'll destroy the city."

"We'll do our best to stop her, but this is no longer a fight you can participate in."

"That's my choice to make, and I'm not going to run away."

"Your choice was taken from you when your mother sent that blast of power at you. I arrived just in time to realize what she had done. I barely got you out of there alive."

"What did she do to me?"

"I'm sorry, Fabian, but she's stripped you of your powers. You're no longer a demi-god."

Fabian shook his head. "She can't do that, *can* she?"

"She can and she has. You are now a mortal man, of around thirty years of age—that's the age I've put on your papers—and you will now live a mortal lifespan."

Fabian took the satchel Caspian handed to him, but he didn't open it. "The Atlanteans were mortal, too. They survived under the ocean. I can do the same."

"I'm sorry, but you can't. Whatever your mother did when she took away your powers, she also made it so you are no longer Atlantean. She has disowned you entirely."

"But Delwyn..."

"He is a merman who has lived his entire life in Atlantis. His place is there, as one of my sister's Oracles."

"His place is with me."

"It's too dangerous for him to leave the city. He would never survive the journey alone."

"You could bring him here instantly, like you have with me."

"He's an Oracle. He *must* remain in Atlantis."

"Then send me back to the Isle of the Gods and I'll live there. He can visit me via the temple whenever he wants."

Caspian shook his head again. "Mortals cannot live on the isle without being bound to a god or goddess, you know this."

"I'll be bound to any immortal you like, if you'll just let me live there. There are mer on the isle. I can help them."

"The mer are there temporarily. As soon as it's safe to return them to the city, they'll be leaving the island."

"I lived there before. I was bound to Cari. I'll swear loyalty to her again, or my aunt Medina."

"You know you can't. A mortal can only ever be bound to one god in their lifetime. Because you were a demi-god you could swear fealty to your mother when you had previously bound yourself to Cari. Now you're mortal and you cannot bind yourself to a god again. Life amongst humans is your only option."

"It can't be. There has to be a way."

"If you don't like this country then you may choose another. I can arrange for you to start your new life wherever you wish."

"Except where I want to be."

"I'm sorry, but there's nothing more I can do. If I had known what Mariana intended when she took aim at you, I would have pulled you out of there sooner. If I'd left you there any longer you would have died, either by drowning or from the pressure of being so far under the ocean."

Fabian began to shake as the reality of what Caspian had said hit him with full force. His mother had tried to kill him. She had taken away his power to survive under the water while he was in Atlantis, knowing he would die.

"Deep breaths," Caspian advised as he rubbed his back.

"She tried to murder me," Fabian gasped out between breaths. "I'm her son and she tried to kill me."

"I know."

Fabian put his head between his legs and drew in one last deep breath. He wouldn't let her win.

"I wish I had better news for you," Caspian said. "If the God of the Sea were awake he could at least give you the ability to survive below the ocean, just as he did for the rest of the Atlanteans. Unfortunately, there is no sign of him stirring and he is the only one with the knowledge of that magic."

Fabian understood, but he had no intention of giving up so easily. He had waited so long for Delwyn to swim back into his life. He had to believe they would find a way to be together.

"A mortal life isn't so bad," Caspian said. "It's just rather shorter than what you would have had."

"That doesn't bother me. I wasn't particularly happy with the idea of Delwyn growing old and dying, leaving me to face centuries of loneliness without him."

Caspian didn't say anything in response.

Fabian belatedly remembered who he was speaking to and grimaced. "Sorry, I didn't think."

"Don't worry about it," Caspian muttered. "Now, there're a few things you need to know before I go back to Atlantis."

"Such as?"

"This," Caspian said as he touched his hand to Fabian's forehead. "Knowledge of English, human customs and modern terminology, at least as much as I know of it. I'm sure there'll always be a few phrases you don't understand, but rest assured, the way the English language is evolving means you won't be alone. You'll learn."

Fabian's mind flooded with knowledge. The volume of things he had to learn and adapt to threatened to overwhelm him. "Thank you."

"And clothes," Caspian said. "While your armor might have been suitable for Atlantis, you'll stand out a little if you wear this in England."

"I left my robes on the isle."

Caspian chuckled. "And you'd draw just as much unwanted attention if you were to wander round town in those. Here."

Fabian's armor disappeared and was replaced with strange garments that clung to his body. His knowledge from Caspian told him the clothing covering his legs was called 'jeans'. He didn't like them. They were too tight and constricting.

"You'll get used to them," Caspian told him.

Fabian stood and brushed himself down. "I guess I need to find somewhere to live."

"There's time for you to do that later. You can stay here until you're more accustomed to this country."

Fabian looked behind him to where Caspian gestured. A huge building stood at the end of the long driveway. "Is this your house?"

"No, it belongs to…" Caspian hesitated as though he wasn't sure how to finish his sentence. "A friend."

"A lover?" Fabian asked.

Caspian glared at him. "No."

Fabian opened his mouth to apologize, but Caspian was already stalking along the path toward the front door. By the time he had caught up to the god, Caspian had rung the bell and vanished.

"Thank you!" he called, though he suspected Caspian hadn't heard him.

Fabian shifted nervously from one foot to the other as he waited for whoever lived in the house to come to the door. He hoped Caspian's friend didn't mind a stranger turning up on his doorstep.

His stomach churned at the thought of how close he had come to dying. As a demi-god, he hadn't worried too much about his own mortality. Death had been a very distant event, not imminent and at the hand of his own mother. He leaned against the wall and drew in a deep breath.

During all his years as a sea dragon, imprisoned by the mer, he had never felt as helpless as he did right now.

"Aunt Medina!" he yelled, knowing she could hear him wherever she was in the world, and hoping she answered.

The goddess appeared in front of him a few moments later. "Fabian, my darling," she said as she pulled him into her arms.

"Can you help me?" Fabian asked. "Please, Aunt Medi. I've never asked you for anything my whole life, but I love him."

"I know you do."

"Then you'll help?"

Medina sighed and sat on the step, patting the stone beside her until Fabian joined her. "Delwyn is bound to Cari. If I were to spirit him here to England, she would do everything within her power to ensure he returned to Atlantis, just as she did when Kai left."

"Then you're saying he has to remain a prisoner there?"

"I'm saying I can't remove one of Cari's Oracles from the city."

"And Cari *won't*," Fabian said. While he had a great deal of respect for the goddess he had served, he was also well acquainted with her stubbornness.

Medina wrapped her arm around Fabian's shoulder and gave him a squeeze. "Cari's Oracles *must* live in Atlantis."

"It's not fair. Isn't there anything you can do?"

Medina stood and brushed off her skirts. "I'm sorry, Fabian, but as long as Delwyn serves Cari, he is lost to you."

Fabian didn't want to believe it. He wanted to argue and rage at the injustice, but his aunt didn't give him a chance to. She vanished, leaving nothing behind but a trace of her perfume.

A few minutes passed, and Fabian was contemplating ringing the bell again when the door opened. He jumped to his feet and turned to see who had finally come to greet him.

A man with short, sandy blond hair stood in the doorway, staring at him expectantly. "You're not the delivery man, are you?"

"Er, no, sorry."

"Can I help?" the man asked.

"I'm not sure. Caspian said I could stay here?" Fabian's words sounded like a question to his own ears and he hoped the god hadn't misinformed him. Thankfully, the man's expression cleared and he stepped back to let Fabian in.

"I should have guessed from the trident," he said. "I'm Jake. Come on in and I'll introduce you to the others. You'll have to excuse us. We're having a bit of a family party this afternoon. You're welcome to join us. We'll put your weapon in the closet, though. It might cause a few awkward questions if you carry it around the garden with you."

"Thank you." Fabian didn't feel entirely comfortable about intruding on a private gathering, but maybe it would help to take his mind off the battle in Atlantis. He didn't know who he was trying to fool. He would worry about Delwyn for the rest of his life. Surely there was a way for them to be together.

Jake stored Fabian's trident and took him through the house and out into the garden at the rear of the property. There were lots of people laughing and talking while music played in the background.

"I'm surprised you heard the doorbell," Fabian commented.

"I didn't. I'd gone through to the kitchen to fetch some more ice. I spotted you through the window."

"Ice?" Fabian said with a glance at Jake's empty hands.

Jake looked down and smacked his forehead with the palm of his hand. "Duh. I'll run back and get some. Go help yourself to some food. I imagine you're probably hungry after your swim here, and from what I've heard there's not much in the local waters worth eating."

"Swim?" Fabian asked.

Jake stopped halfway back to the door. He glanced around the people nearby and when he spoke he lowered his voice. "You *are* mer, aren't you?"

Fabian shook his head.

"Oh, fuck!" Jake looked panic-stricken at his response.

A familiar face popped into Fabian's line of sight as the merman rushed to his host's side. "Jake, are you okay?"

Fabian dropped to one knee and lowered his head. "Prince

Finn, it's an honor to meet you."

When he glanced up again he could see Jake's look of relief, while the prince appeared mildly annoyed. Fabian had a feeling he had done something wrong.

Jake gestured for Fabian to follow him back into the building and the three of them went inside, away from the rest of the crowd.

"Who *are* you?" Jake asked.

"I guess he's one of the mer," Prince Finn said. "I don't recognize him, but I didn't know everyone in the sunken city."

"He just told me he wasn't mer," Jake said. "When he said Caspian had told him to come here, I assumed he was. Then, when he said he wasn't, I thought I'd just revealed the existence of your race to a regular human."

"You're not mer?" Prince Finn added.

Fabian shook his head. "I'm Atlantean. I apologize for my intrusion, Your Highness."

Prince Finn sighed. "Please don't call me that. Around here I just go by the name of Finn."

Fabian nodded. "I'm Fabian, and while I might not be mer, I am something of a fish out of water right now."

Jake waved for Fabian to take a seat. Jake sat on the sofa and Finn curled up beside him. "Can you tell us what's been happening in the sunken city? That is where you've come from, yes?"

Fabian pinched the bridge of his nose and nodded. "Where do you want me to start?"

"Maybe we should fetch Kyle and Marin before he starts?" Finn suggested.

Jake nodded. "Kyle, yes, but I think it best to leave Marin out of this until we know what Fabian's going to say."

Finn hopped up from the sofa and disappeared out of the door.

"Marin's here?" Fabian asked. "How is he?"

Jake shrugged. "He's here, but he's not doing so good right now. How much do you know about what happened

218

to him?"

"Enough."

"I don't recall him mentioning you," Jake said. "Not that he's said much of anything since he arrived."

Finn returned along with the man Fabian presumed to be Kyle. He vaguely recognized him as having served a brief stint in Calder's guards.

Once everyone had taken their seats, the trio of men turned to Fabian with expectant expressions on their faces.

"Where do you want me to start?" Fabian asked again.

"How about with who you are," Kyle suggested. "I understood the Atlanteans were gone from the sunken city, centuries ago, yet clearly you've been there since Finn says you recognized him."

"As I said, my name's Fabian and I'm the only son of the Atlantean Goddess of Sea Creatures."

Finn gasped. "You're a god?"

Fabian gave a nod, then remembered his change of circumstances and shook his head. "I was a half-god, but not anymore. As of the moment I arrived on your driveway, I am no longer a demi-god, or even Atlantean. My mother disowned me and stripped me of my powers. If it weren't for Caspian's quick intervention, I'd be dead."

Everyone went quiet at his words and each of the men wore expressions that were a mixture of sympathy and horror.

"I think you need to start at the beginning," Kyle said.

Fabian nodded and set out for them everything he knew. He told them of his divided loyalties between two different goddesses, the banishment the Atlanteans and his mother's spell to create the sea dragons to circumvent the decree of the God of War.

"You were a sea dragon?" Finn asked. "Is that how you recognized me?"

Fabian smiled at Finn's awed expression. "I was, and it is. I saw you many times, usually sneaking around and getting into mischief. How many times did I see two sets of silver fins disappearing into somewhere they shouldn't?"

Finn grinned widely. "I guess you really were there."

Jake chuckled and Kyle laughed out loud.

Fabian couldn't summon up more than a weak smile. He hadn't told them about Delwyn yet, but even mentioning him so vaguely hurt.

The laughter didn't last long and Fabian hadn't even told them of recent events.

Kyle was the one who asked the question they all clearly wanted to know. "What happened to Calder?"

"How much did Marin tell you?" Fabian asked.

"He's barely uttered a word since Caspian brought him here," Finn said. "I think he's in shock. We would have cancelled the party, but he insisted we go ahead. He's in one of the rooms upstairs. We take it in turns to check on him."

"When I asked where Calder was, he just said he was gone," Kyle explained.

Fabian wasn't surprised to hear Marin wasn't doing so well. Marin had been devoted to Calder for years and the leader of the guards had adored the younger merman. Even when relationships between two mermen had been forbidden in the sunken city, the affection they'd had for each other had been obvious. Fabian had watched them sneak out of the city together on many occasions.

"He died protecting Marin and other unarmed mermen from one of the sea dragons."

"I thought you said the sea dragons were really Atlanteans, like you?" Jake reminded him. "Why would they attack the mer?"

"My mother has no love for the mer and most of her priests do her bidding without question."

Fabian went on to explain what had happened when Urion had become aggressive, the sea-fire hitting his collar, the waking of the goddess and her subsequent attack on the city.

"It wasn't your fault," Jake said.

"How — ?"

"How did I know what you were thinking? It's written all over your face."

"You're wrong," Fabian said. "It *was* my fault. I was already free from my collar and I encouraged the mer to use sea-fire. If they had used regular spears, he would never have been freed."

"How is it you were free already?" Finn asked. "I thought you just said your mother freed all the dragons when she woke, and it was Urion becoming free that woke her."

Fabian had talked all around Delwyn, avoiding mentioning him by name at all. He guessed his time had run out and now he would have to tell that part of his story.

Slowly he explained how it was he had come to be free. He still didn't refer to Delwyn by name, but certainly Finn, and probably Kyle, would know who he meant. There was only ever one Oracle of the past at a time.

He faltered and stumbled over his words as he neared the end of his account. He couldn't accept the idea of never seeing Delwyn again. He refused to believe that what they had shared was over before it had ever truly begun.

By the time he had finished speaking his eyes were watering and he ducked his head to avoid the gazes of the three men.

He looked up when he realized Finn kneeled at his feet.

"Delwyn," Finn whispered.

Fabian nodded.

Finn wrapped his arms around him, pulling him into a tight hug. The gesture sent Fabian over the edge and the tears began to flow.

"I'll die if I try to go back there," he explained between quiet sobs. "I can't survive at those depths anymore. Yet he's an Oracle and the gods say he *must* live in the sunken city."

"The two of you will find a way," Finn assured him. "If I know one thing about Delwyn, it's that he's a hopeless romantic, and now he's found the other half of his soul, he'll work out a way for you to be together."

"You believe in soulmates?" Fabian asked.

"I don't know," Finn admitted. "I have two men of my own, so I'm apparently the greedy type. But it doesn't matter what *I* believe in. What's important is that Delwyn believes in soulmates and I trust he'll find a way to get back to you, even if he has to swim the entire way alone and blind."

"He'll never make it if he tries anything so foolish." Even though Fabian had never made the swim himself, he knew enough about the oceans to know the waters were dangerous even for the most skilled warriors. A lone, blind merman didn't have a prayer.

Chapter Twenty-One

"What do you mean he's gone?" Delwyn asked.

Kai had been giving the rest of them a running commentary on the fight outside the palace.

"He just vanished," Kai said. *"One moment he was there, the next he was gone. His mother sent some sort of blast at him."*

"Sea-fire?"

"No, it was something else. I never saw it before. It was a bright green color and when it hit him he vanished."

Delwyn didn't like the sound of this at all.

"Maybe it just transported him somewhere?" Ula suggested.

"Can you see his future?" Delwyn asked.

If Fabian was alive, Ula would be able to see something.

Ula patted him on the arm consolingly. *"I'm sorry, I've been doing too much. I can't summon enough power to see anything right now."*

"Let me try and find him," Kai said. *"My visions have been limited to the city, so it hasn't used too much of my powers."*

All of their powers could be draining depending on how they used them. For Delwyn, the farther back in time he saw, the more exhausting it was, at least until Cari had helped him with her power boost. For Kai, distance drained him. To see things close by was nowhere near as tiring as seeing something on the other side of the world.

Delwyn waited impatiently as Kai searched for Fabian.

"Well?" he asked as soon as Kai cleared his throat to let them know the vision was over. *"Did you see him? Is he okay?"*

Kai smiled. *"He's alive."*

Delwyn let out the breath he hadn't even realized he had

been holding. *"Where is he?"*

Kai frowned. *"You're not going to like it, but he's in England."*

"England?" Delwyn couldn't have been more surprised if Kai had announced Fabian was on the moon. *"How did he get there? He was here in the sunken city just a few minutes ago."*

"I don't know how he got there, but I'm guessing it was a result of whatever his mother blasted him with. He's with Finn right now."

Delwyn didn't understand what had happened, but whichever god had taken Fabian and deposited him in the land of humans had better bring him right back.

"He'll find a way to return," Kai said. *"He loves you too much to give you up."*

"I hope so," Delwyn replied.

"I know *so,"* Kai countered. *"He's a former Oracle of the present, which means I have his memories."*

Delwyn had forgotten all about that. Even though he too had the memories of all the former Oracles of the past, he hadn't thought of the implications of Kai having Fabian's memories.

Thoughts of what they had done in Fabian's room on the Isle of the Gods heated his face before he recalled that Fabian had renounced Cari by then. Kai wouldn't have a memory of that, but he would know about what had happened on the beach. Delwyn wanted to swim under a rock and hide for the next decade.

Kai laughed and poked Delwyn in the ribs. *"Don't worry, Delwyn. I won't tell anyone what I've seen."*

"What have *you seen?"* Ula asked.

"Not a word," Delwyn warned Kai.

"Tell me later," Ula said with a chuckle.

"What are you all talking about?" Delwyn's mother asked, making his embarrassment complete.

"I think it better not to ask," his father replied.

Everyone laughed apart from Delwyn. It wasn't that he couldn't take a joke at his expense — he was simply too worried about Fabian right now.

224

At Ula's request Kai continued watching the events in the city, reporting back to the others frequently about what was happening.

Through his visions, Kai told them that whatever the Goddess of Sea Creatures had done to Fabian had apparently weakened her. The rest of the immortal allies had her surrounded and were taking it in turns to send blasts of power in her direction.

Unfortunately, while she was weakening, the sea dragons weren't. They continued to bombard the south wing and it wasn't long before the stones crumbled and the entire wing collapsed.

"There's no one hurt in there," Kai said.

Thanks to Ula's vision, there had been plenty of time to evacuate the area, so no lives had been lost.

King Nereus led a team of mermen who were evaluating the structure of the palace, trying to determine the safest place for the mer who had taken shelter within the walls.

While there were plenty of underground chambers, including the private temples of the royal family, it had been decided to keep most of the mer on ground level. If the palace should fall, the chambers below would become a tomb. Only those bound to a god, like the Oracles, would be able to escape, and only those mer in very close proximity could travel to the Isle of the Gods with them.

Otus had, by unspoken agreement, taken over leadership of the guards, though whether the unpopular merman would stay in the position after this was over remained undecided. Despite his lack of social skills, there was no denying Otus was a formidable fighter and the guards he commanded were tireless in their efforts to drive the sea dragons away from the palace.

The sea dragons had soon figured out the mer knew how to send their own sea-fire right back at them and weren't using their fiery breath as much as they could have. Unfortunately, they were still extremely dangerous. More than one swipe of a tail had sent the mermen spinning away through the water.

The immortals who had joined the fight against Mariana hit her with everything they had, but while she was visibly tiring, she clearly had no intention of surrendering.

Kai alternated his visions between various locations around the palace, and as such, he missed seeing what had happened to cause the building to suddenly shake violently.

"What's happening?" Ula asked. *"Has another part of the palace collapsed?"*

"No," Kai replied. *"It's another immortal waking."*

"Do you know which one?" Ula asked.

"Is it the God of War?" Delwyn added.

"No, it's a female goddess," Kai said. *"And she looks furious. The damage done to the south wing was right over her temple. Her statue was broken."*

"Is that what she's angry about?" Ula asked. *"She can fix it just like Medina did when she restored her temple."*

"I have a feeling that isn't the point," Kai replied. *"She's on her way to Mariana."*

"Well, what are you talking to us for?" Ula snapped. *"Take a look and see what she's doing!"*

Delwyn chuckled at Ula's impatience, even though he shared her eagerness.

Kai was still lost within his vision when Cari returned to her temple.

"It's safe now. Mariana has fled the city, taking her remaining priests with her."

"What happened?" Delwyn asked. *"Who was the goddess who woke?"*

"That was Tempest, Goddess of the Storm, and she certainly whipped up a good one today. The damage to her temple was great enough to wake her."

"Will she help protect the mer if the Goddess of Sea Creatures comes back?" Ula asked.

"I don't know," Cari admitted. *"I have no doubt Mariana will return, but whether Tempest will help protect you, I don't know. She has never taken sides in quarrels between Atlantean and mer.*

Her help today was purely coincidental."

"Perhaps she might take kindly to us, if we restored her temple," Ula suggested.

"It can't hurt to try," Kai said, signaling that he had come out of his vision.

"There will be time for that later," Cali said. "In the meantime, King Nereus is arranging a feast in the main audience chamber. I would suggest you all join the rest of the mer and find something to eat."

Delwyn felt the others brush past him on their way out of the temple. He wasn't hungry.

"I know what you're thinking, Delwyn," Cari said. "I'm sorry, but you can't go to land. Your place is here in Atlantis."

Delwyn knew Kai had tried arguing with Cari over this very point but had been unsuccessful in his efforts. Luckily for Kai, Dax had agreed to stay in the sunken city so they could be together.

"Can you bring Fabian back here?" he asked. "Kai saw Mariana send him away, and he says he saw him with Finn. You could go to him and bring him here."

"I'm sorry, Delwyn, but Fabian cannot return to Atlantis."

"Why not?"

"It wasn't his mother's actions that sent him from the city, it was Caspian."

"Then can't he bring him back here?" Delwyn asked.

"He took him to land to save his life. The blast from his mother stripped him of the ability to survive at this depth. She made him mortal."

"No!"

"I'm sorry. If Fabian were to try to return to the city, he would die."

Delwyn wanted to argue with the goddess. He wanted her words to be lies, but he knew she spoke the truth. Fabian was lost to him.

* * * *

227

After Jake and Kyle went back to their hosting duties, Finn took Fabian on a brief tour of their home.

The house was large and contained a huge indoor swimming pool, perfect for the mermen in residence.

Thanks to Caspian's knowledge of the modern world, Fabian knew the function of the majority of the things he saw. He also recognized the animal bounding toward them as being a dog.

"This is Treacle," Finn said. "He's a friendly mutt. He's been shadowing Marin since Caspian brought him here."

A moment later Marin turned the corner and Treacle ran to his side.

"I was just using…" Marin pointed behind him before hurrying through a nearby door.

"As you probably realized, this is the room we've put Marin in. You can use one of the other guest rooms along here." Finn gestured to the door Marin had pointed to. "This is the nearest bathroom. I assume you and Marin will be okay sharing?"

"Yes, that's fine."

Finn opened another door, pulled out various items of linen and put them into Fabian's arms. "Here you go. I hope you're adept at making a bed up, because you'll find your knowledge from Caspian lacking in that aspect, or at least all the rest of us did. Good luck!"

Fabian watched Finn disappear with a cheeky grin over his shoulder. The merman stopped at Marin's room and knocked softly. He poked his head inside briefly but withdrew almost at once. The expression on his face when he retreated was sad.

Alone in the corridor, Fabian went to the nearest door and opened it. The bed inside appeared comfortable and spacious and Fabian put the linen down on the mattress. He would make the bed later. First, he wanted to speak to Marin.

Marin answered his knock and Fabian slipped inside. The merman was curled up on the bed, his arms around his knees. He didn't look at Fabian.

"Hello," Fabian said as he approached the bed. "I'm not sure if you remember me or not, but I'm Fabian."

"I remember you," Marin whispered. "What are you doing here?"

Fabian sat on the edge of the bed. "Caspian brought me here."

"Is Delwyn with you?"

"No. He's still in Atlantis."

Marin didn't say anything, but he curled up tighter at the mention of the city.

"I'm sorry about Calder," Fabian offered. "He was a good merman. He always treated us fairly and kindly. If there's anything I can do to help you, please let me know."

"Is he dead?" Marin asked.

"Who? Delwyn? No, he's alive. I'm afraid my departure was a bit sudden, otherwise I'd have brought him with me."

"Not Delwyn," Marin said. "*Him*. The monster who killed Calder."

Fabian shook his head. "He was still alive when Caspian pulled me out of the city."

"Good," Marin whispered.

Fabian frowned, not understanding.

Marin stared at him, his mismatched eyes flashing with determination. "That means I can kill him myself."

"Sea dragons are notoriously hard to kill," Fabian warned him.

"But they weren't always dragons, were they?" Marin reminded him. "They had a human form, just as you have. Sooner or later, he'll become human, and when the time comes, I'll be waiting."

Fabian could tell it was the grief speaking and he didn't try to argue with Marin. If thoughts of revenge were the only thing keeping Marin going, then he would let him cling to them.

"Can you teach me how to fight?" Marin asked. "I promise I'm not as bad as everyone says. I only messed up a lot so I could spend more time with Calder. I *can* fight, really."

Fabian wasn't sure how wise it was to hand Marin a trident, but he couldn't refuse. "I'll help you."

Marin gave him a weak smile and sat up. "Can we start right away?"

Again, he couldn't say no. Besides, the distraction of training Marin would keep his mind off Delwyn and his own problems.

After retrieving his trident from the closet, they found a large room with no furniture on the top floor of the house. It was far enough away from the party outside that no one would hear them, not even with Treacle barking his encouragement.

Fabian handed Marin the trident and asked him to hold it as he would to defend himself. "Not bad," he praised. "How are you at conjuring sea-fire?"

"Not very good. Calder wouldn't let me use a trident. I only ever did it once, when I took a shot at Otus. I'm not even sure how I managed it."

"Okay, well, you'll be able to summon it whenever you like, because all the mer, along with the Atlanteans, were gifted with the ability to conjure it by the Atlantean gods. Over time, the mer forgot how to do it, but now the gods are waking the power is easier to wield."

"Easier is good," Marin said as he took aim.

"Er, wait a minute." Fabian raised his hand to halt Marin. "Let's find you something to aim at."

As there was nothing in the room, Fabian went to check the other rooms on the top floor. Unfortunately, they were equally deserted.

When he tried the next floor down, he found Kyle.

"There you are," Kyle said. "Is Marin with you?"

"Yes, we're doing some training upstairs. Have you got anything we can use for target practice?"

"Training? Are you sure that's a good idea?"

"Marin intends to go back and kill Urion," Fabian said. "He'll do that with or without my help. The training gives him purpose."

Kyle nodded and took Fabian through to one of the rooms Finn had passed by earlier, merely referring to it as the junk room.

"Anything in here is rubbish. Mostly it's stuff left in the property before we moved in. Too beat up to sell, but not so bad to take it to the tip. It's just sitting here gathering dust until we can think of something to do with it all. I'm sure you can find something in here to shoot at."

"Are you sure? You don't want to check in case we destroy something you might need later?"

"Nah, if it was up to me, everything in there would be long gone. It's just Jake that's sentimental over other people's rubbish."

Fabian grinned. "So it's just Jake I need to worry about, if we blast the wrong thing?"

"You can blame me," Kyle said. "I'll be downstairs if you need me."

Fabian went into the junk room and after a quick search gathered together some broken bits of furniture that might have been salvageable.

He took as much as he could carry upstairs, where Marin waited for him.

Marin was practicing, twisting as he turned the trident in one direction, then another. Fabian watched for a few moments, assessing the merman's skill.

Fabian soon saw Marin had told him the truth. He was a far better warrior than he had led the rest of the guards to believe. He moved with the grace and agility inherent to all the mer.

As soon as Marin spotted him watching he stopped, his face flushed from exertion.

"You really do know what you're doing," Fabian commented. "How did you fool everyone into believing you were hopeless?"

"I didn't convince everyone," Marin replied. "Calder knew, and so did Delwyn."

Fabian wasn't too surprised that Calder had figured it out. He had always been an observant merman. "Why didn't Calder promote you, if he knew what you were capable of?"

"I asked him not to. I was selfish and wanted to stay in training so I could spend time with him. He agreed, since he was a little over-protective. He didn't want me going outside the boundaries, guarding the sea dragons, or doing anything that might put me in danger. Stupid, right? If I hadn't been so selfish he might still be alive."

"You couldn't have known what would happen," Fabian assured him. "You and the others were unarmed when Urion attacked you. You weren't on any sort of duty, and neither were they. Calder died saving your lives, and I have no doubt he would have done the exact same thing no matter whether you were his second-in-command or the worst recruit in the history of the guards."

Marin began to tear up and Fabian thought a change of subject was in order. "Come on, let's set up your targets."

It didn't take long to place the furniture. Fabian placed a small table with one missing leg and one broken one on its side across the room.

"Let's see what your aim is like," he said. "Go for it."

It took a few tries before he managed to raise a spark, but when he did the bolt shot across the room, hitting the table squarely in the center, causing a charred circle to appear.

"Do you think it should be called something else when we're not in the sea?" Marin asked idly as he took aim again.

Fabian shrugged. "It's the only fire that can be sustained underwater. That's why it has the name."

Marin's second shot hit the mark as well and Fabian clapped his hands in praise.

"You seem to have this all sorted," he said. "Are you sure you need any training at all?"

"I need all the help I can get," Marin insisted. "Can you change back into your dragon form?"

"You want to practice on me?" he asked.

"Can I?"

"I'm sorry. The magic that transformed me was my mother's, not mine. I'm totally human now. I also doubt I'd fit in this room anyway."

Marin looked disappointed, but Fabian could do nothing about it.

"I need to get back to the sunken city," Marin said. "Will you take me?"

Fabian wished he could. He wanted to go back to Atlantis more than anything. "I'm sorry, Marin, but I can't."

Marin frowned and Fabian hastened to explain.

"I'm no longer Atlantean. I can't survive under the ocean like you can. I'd be dead long before I reached the city."

Marin was clearly disappointed but he quickly recovered. "Then will you help me talk the others into coming back with me?"

"The others?"

"Jake and the others."

"I thought Jake was human?"

"He is, but Kyle told me he's descended from the Atlantean Goddess of Love. He can survive underwater."

Fabian hadn't realized Jake was Atlantean, or that he was actually a relative, albeit a somewhat distant one. Belatedly, he recalled Delwyn telling him of an Atlantean who lived on land with two mermen. Only now did Fabian realize who Delwyn had been referring to. He wasn't sure how much success he would have in talking them into taking a trip to Atlantis. They seemed quite happy and settled here in England.

"Please," Marin begged.

Fabian found himself agreeing that he would, though he made no promises for his success.

Chapter Twenty-Two

Even though everyone else rejoiced in the defeat of the Goddess of Sea Creatures, Delwyn didn't feel like celebrating.

Since becoming an Oracle, he had often felt more of a prisoner than anything else. Right now the feeling was strong once again.

He didn't want to lose Fabian, but he was gone and would die if he attempted to come back.

If Fabian couldn't live in Atlantis, then Delwyn knew he had no choice except to leave the city and join him.

That was easier said than done.

Kai and Ula were his constant shadows and his mother had practically moved in to the temple, as well. In addition, Cari made daily visits to her Oracles, and Delwyn had a feeling it was to check he was still there. He supposed he couldn't blame her for her vigilance—after all, Kai had managed to sneak out with Dax not so long ago, and had swum all the way to England without her being aware he had left. Of course, Kai and Dax had had some assistance from Medina. The Goddess of Love had shielded them on their journey.

The more he pondered the problem, the more it seemed to him that Medina might be the solution.

"I think I'm going to go for a swim," he told Kai one morning, shortly after they had eaten.

"I'll come with you," Kai offered, though he didn't sound particularly enthusiastic.

"I thought you and Dax were going to go to land this morning?" Delwyn had chosen this time for that precise reason.

With Mariana and her priests still at large, most of the mer were being cautious about visiting the nearby island. They only went in large groups and accompanied by several guards. Delwyn knew Kai had been eager to reconnect physically with Dax for the last couple of days.

"We could always go to land later."

Delwyn heard the hesitation in Kai's voice and used it to his advantage. *"You go ahead. I thought I'd just go for a wander round some of the temples."*

"If you're sure?"

"Yes, you have fun with Dax."

Kai didn't need much persuading to stick to his original plans and Delwyn was soon on his way to Medina's temple, along with his guard.

"You can wait out here," Delwyn said when they arrived at the public temple of the Goddess of Love.

His guard snorted. *"I don't think so."*

Delwyn realized the guard was one of those who had been guarding him and Kai when Kai had slipped out of the city. He apparently wasn't taking any chances of losing his charge this time.

Since he could communicate privately with Medina, just as he could with any of the mer, he decided to go ahead with his plan. He wasn't even certain the goddess would show when he called her, anyway.

Delwyn entered the temple and called for Medina. She responded immediately, almost as if she had been waiting for him to visit.

His guard gave a squeak of surprise before Medina even spoke.

"Delwyn, darling," Medina greeted him with a kiss to each of his cheeks. *"I think I know why you're here."*

"Um, my guard…"

"He won't hear my words if you don't wish him to. Now, what are we going to do about you and my nephew?"

"Can you help him?" Delwyn asked.

"I can't give him the power to survive here in Atlantis,"

235

Medina said. *"Neither I nor my sister know the secret of that magic. The only god who has that sort of power is the God of the Sea, and he is still fast asleep and likely to remain so."*

"Then it's hopeless."

Medina smacked him lightly on the arm. *"Surely you're not giving up so easily?"*

"You know the Oracles aren't allowed to leave the sunken city. Look what happened when Kai left."

"Kai chose to return, but he didn't have to."

"Cari won't allow me to leave. She needs her Oracles here in the city to keep her powerful."

"Yes, she does," Medina agreed.

Delwyn waited for the goddess to give him the solution to his predicament, but it seemed she didn't have one.

"You have the answer already," Medina said. *"All you need to do is follow my nephew's example."*

"I already told you, I can't leave the city."

Medina gave a small giggle. *"That's not what I meant."*

"What did you mean?"

When no answer came he asked again.

"She's gone," his guard said.

"Oh."

Well, he guessed that was as much help as he was going to get from the Goddess of Love.

* * * *

Since Medina hadn't told him anything particularly useful, Delwyn spent the next couple of days moping around his chambers and trying not to annoy his family with his persistent whining about how unfair life was.

He was glad he and Fabian were now living in the same time, and that Fabian was human again, but why did he have to be on land, while Delwyn was stuck at the bottom of the ocean?

In some ways it was worse now than when Fabian had been a sea dragon. At least he had been able to talk with him and knew he was well.

What if Fabian found someone else while Delwyn was still trying to figure out a way for them to be together? Why couldn't Medina have been more specific with her advice? She obviously knew what it was he should do, so why not just tell him?

Two days later, when Delwyn realized what Medina had been obliquely referring to, he cursed his stupidity.

"I am such an idiot!"

Ula laughed. *"Tell us something we don't know."*

Delwyn tried to smack her but missed completely and cursed, causing her to laugh even harder.

He ignored her and swam from the room, directly to Cari's main audience chamber.

The goddess had provided comfortable living quarters within her temple for the Oracles, but the public audience chamber remained much as it had for hundreds of years. When the mer were allowed to approach the Oracles to request a vision, this is where they greeted them. Cari's statue took center stage and Delwyn had seen it often enough in his visions to know exactly where it stood. He approached it nervously, wondering whether he should have discussed this with Kai and Ula.

"Delwyn, what are you doing in here?" Ula asked.

"Just thinking."

"Liar. You shot out of the room like a shiver of sharks were on your tail."

Delwyn tried to think of a reason for his behavior, but before he could speak Ula grabbed hold of his arm.

"No, Delwyn, don't do it."

Delwyn tried to break free of her grip.

"I've seen what you're going to do," Ula whispered. *"Please don't do anything drastic."*

Delwyn gently removed her arm. *"Then it'll work?"*

"You know it will, but Delwyn…"

"I can't stay here," Delwyn said. *"I need to go and find him, and right now I can't. Cari will never allow one of her Oracles to*

leave the city."

"Have you talked to Kai about this?"

"No." Delwyn knew he would try to talk him out of it.

"Kai!" Ula's call screamed through Delwyn's mind and he knew Kai would hear it no matter where he was in their temple. He might even have heard it outside the building, too.

"What are you shouting about?" Kai asked as he swam into the chamber.

"Delwyn is about to do something really important without discussing it with us first."

"Only because you'll try to talk me out of it," Delwyn complained.

"Do you want to tell me what you're talking about?" Kai asked. *"Or am I expected to guess?"*

"Are you going to tell him, or am I?" Ula said.

Delwyn sighed. He wasn't going to be able to do this without the approval of his adoptive family. *"I'm going to renounce Cari."*

"What do you mean?" Kai asked. *"What will happen if you do?"*

"He'll no longer be an Oracle," Ula said. *"He intends to give up his powers and follow Fabian to land."*

"Is that true?" Kai didn't sound happy about it.

"You know Cari won't allow me to leave the city as long as I'm bound to her."

"And how are you planning to get to England?" Kai asked.

"I'm hoping I can persuade Medina to take me there, but if not, I'll swim."

"Swim? Are you out of your mind? You'll never make it."

Delwyn glared in what he hoped was Kai's direction. *"Thanks for the vote of confidence, Kai. You'll remember when it was you planning on making the journey I helped you escape and wished you all the best."*

"I'm sorry, but this is different. I never planned on going alone."

Dax coughed deliberately. *"No, Kai, you just planned on swimming back on your own."*

"You didn't?" Delwyn asked.

"Thanks, Dax," Kai muttered. "I hadn't actually told them that."

Ula gave a strangled scream. "You're both insane."

A tail—most likely Ula's—smacked against his fins and a moment later he heard the impact of her doing the same to Kai. He had no idea how Ula managed to hit her mark while he missed more often than not.

"I'm not asking for your blessing," Delwyn said. "I'm going to do this. I have to. Please don't try to stop me."

"Are you sure about this?" Kai asked.

"I love him, and if he can't live here with me, I have to go to land with him."

Kai pulled him into his arms and hugged him. "I won't stand in your way, but if you're going to swim the whole distance, I'm coming with you."

"We're coming with you," Dax amended.

"Do you honestly think Cari will let you go swimming off again?" Ula asked.

"If she knows it's only temporary, and that we're coming back, then yes, I think she will," Kai replied. "Of course, this is all working on the assumption that Cari will let him renounce her."

"It's not a question of her letting me," Delwyn said. "She has no choice in the matter."

"Delwyn is quite correct," Cari announced from her throne.

"Goddess." Delwyn greeted her with a nod of respect.

"I know there won't be any chance of talking you out of this," Cari said. "And I won't try to stop you."

"Thank you."

"Come here, my Oracle," Cari urged.

Delwyn swam over to her and she pulled him into an embrace.

"Only one other Oracle, in all the centuries I have appointed them, has ever renounced me. I suppose it is fitting that the second one to do this chooses to do so because of his love for the first. Now, say the words and I'll take back my gift. I promise it will be done."

Delwyn swam back a short distance and nodded. *"I renounce you, Cari, Goddess of Prophecy."*

For the first time in years, Delwyn saw something outside of his visions, a shimmering light, hovering in front of his face. He felt Cari reach out to touch him and suddenly his sight was restored completely.

"It is done," Cari said. Her voice sounded weak and she collapsed onto her throne as though exhausted.

"Cari?" Delwyn swam to her and took her hand in his. *"What's wrong?"*

"To appoint a new Oracle in such a way is tiring," Cari explained. *"I'll need to rest soon."*

"Undine," Ula announced.

"A mermaid?" Kai asked.

Delwyn frowned. *"But I thought all Oracles were chosen from those who have yet to experience their first mating season? Undine is older than any of us were when we came into our powers."*

Cari shook her head. *"While I usually appoint those of a young age, it isn't necessarily the case. The reason I previously chose those who were unmated is because of the old law preventing the Oracles from going to land. I did not wish to split up families or part those who had already found love. The law is no longer an issue and I believe Undine may not be opposed to being cursed with infertility. I had hoped to greet her, but I fear I am too weak. I must rest a while. I leave you to welcome Undine to her new home."*

Cari faded out of sight, leaving a few flickering lights, which eventually vanished, too.

Ula chuckled. *"At last there is another female Oracle. Which means for the first time since I came into my powers, the females will outnumber the males."*

Kai groaned. *"Delwyn, look what you've reduced me to."*

Delwyn couldn't help chuckling at Kai's pained expression.

Their mirth was cut short by the arrival of Undine, assisted by an older merman.

"Oh, I thought..." The merman halted as he counted the three Oracles. *"But you're all still alive."*

"Papa, what's the matter?" Undine asked.

"I think you were wrong about what the loss of your sight means. I'm counting three Oracles here. No one has died."

Delwyn swam forward. *"I'm no longer an Oracle,"* he explained. *"Come on in, Undine. I'm sure you know who they are, but let me introduce you properly to the rest of the lunatics."*

This time, when Ula swatted at him, Delwyn swam out of range and she missed.

Even though he was eager to join Fabian, Delwyn decided to stay in the city for a few days to help Undine become accustomed to her new status.

He escorted her to the Goddess of Fertility's temple, where Odessa confirmed Undine had been cursed with infertility, just as the other Oracles were. As Cari had predicted, Undine took the news well, revealing to the others that she had not broken her mating fever since she had suffered a bad pregnancy, resulting in a stillbirth, some years before. To be cursed in such a way was, for this mermaid, actually a blessing.

When he was sure Undine had settled into her new role, and had begun her training in how to recognize the signs of an imminent vision, Delwyn went to see his parents and say his goodbyes. He knew he probably wouldn't see them again. They were both too old to make the journey and it was unlikely the immortals would agree to act as some sort of transportation service.

"Mama, are you here?" Delwyn swam into his parents' quarters in the palace, gazing around the rooms he had grown up in, knowing he would never return after today.

"Delwyn, darling, you're just in time." His mother swam through from the sleeping chambers.

"In time for what?"

"I've just finished installing your new sponge. Your room is all ready for you to move back in."

"Move back in?" Delwyn gaped at his mother.

"Why, yes, dear, of course. Now you're no longer an Oracle, there's no reason for you to stay in the temple. You should be here with your family."

Delwyn let his mother tug him through to the sleeping chamber. She had clearly been working hard to make it as comfortable as possible for him. She had found some of his old treasures and put them on display on the shelves, and his new sleeping sponge had been placed in the center of the room.

"What do you think?" she asked.

"You shouldn't have gone to all this trouble," Delwyn said.

"It's no trouble at all," his mother assured him. *"You're coming home and your father and I both want to make sure you have your own space. Your father thought the new larger sponge would be better for if you want to invite a merman back sometime."*

Delwyn swam over to the sponge and settled on the end. *"Mama, I won't be moving back in to the palace."*

"Why ever not? You're not an Oracle anymore. Your place is no longer in the temple."

"No, it's not," Delwyn agreed. *"I belong with Fabian."*

"The Atlantean? I thought he left the city during the battle?"

"Caspian took him to land to save his life. It wasn't as if he had a choice."

His mother patted Delwyn's arm. *"I'm sorry, darling. I know you cared for him."*

"I love him."

"There'll be other loves."

"Not for me. Mama, I'm going to live on land with Fabian."

"No!" Delwyn cringed as his mother's yell resounded through his head and brought his father swimming into the room at speed.

"What is it?" his father asked.

"Delwyn says he's going to live on land," his mother replied. *"You have to talk some sense into him."*

"Delwyn, is this true?" His father sat on Delwyn's other side. *"Swimming to even the nearest body of land is a dangerous*

journey."

"I won't be swimming," Delwyn explained. *"Fabian's aunt, the Goddess of Love, will take me to him. I won't be in any danger and I'll be with the man I love."*

Delwyn had hoped his words would assure his parents, but the deafening silence said otherwise.

"Mama, Papa, please say something."

"I don't want you to go to land," his mother finally said. *"You're a merman and your place is in the ocean, here in the sunken city, with your family."*

"Other mer have made lives for themselves on land. Finn is happy there, along with his mother and Kyle."

"I can't live on land," his mother said. *"And I don't want you to, either."*

"But I love him, Mama."

"You barely even know each other."

Delwyn took his mother's hand and gave it a squeeze. *"You're wrong, Mama. I love him, and he loves me."*

"How can you be so sure?"

"Fabian gave up his Oracle powers and swore loyalty to his mother, just so he wouldn't lose his memories of me. He's stayed here, a prisoner, watching over the city for centuries, waiting for me. He has loved me all that time. He's given up so much for me. For me to leave the ocean is such a small thing, compared to what he has done to be with me."

"But, Delwyn..."

"No, Mama. I know my own heart. I love him and I'm going to spend my life with him."

"You thought you loved the young prince, too," his mother pointed out. *"The two of you were inseparable, but over time you came to understand that what you felt wasn't love, and that there could be another for you. Your feelings for this Fabian will fade too, and you'll find love with someone else, someone right here in the city."*

"You're wrong, Mama. I did love Finn and he loved me. Our chance to be together might have slipped by, but I still have feelings for him, just as I know he still has feelings for me. But

we didn't fight for our love and we lost each other. I won't let the same thing happen again. I love Fabian and I'm going to do whatever it takes to be with him."

"But, Delwyn, you can't leave the ocean for an Atlantean."

Delwyn wanted to argue, but his father beat him to it. "It's Delwyn's life, and his choice," he said. "If we seek to keep him here, he'll only resent us. He's a grown merman now."

"Thank you, Papa." Delwyn pulled his mother into his arms. "Mama, please let me have your blessing."

"I don't want you to leave."

"I know, and I'm going to miss you, both of you, but I have to go to Fabian."

"You have our blessing," his father said, but Delwyn needed to hear it from his mother, too. "Just know that if things with Fabian don't work out, you're always welcome to come back home."

"Mama?"

His mother nodded and rubbed at her face. "Do you truly believe the Atlantean can make you happy?"

"Yes, I do."

"And you'll be careful on land, making sure no one sees what you are?"

"My fins will be well hidden," Delwyn promised.

"Then I suppose we have no choice except to wish you all the best and say goodbye."

Delwyn gave his mother a peck on the cheek. "I don't have to leave immediately. I can stay a little while longer."

"He must have caught sight of the welcome home dinner," his father teased. "Though I suppose now it should be called a goodbye dinner instead."

Delwyn chuckled. "I might have spied my favorite meal all laid out in the other room."

"Then let us eat and enjoy the time we have left together."

He stayed with his parents all day, discussing his hopes for the future and reminiscing about the past.

Finally, the time came for him to leave, before it became too hard to say goodbye.

"I'm going to miss you, Mama," Delwyn said as he let his mother hold him for several long minutes. Under the water, it was hard to tell when someone was crying, but he knew she was from the quivering of her body.

His father didn't cry, but Delwyn could tell from his downcast eyes that he would miss him just as much as his mother.

"You take care of yourself," his father ordered.

"I will, Papa."

Delwyn drew back from his mother's embrace, gently disentangling himself. "I love you both."

"We love you, too," his mother said. "Don't forget us."

"Never. If I can visit, I will."

"You are not to make the swim alone," his mother ordered. "Promise me you won't, and that you'll stay safe."

"I will, Mama, I promise."

Delwyn hugged his parents one last time before swimming back to the temple and his other family.

Saying goodbye to Ula and Kai was almost as hard as departing from his parents.

They swam to Medina's temple with him. Although he suspected Cari would have taken him to land if he had asked, they had not seen the goddess since the day he had renounced her. During a brief visit from Caspian, the god had informed them Cari needed to rest before she could appear again. She wasn't in stasis, as the other immortals had been, but if she tried to do any form of magic it would send her into that state.

Delwyn understood now why she had been so set against her Oracles giving up their powers. He was sorry it had taken such a toll on her, but he didn't regret his decision.

As they entered the temple of the Goddess of Love, Delwyn found Medina waiting for him.

"There you are," she said, greeting him with a smile and a kiss on the cheek. "I expected you days ago."

"It took me a couple of days to figure out what you meant," Delwyn replied. "Why didn't you just tell me I had to renounce

Cari?"

"It's strictly forbidden for a god or goddess to actively encourage the followers of another deity to turn away from the one they are sworn to serve. The only reason my sister could do so with Fabian is because he is her son. I couldn't tell you directly without risking the wrath of the other gods. You already had the knowledge of what you needed to do. I simply gave you a nudge in the right direction. I'm very glad you figured it out because Fabian is desperate to see you again."

"Are you able to help me travel to England?" Delwyn asked.

"Of course, my darling boy," Medina replied. *"Why else do you think I'm loitering around in this temple?"*

"I wasn't sure," Delwyn admitted. *"You made Kai swim there."*

"Well, that was because Kai's journey was important. You've already won the heart of my nephew. To keep you from him while you swim the whole way would be too cruel. Now, are you ready?"

Delwyn faced the Oracles who had been his family for so long.

Ula moved first, dragging Delwyn into a tight hug. As always, her accuracy in finding him was perfect. He hugged her back.

"Goodbye, my brother," she whispered. *"I know you'll be very happy."*

"You do?"

Ula gave him a knowing smile. *"Did you think you could swim out of our lives without my peeking into your future?"*

"I guess not."

"I had to make sure you were making the right choice."

"And if I weren't?" Delwyn asked quietly.

"I would try to talk you out of it, of course." Ula gave a bright smile. *"But I see much happiness in your future, so there is no need for warnings and all I have to do is wish you well."*

"Thank you, my sister."

Delwyn gave Ula one last hug before he turned to Kai.

"I suppose it would be pointless to ask if you're sure," Kai said.

"It would," Delwyn agreed.

"Then come here and let me say goodbye properly." Kai didn't wait for Delwyn to move to him. He swept Delwyn into his arms and kissed him soundly on the lips. Over the years, they had shared many kisses, some soft and teasing, others passionate and consuming.

"I love you, Delwyn," Kai said as he continued to devour Delwyn's mouth.

"You do remember your own lover is right here in the room?" Delwyn teased, though he made no effort to break the kiss.

"I remember, and he's enjoying the show," Kai replied. *"Later, when we're on the beach, he'll tell me how much."*

Delwyn laughed as he ended their embrace. *"You're dreadful, Kai."*

"I know, but that's why you love me, right?"

Delwyn looked at Dax over Kai's shoulder and smiled. *"Maybe I should have joined you on the solstice after all."*

"Perhaps you should," Dax agreed, *"but we understand why you didn't. I hope Fabian knows how lucky he is to have you."*

"He knows," Medina said. *"And if he should ever forget, I'll be sure to remind him."*

Delwyn swam over to Dax and pulled him into a hug as well. *"You had better not forget how lucky you are to have Kai, either. If I hear otherwise, no ocean will be large enough to hide you from my wrath."*

"Is that right?"

Delwyn made sure his next words went only to Dax. *"If you hurt him, I will track you down. I'll do more damage to you with one trident than a hundred sharks could accomplish. Then I'll take you to land and make sure you never enjoy another mating season for as long as you live. Do you get the picture?"*

"Oh yes, I understand perfectly," Dax replied. *"But I promise, you have no need to worry. Kai's heart is safe with me."*

"It better be," Delwyn warned.

He pulled away and after giving Kai one last quick hug he swam to Medina and took hold of her outstretched hand.

"I'm ready," he said. *"Goodbye, everyone."*

The last thing he heard was their replies and wishes for

his happiness, echoing in his mind as the room vanished around him and another appeared in its place.

Chapter Twenty-Three

"Where am I?" Delwyn gazed around the strange room. He was still in his mer form as he sat on the bed. "Where's Fabian?"

"Oh, he's around here somewhere," Medina said. "Let's get you ready for him. First things first."

Medina tapped him on the forehead.

"What was that for?"

"Just a little something you'll need," Medina replied. "The knowledge of English and all those quaint human customs. You'll find that while everyone in this house can speak mer fluently, the rest of the country is quite lacking in that respect."

The goddess tossed Delwyn a towel and he used it to dry his fins and restore his human legs. When he tried to stand, Medina urged him back onto the bed.

"Sit back there, that's it," she advised him. "Place your feet flat on the mattress. No, not like that with your knees together, you need to display yourself for him properly."

Delwyn scowled at the goddess. As grateful as he was for her help, it was all a little ridiculous, posing on the bed. He wanted to go and find Fabian, not sit around waiting for him to show.

"I'm trying to help you," Medina said. "By the time I'm finished with you, you'll appear sexy and Fabian won't be able to resist you."

"I don't think Fabian will care about how I'm positioned on the bed."

"Oh, you silly boy." Medina chucked him under the chin. "Every man likes to look gorgeous for the one he loves.

Fabian will appreciate the vision of sexiness you'll be."

"I'd rather just go and find him."

"Don't you want him to come in here and ravish you?"

Delwyn frowned as he considered the question. He could tell Medina expected him to answer yes, but he wasn't sure he wanted to. This would be his first real time with Fabian and he wanted it to be special. He might be a foolish romantic to even consider such things, yet he couldn't help himself.

Medina took his silence as assent and set about bossing him around once more.

Delwyn had just got his voice back when the door to the room opened and a man he recognized as Finn's human lover entered.

"Medina, what are you doing here?" The man gestured at Delwyn. "And who's this?"

The goddess smiled and glided across the room, kissing the man on each cheek. "Jake, my dear, let me introduce you to the most recent addition to our little family."

"What are you talking about?" Jake asked.

"You, me, Fabian, and now Delwyn," Medina said.

"Delwyn?" Jake gaped at him and Delwyn gave him a nod. "Let me go and find Fabian. He'll be delighted."

Jake dashed out of the door, leaving Delwyn to stare after him.

"I'm sorry for his rudeness," Medina offered. "Not even properly introducing himself. Whatever must you think of him?"

"He was probably a bit surprised to find a naked man in the room."

Medina snorted. "He shares his bed with two other men, as I'm sure you already know. He is quite accustomed to the sight of cocks."

"I just meant…" Delwyn shook his head and didn't bother finishing his sentence. He doubted Medina would understand his point and he didn't wish to annoy her. With Fabian so close, he had no intention of giving the temperamental goddess an excuse to separate them. He fidgeted nervously, staring at the door in eager anticipation of the arrival of the man he loved. He tried to settle himself more comfortably, and so he appeared a little less ridiculous-looking, but every time he moved a muscle Medina noticed.

Medina sighed and tutted as she gestured for him to get back into place, before heading across the room to mess with the curtains, muttering something about the right lighting.

"Delwyn!" Fabian burst into the room and threw himself onto the bed and into Delwyn's arms. "I thought I'd never see you again. What happened?"

Fabian prevented him from replying with a kiss, thrusting his tongue into Delwyn's mouth and pushing him back onto the covers. Only Medina's presence halted Delwyn from enthusiastically participating in their kiss.

"Aww."

Fabian froze and pulled away just far enough to speak. "We're not alone, are we?"

"Sorry, Medina brought me here."

Fabian twisted round to look over toward the window. "Aunt Medi, do you mind?"

"Not at all," Medina replied. "I'll be gone in just a few seconds. I just wanted to say hello to my favorite nephew, then I'll disappear."

"You've said it now," Fabian said. "Was that all?"

"You could try to sound at least a little pleased to see me. Here I am, busy making sure Delwyn looks as attractive as he can for you, and you don't seem to appreciate my efforts at all."

Fabian rolled his eyes and climbed off the bed. "Aunt Medi, I am forever in your debt for bringing Delwyn to me, but if you don't get out of here, right now —"

"I'm going, I'm going," Medina hurriedly assured him.

She rushed to the bed and gave Delwyn a quick hug. "Welcome to the family."

"Aunt Medi," Fabian warned.

"I'm gone," Medina said as she vanished from the room.

"No other immortals are going to interrupt us, are they?" Fabian asked. "Cari isn't going to suddenly appear and whisk you back to Atlantis or something?"

"No." Delwyn grinned widely. "Not a chance. I renounced her."

"You did?" Fabian sat on the edge of the bed. "How did she take it?"

"She understood my reasons, though it weakened her to appoint a new Oracle in my place."

"And you're happy with your decision?"

"Yes, I am. I never wanted to be an Oracle in the first place. I didn't choose it, not like you. For the first time in years, I don't feel like a prisoner. I'm on my own path, one of *my* choosing, and I will never regret choosing you."

Delwyn held out his hand for Fabian and guided him back down on top of him. "Now, how about we start making up for lost time?"

"What do you have in mind?" Fabian teased.

"Well, for a start, I do believe you're wearing far too many of these human clothes."

"I think you may be right." Fabian pulled his shirt over his head and threw it onto the floor.

Delwyn took in Fabian's well-defined chest and drew a sharp breath. He ran his fingers lightly over his flesh, taking the time to appreciate the sight. This wasn't going to be a rushed encounter like the last time they had been together. He wasn't sure yet what they were going to do, but whatever it was, Delwyn intended to take his time and savor his man.

"What do you want to do?" Fabian asked.

"I'm not sure," Delwyn admitted. "I've waited so long for this, I don't know what it is I want the most. I don't even know what my trigger is during the mating season."

"It's months before the next solstice," Fabian said. "We've plenty of time to explore the possibilities between now and then."

Delwyn nodded. "Kiss me?"

Fabian leaned forward to do as he asked.

As Fabian pressed down on him, Delwyn groaned. The material of Fabian's clothes was deliciously rough against his skin.

Delwyn wrapped his arms around Fabian and held him in place. Now they finally had the time to explore each other, he had no intention of hurrying.

Fabian trailed kisses along his jaw. When he reached his ear he sucked the lobe between his lips and Delwyn gasped in response.

"I'm going to taste every inch of your body," Fabian whispered.

Delwyn's heart raced and his cock rose, nudging Fabian in the process.

Fabian grinned at him. "And I'm leaving *that* part until last."

"Tease!"

"Yes, but I promise it'll be worth the wait."

Fabian lowered his head and sucked on Delwyn's neck, hard enough to leave a mark.

Delwyn groaned and tilted his head to give Fabian better access.

Fabian alternately licked and sucked at his neck while Delwyn moaned beneath him.

Finally, Fabian finished his work on that part of Delwyn's body and he moved a little lower. He dropped soft kisses on his chest until he reached one of his nipples.

When he took the bud between his teeth and nipped it, Delwyn thought he might just come on the spot. He dug his heels into the bed and held on to the covers with a death grip.

Fabian seemed to realize how close he was and he reached between Delwyn's legs, taking hold of his throbbing erection in a firm grip.

If Delwyn had thought Fabian intended to stroke him to completion, he soon realized he was wrong. Fabian squeezed him at the base and Delwyn's climax receded for the moment.

"Not yet," Fabian said. "When you come, I intend for you to be in my mouth."

Delwyn gaped at Fabian, his mouth open in a small 'oh'. Fabian kissed him briefly on the lips before he returned to his chest, this time giving his second nipple the same treatment the first had already received.

Fabian took his time, driving Delwyn to the brink with only his lips.

"What about you?" Delwyn asked after Fabian had staved off his orgasm for the second time. "I know I don't have as much experience as you—or any, really—but you shouldn't be doing *all* the work."

Fabian laughed loud enough that the others in the house probably heard him.

Delwyn scowled for a moment, but Fabian removed his frown with a peck on the lips.

"You think this is work?" he teased. "I'm enjoying this as much as you are."

Fabian took Delwyn's hand and held it to his groin. "Feel how hard you make me?"

Hesitantly at first, then with increasing eagerness, Delwyn traced the hard line of Fabian's shaft, still trapped within his human clothes.

Fabian pushed Delwyn's fringe back from his eyes and smiled at him. "You don't need to have experience to bring me pleasure. All you need to be is here, in my arms. Now close your eyes."

"Why?"

Fabian grinned. "Because I don't want you to see what I'm going to do next."

Delwyn did as Fabian asked and waited to see what he had in mind. Since he had been working his way down his body, he half-expected him to direct his attention to his stomach, but instead Fabian moved his legs apart.

When Fabian swiped his tongue along Delwyn's inner

thigh, he nearly bucked him off the bed. Fabian's strength, holding him in place, kept him from going tumbling off the mattress.

Fabian kissed his thigh, from the top down to his knee then down his shin, all the way to his foot.

When he discovered the soles of Delwyn's feet were ticklish he spent a dreadful amount of time teasing him with licks in between sucking on his toes. Only when Delwyn nearly kicked him in the face did Fabian move his kisses elsewhere.

He worked his way back up Delwyn's other leg, this time, giving his foot a lot less attention than he had the other.

As Fabian worked his way closer to his groin, Delwyn shivered in anticipation.

Yet Fabian seemed determined to keep him waiting, bypassing his erection again and instead kissing his hip as he nudged him over onto his side first, then his stomach. He grabbed a pillow from the top of the bed and placed it under Delwyn, raising his arse.

When Fabian spread his cheeks and licked along his crease Delwyn began to pant and whimper.

He had seen other men doing this, but not as frequently as he watched them doing other things together. Even knowing what was about to happen, he wasn't quite ready for the sensation of Fabian brushing over his taint and teasing his hole with his tongue.

Delwyn clung to the pillow at his head and moaned into the fabric. He ground his hips into the other pillow before pushing back toward Fabian's face.

He was going to spill, he knew it. He couldn't contain himself any longer. Fabian was just too skilled.

Then Fabian's tongue was gone. Delwyn panted desperately as Fabian turned him onto his back once more.

Fabian kneeled between his spread legs and rubbed his hands along Delwyn's inner thighs, inching closer to his aching shaft with each sweep of his fingers.

Delwyn gazed at Fabian with heavy-lidded eyes.

Fabian licked his lips and took hold of Delwyn's hips in a firm grip. He bent his head and licked the tip of Delwyn's cock, swiping the pearly bead from the end.

The tiny touch of Fabian's tongue against his shaft was enough to send Delwyn over the edge and he came hard and fast.

Fabian managed to get his mouth round him just in time to drink down Delwyn's seed.

Delwyn cried out as he thrust his hips. Fabian sucked his sensitive flesh, taking him so deep Delwyn could feel his throat around his member.

When Delwyn had been reduced to a quivering mass of nerves Fabian released him from his mouth and crawled up his body to kiss him again.

Delwyn could taste himself on Fabian's lips and he found he liked it. He wondered if Fabian would taste the same. He intended to find out as soon as he had recovered his senses enough to move.

Fabian didn't seem to be in any rush to finish undressing, but Delwyn had every intention of speeding the process along, just as soon as he could move his limbs. He said as much to Fabian, who laughed and kissed him again.

Finally, Delwyn recovered sufficiently to sit up and tackle the fastenings on the strange human clothes.

Fabian smiled at him as Delwyn undid first the belt, then the buttons of his jeans and pushed the fabric aside. He wasn't wearing anything under the jeans, though Delwyn did have some vague knowledge in his mind of undergarments that most humans wore.

Delwyn moved between Fabian's legs and nudged them apart. Fabian put his arms behind his head and leaned back, letting Delwyn gaze upon him as much as he wanted.

Fabian's erection sprang free from the opening in his jeans. He was long and thick and Delwyn wondered how he would ever manage to take him up the arse.

Something of his concerns must have shown in his expression, because Fabian eased himself into a sitting position and took Delwyn's face between his hands.

"We don't have to do that if you don't want to," he said.

"Isander appeared to enjoy it," Delwyn reminded him. "And you seemed to like being inside him."

Fabian tapped him on the chin to force him to meet his eyes. "Isander is my past. What we did together has no bearing on what *we* do."

"But if we don't do that, won't you miss it?" For the first time in his life, Delwyn regretted how he had watched others having sex in his visions. Thanks to his observations, he worried he wouldn't be able to live up to Fabian's expectations.

Fabian wrapped him in his arms and pulled him so Delwyn straddled his legs. Delwyn began to harden again and their erections brushed against each other.

"Delwyn, listen to me," Fabian said quietly. "There are many different ways we can be together, most of which don't involve anal sex. Yes, Isander liked it when I took him that way, but that doesn't mean you will. You have *nothing* to live up to."

"But what if I'm not enough for you?" Delwyn asked.

Fabian laughed. "Just having you in my arms is enough to push me to the edge. When I kissed you, I nearly came in my nice new jeans. You are more than enough for me. Besides, you're a merman and when the mating season comes around I'm pretty sure you'll exhaust me thoroughly."

"Then it doesn't matter if we don't, you know…?"

Fabian shook his head and eased Delwyn out of the way so he could take off the rest of his clothes. When he was naked he tugged Delwyn back into place on top of his thighs.

"Kiss me," he said.

Delwyn pressed their lips together and as he stroked his tongue over Fabian's, the first spurt of the hot seed of Fabian's pleasure spilled onto his skin.

He rocked against Fabian, grinding their bodies together, his own hardness pressing into the stickiness on Fabian's belly.

Fabian gripped his arse with his large hands and for a moment Delwyn thought he might slip his fingers between his buttocks, but the moment passed and he realized Fabian had no intention of pushing him toward something he wasn't ready for. Something he might never be comfortable with.

Instead of trying to manipulate him into giving more than he could, Fabian simply held Delwyn in place as they ground together, slick with sweat and tacky with their semen.

Delwyn moaned into Fabian's mouth, and when he came for the second time Fabian was right there with him.

They fell back on the bed in a tangled heap of limbs, panting and gasping as they struggled to catch their breath.

Delwyn rolled into Fabian's arms and relished the feeling of being held in his embrace. He knew they couldn't stay here forever, but he intended to make it last as long as possible.

* * * *

When Delwyn and Fabian woke the next morning, they found a strange box sitting on the table at the end of the bed.

"Where did that come from?" Delwyn asked.

"I don't know."

"Do you think we should open it?"

Fabian didn't waste time answering. He lifted the lid and gasped when he saw the contents.

"What is it?" Delwyn approached the end of the bed.

"It's my belongings from the Isle of the Gods," Fabian said. "My ornaments, gifts from my Aunt Medi, even my scrolls."

"Do you think Medina left this here?" Delwyn watched Fabian continue to rummage through the box.

"I doubt it," Fabian replied. "She would have left a note

so we knew it came from her."

"Then who?"

Fabian picked up a folder he didn't recognize and opened it. Inside were identification papers for Delwyn, along with various qualification certificates and other essential items he would need in England. "These are yours," he said. "I think this must be Caspian's work."

"Why do you think that?"

"Because he gave me a similar set of papers when I arrived here."

Delwyn flicked through the papers, trying to make sense of what they meant, but with little success.

"This is yours, too," Fabian said.

Delwyn put aside the papers to see Fabian holding a small box out to him. He took the box and lifted the lid. Inside was a single flower with petals the colors of the rainbow.

"I think Caspian might have had a hand in keeping it alive after my mother stripped me of my powers," Fabian suggested.

Delwyn shot Fabian a doubtful glance. "That doesn't sound like him."

Fabian chuckled. "I've known Caspian my entire life, and while he isn't always the most romantic of men, he does have his moments. I think this might be one of them."

Delwyn sniffed the flower one last time, before placing it carefully on the bedside table. The precious bloom, a gift from a century long ago, kept alive throughout the years by Fabian's magic, was now finally back where it belonged.

When Fabian pulled Delwyn into his arms and kissed him, the merman realized he was exactly where he was meant to be, too.

Dangerous Waves

Excerpt

Chapter One

Present day

Cari sipped her drink, savoring the sweet nectar of the gods. The secret ingredients of the nectar had been stolen long ago from the Greek pantheon, and in her opinion was the best acquisition the Atlantean gods had ever made.

Her quiet contemplation was rudely interrupted by the arrival of the most powerful goddess currently awake. Medina, Goddess of Love, appeared in the garden amid flashes of lightning and a flurry of pale pink silk robes.

"Ah, there you are." Medina didn't bother waiting for an invitation. She sat on one of the cushioned chairs and helped herself to a drink. "This modern world is so vast, don't you think?"

"The world itself is the same size it's always been. There

are merely more humans inhabiting the planet than there used to be." Cari wondered what Medina wanted. She doubted it was a pleasant chat about the changing times. She didn't bother to ask, Medina would reveal the reason for her visit in her own good time.

"Have you been to Greece recently?" Medina inquired.

"Yes. I enjoy eating Greek cuisine in its home country."

Medina waved her hand in dismissal. "You can keep the food. Have you seen what's become of the temples?"

"Times have changed. The old gods are no longer worshipped as they used to be. It's not just Greece. The Roman ones, the Norse, so many of them are mostly forgotten in these modern times. Only scholars of history even know their names, and they don't truly believe."

"The people have forgotten us. Even in Atlantis they don't recall us. Most of the mer call the place the sunken city."

Cari shrugged. She had long since resigned herself to never enjoying the power which came from having thousands of followers. Unfortunately for Medina, the goddess of love had been sleeping for centuries and had only recently awoken. Cari supposed it had been a shock for her to find what had become of the world they had once known.

"If they were to remember," Medina continued, "our powers would eclipse those we once had. Imagine the benefits of being worshipped by even a fraction of the current population of this new world."

Although Medina's tone was mostly wistful, Cari detected a sense of purpose there too. The goddess of love was never going to be happy with merely a handful of followers.

"How it is you didn't sleep like the rest of us?" Medina asked. "What kept you in this realm?"

"My followers were not composed of Atlanteans alone," Cari replied. "Many of the mer already believed in me on that fateful day. Even though they didn't worship me in my temple, they had seen the power of my Oracles with their own eyes."

"The mer believed in me too," Medina pointed out

impatiently. "I still slept."

Cari knew what Medina asked. She had a few ideas about why some had slept and others had remained in the world, though they were only theories. "You'll recall you performed some powerful magic in the weeks before you slept?"

Medina tapped her lip. "Are you talking about the little spell I put on Caspian?"

Cari snorted. "*Little* spell? Yes, I *am* referring to that. It would have taken a lot out of you to put a love spell on a god as powerful as Caspian."

"It shouldn't have taken that much power to put him under the influence for less than a day."

"Had you done other magic on other gods in the days leading up to our fall?"

"Yes, of course, the gods often came to me for assistance with matters of the heart." Medina huffed. "So, are you saying my good deeds are the reason I was too weak to stay awake?"

Cari ignored the remark about good deeds. She was certain Caspian didn't see her meddling that way. "It's as good a theory as any."

Medina took a sip of nectar. "So, now you choose your trio of Oracles from amongst the mer."

"Yes."

"Interesting."

Cari frowned at the direction the conversation was taking. "We all needed followers to stay in this realm."

"And lucky you, the mer were ready to fall at your feet. Rather a shame you couldn't have warned the rest of us so we could take similar precautions."

"I didn't know what would happen."

Medina laughed in obvious disbelief. "The Goddess of Prophecy didn't see the biggest disaster to befall our kind before it happened? Forgive me if I don't believe you."

Cari glared at her uninvited guest. "You know as well as I do, our powers are useless within the temple of another god. I could not see what would happen. If I'd had any idea, don't you think I'd have done everything in my power to stop it?"

Medina nodded and lowered her eyes. "Whatever our differences, I know how much you care for your brother."

Cari took another drink and wished it were something stronger. "What transpired weakened me too. It nearly drained me to appoint new Oracles."

"Humph."

Cari waited, her patience wearing thinner by the minute, wondering what Medina wanted from her. She tapped her manicured finger on her glass, subtly hinting for the goddess to get to the point.

"Your current Oracles are all untouched," Medina commented.

"Yes, I know."

"You used to take most of your Oracles to your bed," Medina continued. "The men at least. Are you losing your touch, or don't you like the idea of letting a half-human fuck you?"

"I'm not prejudiced against the mer. I've invited some to my bed over the years, just not my Oracles."

"Is there any particular reason why not? What's changed since I was last here?"

"The Oracles are forbidden to have sexual relations with anyone. Not that any of the present ones would accept an invitation from me anyway, both Kai and Delwyn are what humans these days call gay."

"What?" Medina's jaw dropped and she placed her glass on the table with a shaky hand.

"You heard me," Cari replied. "They're homosexual. It's really not so unusual."

"That's not the part I'm shocked at. You've forbidden the Oracles to enjoy sexual pleasures?"

"Yes."

"Why?"

"It would appear the power of sight carries down through

the generations now."

"It never used to, did it?"

"No."

"Then how did that happen?"

Another question Cari didn't have an answer for, though again she'd had plenty of time to formulate her own theory on the matter. "I suspect it was a side effect of my mother's interference with the mer physiology."

Medina snorted in a thoroughly unladylike manner. "Your mother seems to be at the bottom of all our troubles, doesn't she?"

Cari smiled softly. "Oh, I think there's plenty of blame to be left at other doors as well."

Medina grimaced. "So, because the powers you gifted on the Oracles are hereditary, you've forbidden them to have sex."

"It's for the best."

"To live without love is never for the best."

"The descendants were discovered to inherit more than one gift if there were two or three different Oracles in their line."

"Ah, now I see what the problem is. If a humble little mermaid or merman could see more than you intended they might rival your own powers. Only *you* are permitted to see everything. Rather selfish of you, don't you think?"

Cari bristled at the accusation. "Many years ago there was a mermaid who did see all. She saw the past, the present and the future and was driven crazy by the visions. She didn't even live to see her first mating season. We imposed the rule to prevent the same thing happening again."

"I'm surprised it wasn't already too late. How many mer had powers by the time this was discovered?"

"A great many, I'm afraid. Relations were banned for all of them so each line ended with them."

"Could you not have simply removed their powers?"

"I tried, but it didn't work. My Oracles are appointed automatically. When one Oracle dies, another comes into their powers without my doing a thing. When I undid the original spell, my appointed Oracles lost their powers, but those who had been born with the powers retained theirs. The law was the only option. I cast my original spell for the final time."

"The final time?"

Cari sighed. "I cannot undo the magic and start over. As you have already seen, we don't have the followers we used to, or the powers our believers instill in us. I think I would have the strength to remove the powers of the present Oracles, but I wouldn't be able to cast the spell again."

Medina nodded. "Yet I still don't like the idea of your Oracles being unable to love, especially considering they are mer, and as you know, go into heat twice a year. Surely it's painful for them."

"They have learnt to cope with the solstices."

"And how do they *cope* with a life without love?"

"They know it's for the best."

Medina waved her hand and a vision appeared in front of her. Cari recognized the two mermen at once, Kai and Delwyn, her Oracles of the present and past. They were under the water, where they stayed, and Delwyn had curled up in Kai's arms. They were stroking and kissing. It was nothing Cari hadn't seen before.

"They are not soulmates," Medina commented. "Although they are close, their souls don't cry out for each other."

"That would be a good thing," Cari replied. "Were their souls bound, it would make their solstices even more unbearable."

"Then you admit they struggle on the solstice nights?"

"Yes, of course they do, as does any merman or mermaid who doesn't find relief in the mating season."

"You don't think it's wrong to stop your Oracles finding love?"

Cari stood and stalked toward the vision, shattering the image as she approached. "It's not ideal, but right now there's nothing to be done about it."

"Kai's soulmate will soon be on his way to Atlantis, and Delwyn's is already there."

Cari used her powers to see into the future. "Oh, damn."

"You see him?" Medina asked.

"They must not meet. It would make Kai's mating seasons unbearable."

Medina laughed. "No one can avoid their fate. Surely you, of all people, know that?"

"Destiny is not a set course. You must help me to stop them meeting."

"Must?" Medina rose and glided over to Cari. "I am the Goddess of Love and the only thing I must do is right this wrong you have inflicted on your Oracles."

"You can't interfere!"

"Of course I can, and I will."

With a gloating smile Medina vanished.

This was not good at all. Cari didn't need Medina meddling in the lives of her Oracles. They were protected in Atlantis and it was where their powers were most potent. They could not be allowed to leave.

* * * *

The heat of the sun warmed Dax's bare back. He hadn't moved from his spot on the sand in nearly an hour. Most of the clan had congregated a little way down the beach, but he was reluctant to join them. He knew he was simply putting off the inevitable, yet he couldn't seem to help himself.

Nearly three years had passed since he had parted ways with the clan he had grown up with. In that time he had traveled with any clan who would let him. Most merpeople he came across happily welcomed him into their group, though there was the occasional tight-knit clan who were reluctant to let him travel with them for more than a few days.

Dax had been with the current clan for nearly eight months, but the time drew near when he would have to move on. Like so many small communities, they talked about traveling to the sunken city, the most secure colony of merpeople in all the oceans. His original clan had decided to go there, and considering the dangers of the oceans, Dax couldn't blame any leader for making the decision to seek sanctuary there.

Unfortunately for Dax, the laws of the sunken city were strict and rigorously upheld, and one in particular made his skin cold and his fins shudder. There were no same sex relations allowed by those who chose to reside there. As a merman who found pleasure with other males, Dax had no choice except to bid farewell to any clan who chose to seek refuge in the sunken city.

Cale, the scout who had been sent to the city in advance, had returned earlier in the day. Dax didn't need to hear what he had to say. He knew the report he would give all too well. It would be the same as the one from the last clan's scout, and all the ones before.

Malka, the leader of the clan, had been in seclusion with the scout ever since his return. Dax knew from previous discussions that Malka already leaned toward the idea of moving to the sunken city. She had been in charge since her mate's death ten years ago, and although she had kept the clan together, from what Dax had heard and seen, she had grown tired of the continuing struggle some time ago.

As soon as she made the announcement to swim to the sunken city, Dax would part company once more and seek out another clan to travel with.

"Dax!" Keshet's shout startled a nearby bird. Dax lifted his head and smiled as his lover approached.

"Any news?"

Keshet nodded as he dropped down onto the sand. "Malka has ordered everyone here to the island by dusk. She's going to make an announcement."

Dax sighed. He hadn't spoken to Keshet about the law in the sunken city yet. He guessed now was as good a time as any.

"What is it?" Keshet asked. "Do you think they won't want our clan in the city?"

"Where's Gilad?" Dax replied, avoiding the question for the moment. Their other lover should hear what he had to say too.

"He was relaxing in the rock pool last time I saw him. Do you want me to fetch him?"

Dax stood and brushed the sand from his body. "No, let's go to him. It'll be quiet there."

Keshet frowned and furrowed his brow. "You want to fuck?"

Dax chuckled. He couldn't blame Keshet for the conclusion he had come to. Usually when the three of them spent time alone together sex was their favorite activity. Dax would always be grateful for the way Keshet and Gilad, the only homosexual mermen in the clan, had invited him to join them. Even though the two mermen had been in an established relationship for several years, they hadn't hesitated to assure him they wouldn't let him suffer through the solstice alone.

"You know you don't have to wait until the solstice if you want a little relief," Keshet continued as they slipped away from the beach. "Gilad and I are happy to have you join us whenever you want."

"I don't wish to intrude on your time alone too much," Dax reminded him.

"It's not an intrusion. You know both of us would consider making this thing between us more permanent?"

"I know, but I'm a selfish merman. I want someone all of my own. I don't like to share."

Dax caught Keshet's roll of the eyes. "You don't seem to be doing a bad job of sharing, if you ask me."

"I do what I must to survive the solstice without the pain that comes with abstinence."

"Is that all we have together?"

Dax shrugged. "You and Gilad have a connection, a closeness, something special."

"I love him.

"Yes, and he loves you."

Keshet smiled and a dreamy expression spread over his face. Dax had no doubt about his two lovers' feelings for each other. A part of him wished he shared those tender feelings, but he didn't, and no matter how good the sex was with the two of them, Dax knew he never would. His heart wasn't involved. He suspected it never had been.

They found Gilad right where Keshet had said, reclining in the rock pool, his orange fins mostly hidden beneath the water. Gilad grinned up at Keshet, barely casting a glance at Dax. Keshet climbed into the pool, transforming into his mer form and swimming into Gilad's arms. They kissed languidly as they wrapped their arms around each other.

Dax could tell he had been momentarily forgotten and he stifled a twinge of envy.

"Aren't you going to join us?" Gilad asked once they had parted.

"Dax has something he wants to talk to us about," Keshet explained.

Gilad's face lit up with a bright smile. "He's decided to join us permanently?"

"No." Dax immediately shut down that line of conversation. "It's about the sunken city."

"Has Malka made a decision yet?" Gilad asked. "Most of the clan are eager to go there, especially if it means safety for the youngsters."

Keshet answered before Dax could say a word. "It's not been announced yet, but I think we all know we'll be heading to the city before the next solstice."

"It's the best decision for all of us," Gilad said. "Even when a clan has been traveling for as long as ours, it's no good upholding the nomadic traditions when the result is there's no one left to do so."

"I think we all know what she'll say," Dax agreed. "The scout will no doubt be reporting to her that the sunken city will welcome us there, they always do."

"What do you mean?" Keshet asked.

"My first clan reported the sunken city welcomes all mer there, and so has every clan I've traveled with since."

"You've been with a lot of clans, haven't you?"

"A fair few," Dax replied. "They all eventually seek shelter in the sunken city. I'm sure Malka will be doing the same soon enough."

Keshet gazed at him steadily. "You won't be coming with us, will you?"

"No."

"Why not?" Gilad asked. "Surely the city would be safer than traveling the oceans on your own?"

"That's what I want to talk to you about," Dax explained. "There's something you need to know about the laws of the sunken city."

"Yes?" Keshet prompted when Dax struggled to find the words to break the bad news to his lovers.

"Sexual relations between two mermen, or two mermaids, are strictly forbidden," Dax finally blurted. "None of us would be allowed to have sex together if we were to go there."

"But what about on the solstice?" Keshet asked. "My mating season fever breaks when another merman takes me."

"And mine breaks when I fuck another merman," Dax added. "That's why I've not gone to the sunken city and I never intend to. My clan was a small one and, try as I might, I couldn't find my release with a mermaid. I suffered through several mating seasons without release until Kyle, my first male lover, reached maturity."

"Where's Kyle now?" Gilad asked. "Surely he didn't go to the sunken city if he needed a merman to break his fever?"

"He had no choice," Dax explained. "When his father died in the final shark attack that decimated our clan, he became leader of our people. He made the only decision he could for the safety of everyone."

"Couldn't he have left the city after seeing your people to

safety?" Gilad asked. "Why would he want to stay there if he couldn't break his fever?"

"He wouldn't have left his family." Dax had no doubt Kyle would have stayed in the sunken city, no matter the cost to himself. He was that sort of a merman, and his selflessness was one of the reasons Dax loved him. He just wished he had told him as much before he'd left. Instead, he had convinced Kyle all they had shared together was a mutual need to get off during the solstice. Perhaps sex was all it had been for Kyle, but Dax knew his own feelings had run a little deeper.

"Perhaps you could come to the sunken city with us and see whether Kyle is prepared to leave with you now?" Gilad suggested.

"He'll have settled into his new life after all this time."

"How long has it been since you saw him?" Keshet asked.

"Nearly three years."

"Well, there you have it," Gilad declared. "That's plenty of time for his people to build lives in the city and for him to swim away with the love of his life."

Dax laughed and shook his head. "I'm not the love of his life. We just used each other during the solstice. We never even sought each other out the rest of the year."

"I bet you wanted to," Gilad teased. "You enjoy sex way too much to be celibate all but two nights of the year."

Dax ducked his head to avoid the knowing gaze of his lovers. They were right, of course. Dax had never been with Kyle outside of the mating season, but he had been tempted. Only Kyle's youth, and the niggling doubt about his lover's feelings for him, had stopped him from being with him every night of the year.

"If you're right about the city, then perhaps it's not the right place for us," Keshet suggested. "The three of us could travel on after we reach the city, and perhaps bring your Kyle along for the journey."

Dax couldn't prevent his smile at the idea of the four of them starting a new clan. Maybe he would travel to the sunken city after all. He could at least see Kyle and his other friends before making his decision.

* * * *

Kai, Delwyn, and Ula swam into the quarters of Justin, heir to the throne of the sunken city, and his lover Lucas. They had been invited over for dinner and Kai looked forward to the break from their normal routine.

As Oracles they spent most of their time in their temple, and although they sometimes ventured out to the market or the temples of other immortals, they never traveled past the boundaries of the city.

Ula and Delwyn spent most of their days secluded in the temple. For Delwyn it was a chance to study the old texts and writings on the walls of the building. Ula meanwhile chose to hone her skills in music-making with a variety of shell-made instruments. Kai had no interests in the ancient inhabitants of the city and had no talent for music or other restful pastimes. Of the three of them, Kai found his imprisonment the most confining, and escaped the temple whenever he could, though a guard always escorted him wherever he swam. More often than not, Kai chose to swim to the barracks, using his powers to see the trainees going through their drills. His dream had been to become a warrior, yet now that had been dashed upon the rocks. His spear had been taken from him before he'd arrived in the city, his mother convinced he would do himself harm with the weapon.

Kai spent most of his days in boredom and restlessness, watching others live out his dreams, forever wondering what might have been, had he not been inflicted with the curse of being an Oracle.

The opportunity to leave the temple, even if just for an hour or two, was one he never missed.

Kai didn't need to use his powers to see their ever-present guards with them. Under the pretext of escorting the blind mermaid and mermen, the guards watched them constantly whenever they left their home in Cari's temple. Kai tried hard not to think of the temple as their prison, but he found it almost impossible to do so.

Justin, recently blind, still struggled with traveling about the city, but Kai was pleased to see he had become more adept at navigating his own suite of rooms.

Today Justin was telling them how he and Lucas had met. Kai had heard some of the tale before, but he was always happy to hear the story again. The knowledge that Justin and Lucas were allowed to be together in the sunken city gave him hope that one day another law might be changed, the one stopping the Oracles from enjoying the pleasures of love.

"I guess Medina isn't so bad," Justin said. *"Though getting on the wrong side of her is definitely not recommended."*

Kai chuckled. The Goddess of Love certainly had a temper, as Justin had learned the hard way.

"You're quiet this evening," Delwyn commented, his voice in Kai's head concerned. *"Are you well?"*

"Just thinking."

"About what?"

"We all know the old Atlantean gods and goddesses are waking, yes?"

"What of it? It's not as though the mer worshipped them. Why should their rising make any difference to us?"

"Maybe if we did go to them things would be different," Kai suggested. *"What if we were to go to the Goddess of Love and ask her for help?"*

"Help with what?"

"Finding love, of course," Kai replied.

Delwyn sighed. *"Finding love isn't the problem. It's the whole being trapped underwater during the mating season. Falling in love with someone will only make our situation worse."*

Kai knew Delwyn made a good point, yet he couldn't help wondering whether Medina might be able to assist in that regard too. From what Justin and Lucas had told them, the goddess was extremely powerful. Could she be the answer to their problem?

More books from
L.M. Brown

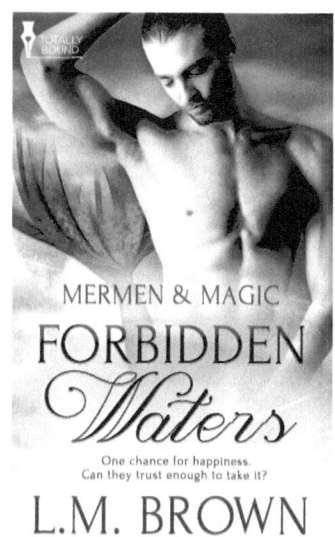

Book one in the Mermen & Magic series

For the dying race of mer people, homosexual relationships are prohibited. When Kyle falls for Prince Finn he knows he is navigating forbidden waters.

L.M. BROWN

FALLING INTO DARKNESS

Their love could save the soul of a fallen angel
or damn an archangel to an eternity in hell

*Their love could save the soul of a fallen angel or damn an
archangel to an eternity in Hell.*

Book one in the Heavenly Sins serial

*When an angel and a demon fall for the same mortal man
there is only one solution…share him.*

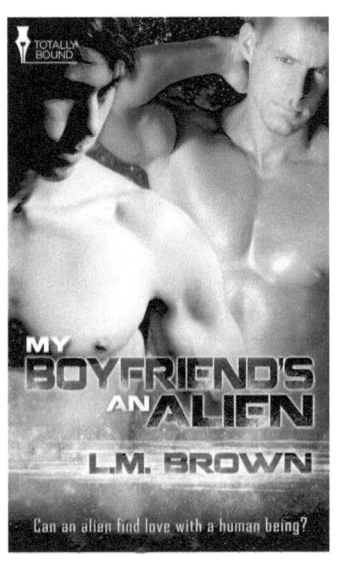

*Can an alien with no knowledge of humans or concept of
sex find lasting love with a human man?*

About the Author

L.M. Brown

L.M. Brown is an English writer of gay romances. She believes that there is nothing hotter or sweeter than two men in love with each other… unless it is three.

When L.M. Brown isn't bribing her fur babies for control of the laptop, she can usually be found with her nose in a book.

L.M. Brown loves to hear from readers. You can find contact information, website details and an author profile page at https://www.pride-publishing.com/